Ewan Lawrie is the author of *Gibbous House*, also published by Unbound. He is one of a small team of editors for the writers' website ABCTales.com.

Whilst serving twenty-three years in the Royal Air Force, including ten in Cold War Berlin and twelve more flying over the rather warmer conflicts that followed, Ewan began writing. In the main this was to pass the time during long, boring flights over desert countries. After a while, this way of killing time developed into a passion.

Until recently Ewan lived in the south of Spain, inland from the Costa Del Sol, where he used to enjoy an occasional beer in bars where no one spoke English, at least not to him, in case they ended up in his notebook or somewhere worse. When not doing that he used to write, but occasionally he taught English to Andalucians and other hispanophones.

Having spent nine months renting in Manchester's hipster equivalent of Shoreditch, West Didsbury, Ewan is now living in Elland in the Calder Valley, where the scenery is as inspiring in its way as that of Spain and the beer is cheaper than in Manchester.

Please Allow Me Inc. represents Ewan Lawrie for marketing purposes. However, since it is an entirely fictitious business, good luck with contacting them. (They often post on Facebook, all material should be consumed with generous portions of Saxa – other condiments are available.)

He has had stories and poetry published in several anthologies. His first poetry collection was published by Cerasus Poetry in October 2018. *No Good Deed* is his second novel.

No Good Deed

No Good Deed or What Moffat Did Next

Ewan Lawrie

unbound

This edition first published in 2021

Unbound
TC Group, Level 1, Devonshire House, One Mayfair Place,
London, W1J 8AJ

www.unbound.com

ISBN (eBook): 978-1-78965-092-1
ISBN (Paperback): 978-1-78965-091-4

Cover design by Mecob

Printed and bound in Great Britain by Clays Ltd, Elcograf S.p.A.

Many thanks to Tony Stowe, an old, bold friend,
for believing in this book, Moffat and me.

Super Patrons

A Silly Twisted Boy!
Richie Allport
Arabist
Henry Crun and Minnie Bannister
Andy Barber
Barnacle Bill the Sailor
Bill Biggles
Black Puddng Bertha
Major Bloodnok
Bluebottles Stage Directions
Sean Brady
Martin Brennan
Brian, The Very Naughty Boy
Bumpy Go Cart
Stephen Calvert
Lisa Campbell
Mark Charlton
Tony Cook
Johnny Cougar
Count Jim Moriarty's Belligerent Cousin
Joe Cowan

Andrew Crawford
Mr Creosote
The Crimson Pirate
D'Ogtanian
Dick Dastardly
Colin Davies
Jackie Davies
Alexander De Pfeffel
Jimmy Dean
Darren Dix
Teresa Dixon
Steve Doane
Charles Lutwidge Dodgson
Sue Dunnim
Paul Dunseath
Eccles
Jared Ely
David Escolme
Kerry Fagg
David Fairhurst
Simon Few
Tom Finn
Neil Flather
Andy Forrester
Adam Garland
Cosy Gray
Dervita Gribble
Hercules Grytpype-Thynne
SJ Gumby
Fiona Gwinnett
Crozier Hackett
Jay Hamilton
Jeanette Hamilton

Richard Harmer
Captain Hastings
Johnny Helmo
Robert Herbertson
Craig Hornsby
John Huffam
Mr Humphreys
Vladmir Ilyich
Professor Jedermann
Jonathan Jenkin
Trev Jones
John Keki
Kenicki's Secret Girlfriend
Patrick Kincaid
Pete Langman
W Tom Lawrie
Isabella Lawrie
Alasdair Lawrie
Tracey Lawrie
Claudine Lazar
Miss Lemon
David Llewellyn
George Mainwaring
Gautam Malkani
Richard McDonough
David McRitchie
Tom Meiklejohn
Ginge Miller
Alasdair Moffat
Peter Moore
Frank Morley
Morven Morley
Stephen Morley

James Morley
The Count of Mouldy Bisto
Mike Murtagh
Marie-Jose Nieuwkoop
Anson Northrup
Dr Winston O'Boogie
Andrew O'Brien
Jack O'Donnell
Ariadne Oliver
Ann Onnymus
John Owen
The Owl of the Remove
Michael Paley
Ellen Pardoner
Pathos
Alexandra Constance Ellen Paton
Davie Paton
Jennifer Pickup
Frank Pike
Penelope Pitstop
Porthole
The Duke of Prunes
Sir Henry Rawlinson
Edgar Rice Burgers
Paul Richardson
Janice Ridley
Jane Roberts
Joanne Rogerson
Rebecca Rose
John Rosie
Kev Ross
Chief Running Gag
Tony Ryan

Ron Saint
Huck Sawyer
Ivan Scovinsky Scovar
Neddy Seagoon
Mrs Slocumbe
Roger Smith
Peter Stokes
Michael Stowe
Tony Stowe
John Stowell
Stephen Thom
Kevin Thompson
Trelawney of the Guards
Alf Tupper
Rudolf Valentino
Apollo C. Vermouth
Rick Wadmore
Ian Warner
Julie Warren
Stuart Watt
Nancy Coco West
Esther Rene West
Gavin White
Billy Whizz
Suzie Wilde
Steve Willett
Neil Williams
Arthur Wilson
The Wolf of Kabul
Laura Wood
Duncan Woodward

1

It was a relief to take my seat inside the coach, if only to escape the ripe odour emanating from the driver and, indeed, to leave behind what passed for a town in southern Missouri. My two fellow travellers proved notable for their peculiarities. They were fellows of similar age, neither seeming more than thirty. Both were possessed of prodigious moustaches and dressed in what I had come to view as the colonial style. This seemed chiefly to consist of wearing any mismatched colours and cloths cut in unflattering imitations of earlier fashions from London, except for the matter of what one wore on one's feet and head. They each wore the ubiquitous boots and a most unusual hat. It came as some surprise when one of these fellows thrust out a hand and bellowed over the rattle of the wheels, 'Clemens! Both of us, that is. Pleased to meetcha!'

I took the proffered hand. It was not calloused, but the grip was firm and recognisably on the square. He held my eye as I switched my handshake to what was clearly his brother's hand and gave the name that had served me best.

'Moffat, at your service.'

It transpired that this Clemens and his brother were bound for the Nevada Territory.

'Orion has become part of the grand orchestra of the State,' Clemens said.

I enquired as to what instrument he played.

Clemens' laughter took some time to subside, before he enlightened me further. 'Hell, no! Orion's on his way to a job as Secretary to the State Governor. Imagine that! My own brother a durned parasite.'

His brother gave him a look of affection rather than distaste, which I found surprising.

Out of manners and nothing more, I enquired, 'And you?'

His eyes gleamed: there was something puckish about the fellow, as though he found me, his brother, the world at large – and even himself – a rich and satisfying source of amusement.

'Silver!' he said. He swept off his peculiar, high-crowned, broad-brimmed hat. The hat was ugly and hardly suitable for a gentleman. It would not have surprised me to learn that the Clemens brothers had been the only purchasers of this innovatory item. Evidently, Mr Clemens was possessed of an unseemly curiosity, for he chose to enquire of me, 'What brings you here, Mr Moffat? You ain't a prospecting type, I reckon.'

'Prospects interest me, not prospecting,' I said.

It was a foolish answer to give such a curious fellow.

'I can tell you're a swell feller, ain't he though, Orion? I reckon we'll rub along fine with him.'

I was unsure whether the fellow could be quite such a pudding-head as he appeared.

Over the next few hours, Mr Clemens junior kept a running commentary of the things he expected to do, and the enormous fortune he expected to make, in the booming frontier towns of Nevada. This fascinating subject exhausted, he began to regale me with the qualities of the wondrous seven-shot pistol he had brought along to defend himself on the wild frontier. He avowed it to be a marvel of engineering so sophisticated that it had taken two fellows to design it. A Mr Smith *and* a Mr Wesson. He was so enamoured of it that he declared himself prepared to overlook its only fault: that one was unable to hit anything with it. Almost every anecdote provided him with an opportunity to blow such gales of laughter as ought to have despatched his sibling's ridiculous hat out of the stage-coach window. I began to look forward to our arrival in St Louis. Mr Clemens informed me that the next stage of their journey would be by steamboat from thence to St Jo, where they would once more try the overland stage.

In St Louis, the Brothers Clemens made for the wharf to arrange their passage and I looked for the nearest place to partake of something to drink. My throat was as dry as if I had been the blowhard and not his victim. I fell into company in what they were pleased to call a saloon bar on Laclede's Landing. This area was dedicated to trading and traders associated with the great river. There were two or three longshoremen, a Polynesian sailor and a smartly if gaudily dressed fellow who appeared to be observing the rest of the company with some disdain. It had taken me some time to become accustomed to the American's disregard for social nicety. Every restaurant, bar or hotel was an egalitarian hodge-podge of strange and ill-met fellows. It was not at all a question of the quality visiting a pot-house of the stews, being desirous of entertainment. It was merely a peculiarity of colonial society. Or so it had seemed to me ever since I had stepped off the SS *Iowa* in Newport News, more than a decade before.

The dandy was wearing what he no doubt would have termed 'a vest': this was a waistcoat, more or less. However, it appeared to be of woven silk, and bore a busy design representing the four suits of playing cards over and over. He had a large cigar clamped between his teeth and was listening to a discussion between the longshoremen and the Polynesian as to the location of the cheapest brothel in St Louis. One and all were drinking a dreadful approximation of whiskey, a libation that I had never found to my taste. There was a tricky moment when I tried to insist on the Polynesian purchasing a brandy for me. It was alarming to think he had been able to conceal so large a blade about his person. The whiskey was best drunk all at once, thereby evading the necessity of actually tasting it, I found.

The Polynesian stepped outside with the longshoremen at some point, presumably to settle their difference over one of the seaman's tattoos. He had been claiming it was a particularly life-like depiction of a beautiful mermaid. This had provoked fits of laughter in the others, who then counter-claimed variously that it was in fact a manatee or one of their mothers-in-law. A secondary dispute had ensued with each of two of the dock workers insisting that their own was the uglier and clearly had been the model for the tattoo. Tiring of this entertainment, I returned to the bar. None of the four returned from their open-air discussions and I could only assume that they had ended badly.

Naturally this left me in the company of the fellow in the extravagant waistcoat. I suggested a brandy, and he informed me that nothing we might buy in the establishment would truly deserve the name. He winked and said that he had something special in his room upstairs. I refused, saying that I hardly knew him. He looked a fine figure, perhaps ten years younger than I. At least, if I had not but recently travelled by stagecoach. It was important that I consider what this man saw in his regard of me. A man of around forty-five – though I looked nearer my true age that day – vigorous, if a little tired. Clean-shaven, yet blessed with a head of hair. I wondered if I had judged his interest correctly.

He did not seem unduly discommoded by the rebuff.

'Better stick to the whiskey, sir... or we could try a beer?' he enquired.

'A capital suggestion, my throat is still quite as dry as dust.'

He ordered the beers with a click of his fingers. We were standing alongside a long counter that served as the bar. There were tables in rough deal aplenty, but few were occupied. The majority of trade was carried out at the bar. Of the occupied tables, one had a game of cards in progress and at the other two military fellows in a grey uniform were sprawled insensible across it. My companion eyed me over his glass.

'Long way from home.'

It did not sound like a question. I answered, after a fashion, nonetheless.

'Somewhat.'

The beer was light and tasted nothing like the porters and ales of home. I made pretence of clicking my fingers, ensuring that this gesture was not seen by the man behind the bar. The man in the waistcoat clicked his own and we were provided with two more glasses of the gold-coloured liquid.

'I am indebted to you, sir. I did not catch your name, earlier,' I said.

'Didn't give it, is why.'

I held out my hand and gave the name, 'Moffat.'

He looked at the hand for a moment, then shook it.

'Anson Northrup.'

He was of a size with me, perhaps larger, due to the fact that I cut a more slender figure since arriving in the Americas. He asked me what had brought me to the New World.

'Necessity,' I said.

'The mother of invention, it's a fact.'

Evidently he was a man of few words. We took several more of the beers. They had no more effect on myself than a cordial. As for the other he became a little more animated, but not a great deal more talkative. Even so, I was able to convince him that he inveigled me into his room and not vice-versa.

We passed an enjoyable hour and it was with some regret that I used a yellow scarf to choke the life out of him. I assumed his clothes and saw with regret what little money he had in his purse. His body I folded into a chest and covered it with my dusty attire. I took the only other item in the room: it was a bag, about the size of a sailor's bag although it had handles for transportation. It had been fashioned from a violently patterned oriental carpet. It was a hideous thing, but what was a man without baggage? Looking around the room, I thought again that it was a pity our acquaintance had been so short.

Still, as he himself had said, 'Necessity is the mother of invention' and, besides, such a personage must surely be wedded to the Father of Lies.

2

Twilight allowed the street outside the groggery a charm that daylight had not afforded it. I resolved to depart before the dark of night rendered it dangerous, feeling less confident in this new town. It had been difficult to survive thus far. A cutpurse might have survived in one of the larger cities, New York, perhaps, but I had washed up in Virginia over ten years ago. Crime was an altogether different profession in the New World. How I had wished for the gas lighting that illuminated London. The shadows between the lit places hid so much more. There had been various schemes that had seemed promising and indeed a few were lucrative in the short term. However, my luck had deserted me in large degree ever since I had left the Sceptred Isle. My last dollar had disappeared into the grubby stagecoach driver's pocket. The relative riches I had brought from England had melted away like April snow. It was hard not to appear a gull for every thief and, in the local vernacular, hornfuggler, when the moment one's mouth opened, one was taken for a fresh fish just landed off the boat.

The relief I felt at discarding the very last of my Northumbrian-tailored clothes was more than palpable. It might even be said to have been olfactory. I thought, of a sudden, that I might explore St Louis in the guise of Anson Northrup, and if my accents were at odds with my dress, what of it? Perhaps I was a moneyed layabout recently returned from Europe, or even Philadelphia, whose citizens were often accused of aping the characters to whom Mister Dickens had introduced them, on the occasion of his theatrical tours. Someone had once been at great pains to inform me that clothes maketh the man. I meant to test this theorem to its limits.

Having walked a few furlongs, I found myself at the corner of Olive and Fourth Streets. Some rails adorned the surface of the road, there was a loud clanging bell and a horse-drawn railway carriage blew past in a whirl of dust. I had heard that London had such things by that time but was greatly surprised to see one in St Louis. The horse-drawn car screeched to a halt some way down Olive Street and I saw several persons embark. By running at a pace sufficient to shorten my breath considerably, I managed to swing onto the rear access just as the vehicle set off. The acceleration of the vehicle made sitting down a more violent occupation than expected and I was still gasping, when a uniformed fellow accosted me and grunted, 'Whereyagoin'?'

He held a hand out, palm upward, and I presumed he was seeking a fare.

'End of the line, if you please?' I said.

The man had a full beard and bushy moustaches, which were both stained with some brownish liquid.

'A quarter,' he said and he let out a jet of tobacco juice which struck the floor of the vehicle scarce an inch from my recently acquired boot.

I laughed in his face and hooked a coin of much smaller denomination from a tiny pocket in the gaudy waistcoat. I dropped the battered metal into his hand and said, 'Not today, sir. Not today.'

He spat again, this time striking the upper of my left boot, but I let it pass. Opposite me sat a woman of about five and twenty, decorously dressed, but unescorted.

'If you please,' I was at a loss how to address her, I admit, 'could you tell me if all of these contraptions proceed at this breakneck rate?

'I believe the driver is on his way to the Yaller House.' She made a face suggesting that this was some euphemism for the most repugnant of outhouses.

'I'm sorry, but what exactly might a "Yaller House" be?' I thought it a civil enough question.

The young lady sniffed and said, 'Yaller, like the colour, Mister.'

I resolved to stay on the car until the end of the line, or at least until the driver was relieved. The Yellow House had received the most approving comments during the longshoremen's discussion of whorehouses.

The horse-drawn vehicle came to a precipitate halt at the corner of 21st Street. Up ahead Jefferson Pratte Avenue crossed Olive Street; it looked a more likely place for a sporting establishment than anything immediately visible. The driver leapt from the cab, tossing the reins to the fellow who had taken my money. I disembarked myself, proposing to follow the driver. First, however, I approached the fellow newly charged with the responsibility for the vehicle.

'This seems a strange way of operating transportation, sir,' I said.

'Conductor got the money, friend, may as well give him charge o' thuther val-ya-bles.'

How bizarre I found this American trait of appropriating the musical for almost any purpose. A jog trot sufficed to place myself close enough to the delinquent driver to follow without arousing too much suspicion. My quarry, head well forward and shoulders hunched, walked as though in a hurry for some appointment, looking neither left nor right. 21st Street became Mercer Street and the man passed someone who might well have been his twin, judging by the clothing and demeanour. Each growled a greeting to the other and within short moments my fellow had entered a building on the left. I found myself at the threshold of a house that most assuredly was not yellow.

It was brick: dull, smoke-discoloured, common brick. The building, had it been named for any colour, would surely have been 'The Bistre House'. Grey pilasters flanked a less than ostentatious door. There was no handle or knob to the exterior, nor any nameplate. Two brass digits were affixed to the un-prepossessing brick on the left of the door. Below the number 13 was a bell-pull. Operation of this rewarded me with a wait of some minutes, whereupon the door opened to the minimum extent required for a walleye to take account of the figure before it.

'I am informed that these are the premises known as The Yellow House, is it so?'

The eye disappeared with the closure of the door. This state lasted no more than the blink of a more pulchritudinous eye than the one recently encountered.

The door opened wide to disclose a woman. Tall, by any estimation, she was elegantly dressed by the standards of St Louis. A long skirt with a minimum of crinoline, with much less flare than would be considered usual in Paris or London. It gave a pleasing bulk to her figure in the appropriate places and flattered an already slim waist. A face belonging to a woman of relatively mature years crowned this impressive shape, but that was not the most striking thing about the woman. Her complexion was a thing of beauty, no artifice – whether cream or powder – hid any blemishes, for there were none. And the colour was beautiful – that of amber sand. The establishment had been named in her honour, then.

Her voice was like the mellow tones of an oboe.

'Welcome stranger, we are glad you did not pass by.'

Quite to whom this pronoun referred, I was not sure. The owner of the alarming walleye was not in evidence, nor was anyone else, aside from the elegant lady herself. I had been admitted to a darkly dusty vestibule. Lighting was afforded by a damnable few candles. Some stood in candelabra on whatnots hard against half-panelled walls, others were in sconce-like affairs affixed at uncertain angles upon the walls themselves. The woman crooked a finger and I enjoyed the grace of her movement from the rear aspect as she led me to a further door at the end of the vestibule.

She ushered me through the door into a large salon. There were numerous chaises longues and many odalisques to decorate them. Again, I was struck by the rich variety of customer: my erstwhile driver was not the only horny-handed working man on display. Even so, I saw one or two exceptionally well-dressed gentlemen. Admittedly, they were each in the company of more than one of the more beautiful jewels of the establishment, whilst the driver was in the company of a most broken-down jade.

'Take a seat, if you would prefer. Someone will provide you with refreshment, in any event,' the woman said, and she floated away. My eye caught a portly fellow lighting a cigar for a statuesque female companion. To their left was a diminutive fellow who was burying his head in the navel of a young woman whose skin was of a singularly cuprous hue.

I stood a little awkwardly under a hundred-candle chandelier in the middle of the large room until a sweet young lady of little more than fourteen approached.

'Would yuh like somethin'?' She drew a toe back and

forth along the carpet and looked up at me from under her bangs.

'I'd like a brandy if you have such a thing.'

She twisted a finger in a curl at the side of her head. 'Anythin' else?'

'A woman of mature years for preference.'

She made what she doubtless considered an attractive pout and then her way to a small bar in the corner, where she instructed the man behind it to affect at least the first of my requirements.

One of the better-dressed fellows caught my eye and beckoned me over.

'First time, sir?' he said, in a booming voice that ought to have caused every head to turn. They did not, but then I supposed any bawdy house lived by discretion, even in St Louis.

'I am newly in St Louis, sir.'

He was a stout fellow, with a high forehead and the thin-lipped mouth of a lawyer. Clean shaven, his jowls indicated more than fifty years of living well. He pointed to the woman on his left, an Hispanic-looking woman who reached no higher than his shoulder. Heavily rouged and powdered, nonetheless the most striking thing about her appearance was her hot-eyed gaze.

'This is Lola Montez.'

I looked from the woman to him and back again.

'Aw hell, she ain't the real Lola, that's just her nawm de ploom,' he guffawed. 'And this is Muskrat Jaw Jean.'

On his right stood as mannish a figure as ever I had seen in female attire, outside of a few specialised houses in Holborn. Aside from the absence of curves, her visage gave indication as to the origin of her sobriquet. The poor woman was entirely deficient in the matter of a chin, to the extent that she appeared to have no lower mandible at all. I imagined that this made it difficult for her to speak and perhaps that was her attraction.

The man thrust out a somewhat meaty, and, as it proved, clammy hand. 'Claiborne Fox Jackson, Governor of Missouri,' he said.

'Anson Northrup, gentleman-at-large.'

I could not imagine why he felt it acceptable to laugh quite so loud at this point.

A moment later we were approached by the Madame, if such she were. She handed me a balloon of what I hoped was brandy. She arched an eyebrow and said, 'Might I relieve you of your burden, sir?'

I followed her gaze and realised that I was still carrying the carpetbag. Perhaps this incongruity had occasioned Jackson's laughter. She grasped the bag, making light of its weight, and enquired as to whether she should place it in one of the guest rooms. I replied in the affirmative.

Turning to Jackson, I asked him, 'Who is that woman?'

'She's the Yaller.'

'The Yellow?' I knew well what he meant. However, I was intrigued to see how the Southron might elaborate.

'She's an octaroon – and a free person of colour,' his lip curled in a sneer.

'Does she have a name, sir?'

'Some call her Zoe Terrebonne. I reckon she gave it herself,' the politician replied.

I took a sip of the brandy, it was a fine Armagnac, if I was not very much mistaken.

'What brings you to Missouri, Northrup?' Jackson asked. The two women remained silent, occasionally stroking some part of the Governor's person as the whim took them.

'Recently having returned from England, I am travelling my native land, the better to acquaint myself with it.'

'How long didya spend over there, Northrup? I swear you talk just like a Britisher.'

'Twenty years. It was indeed an education.'

Jackson let out a snort worthy of a barrow. I reflected it was not the only touch of the porcine about him.

'Edyoo-kay-shone, bah! Well you know what we say in Missouri about soap and education!'

As it happened, I did: it was one of several flippant remarks made by Mr Clemens during the interminable stage-coach journey.

'Anyhow, I won't hold neither agin you, if you'll join us.'

The two women smiled at me; Muskrat Jaw Jean's attempt was fascinating, if repellent. I made a bow to Lola and Jean and said that I'd be delighted. This minor lie was punished almost immediately by a lengthy lecture by Jackson on Missouri politics. The man was at particular pains to confirm that something called 'secession' was both inevitable and imminent. It sounded to me like some religious business.

In my thus far brief dealings with the natives of Missouri, I had noted a preference of the indigenous population to pronounce the name of their state as 'Mizzoo-ruh'. This and their propensity for anecdote and aphorism made them profoundly irritating. Extrication from this deadly company was not effected by me. My salvation occurred when the politician took himself off to the stairs beside the bar in the company of Lola Montez. Reasoning that any overnight use of the 'guest rooms' would necessitate the company of one of the establishment's employees, I informed Muskrat Jaw Jean that I should be delighted to make her closer acquaintance. In my heart of hearts I would have preferred to invite Miss Terrebonne to accompany me. Doubtless the invitation would have been refused.

I closed the door of a small, but surprisingly clean bedroom behind us. The carpetbag stood unopened on the floor-boards beside an iron bed. It would be a night relatively free of insects, at least. My intention was to pay for the girl's company without recourse to her charms, chiefly with the goal of exploring the bag's contents. It was not to be: Muskrat Jaw Jean was enthusiastic in her work. Moreover, her mandibular deficiency permitted her to demonstrate several tricks that excited even my own jaded palate.

My opportunity to study the contents of the carpetbag was not entirely lost. Miss Jean's eponymous peculiarity occasioned a deal of snoring and whistling sufficient to rival a large steam engine. I slept not long, but deeply. When I opened my repeater watch, once the property of one late Reverend Parminter, the time was a quarter of four. Having performed my ablutions, excepting a much-wished-for shave, I dressed to the accompaniment of Muskrat Jean's unusual symphony.

Upon opening the bag I found a frock coat identical to the one I was wearing. Close inspection revealed hidden pockets in sleeve linings and sundry other locations. A dozen unbroken packs of playing cards had been covered by the coat. Next to the playing cards was a box about the size of a writing slope. Made from walnut, it had been polished to a high sheen. It was not locked. I opened it. Miniature bottles, a round two dozen of them, nestled in especially fashioned compartments in a velvet lining. The bottles were each and every one stoppered with tiny corks and bore a numbered label. Removing a cork at random, from a bottle numbered 13 as it transpired, I sniffed and smelled an alcoholic aroma. A sip was sufficient to provoke a choking such as a soup-ladle full of mustard might have done. In the lid of the box was a pocket. I pulled out a folded sheet of yellowed wood-pulp paper. It listed the contents of the bottles. No 13 was named as 'Kentucky Corn Whiskey'. Alongside this appellation, in a different hand was written, 'Davis, Todd County: For sale west of the Brazos only'. A dreadfully wild location it must have been, at that.

A creased and grubby card had fallen out as I removed the list of contents from the pocket: '*Anson Northrup: Purveyor of Fine American Whiskeys*'. On the reverse side of the card, the annotating hand from the list of contents had written, '*Knights of the Golden Castle. Copperheads?*'

I replaced the list and the card, although there were more respectable examples of it in the inside pocket of the frock coat.

The last remaining item in the bag was a tiny pistol, of the type I believed was known as a derringer. It was holstered in a contraption apparently designed to be strapped around the forearm and concealed by a roomy coat sleeve. I removed my frock coat and strapped the peculiar holster to my lower arm. Not surprisingly, it was well concealed and no more uncomfortable than a tight shirtsleeve.

I shook Muskrat Jean awake, gave her a silver dollar and made my way downstairs.

Mme Terrebonne was behind the counter of the bar, a brandy glass before her. She placed another next to it on noting my arrival. The salon was otherwise deserted. She poured two generous measures of spirit into the glasses. I picked one up.

'Your health, Mme Terrebonne!' I said.

'Your bill, sir. Five dollars.'

I had but four left in Northrup's purse. She proved herself most perspicacious for she added, 'Or you could do something for me.'

My hopes were cruelly dashed when she handed me a packet about the size of a journal or notebook.

'It needs to go to Hannibal,' she told me.

'Who is that?' It seemed a reasonable question.

'Hannibal, Missouri. A hundred miles upriver. You'll be on one of the riverboats soon enough.'

'Will I?'

She nodded at the gaudy waistcoat, 'Where else would someone like you be headed?'

'If I do, to whom shall I deliver the packet?' I asked.

'Winona Shepherd. She will be on the shore when your riverboat docks.'

'How does she know which boat I will be on?'

'She meets them all, Mr Northrup. She will ask for news of Levi Coffin, just hand over the packet when you are asked about him.'

Since surely the Brothers Clemens had long since caught an earlier riverboat, I thought it might be safe to play the gambler aboard another. A little practice with the concealed pockets and I felt sure I could make shift to earn some money. I asked the madam to advance me the riverboat fare. She fished in a pocket in the side of her skirts, tossed a double eagle onto the polished wood of the bar and motioned me to the door with one hand, whilst removing the brandy glass from mine with the other.

3

On Mercer Street, the cold was little mitigated by a brittle sun. Deciding to forego the pleasures of the horse-drawn streetcar, I commenced walking riverward. Towards the commercial wharves I stopped at the sign of a striped pole. Not one customer was inside the barber's; the aproned one himself was asleep in the customary high chair. The fellow's skin was mighty scrofulous and no great advertisement to his skills. His snores resounded through the empty shop. I was already turning away, when a dark-skinned hand's finger beckoned me out of the establishment's door once more. Once outside I was confronted by a handsome black man in new leather boots and ragged hand-me-downs of uncertain fit.

'Haircut, suh?' he asked, giving my waistcoat a keen look.

'It is a shave I need, young man.' I rubbed a hand along my jaw, it rasped like a lucifer on sandstone.

'Yuh goin' on the boats?'

I almost changed my plans on the basis of yet another assumption made about them. On reflection, I decided that I should change the waistcoat for another at the earliest opportunity.

'That I am, though what business it is of yours, I cannot say, boy.'

'Boats got barbers, suh. Mah brutha is barber on the *Gran' Turk.*'

I laughed, admiring the young man's enterprise.

'Let us go, then, to this *Grand Turk.*'

Thus, passage paid, I sat two hours later in the barber's chair aboard the *Grand Turk*, steam-driven riverboat, bound upriver along the Mississippi out of St Louis. The boat itself had lost any pretensions to its title, if ever it had had any. Alongside, it had looked of middling size amid the many vessels intent on navigating the big river. The superstructure was badly in need of a coat of paint, the colours being the faded tones of a down-at-heel fairground attraction. There was little to see of the hull, for – in common with the other boats in evidence – it appeared to have little draught and no great evidence of any hull above the waterline. The paddles looked in poor repair; I noted the odd missing spoke in the great wheels.

The barber, sprucely turned out, was a tiresomely self-important fellow, much enamoured of recounting the peccadilloes of such passengers of quality as had travelled aboard the *Grand Turk*. Amid his salacious digressions, I learned that the tub was out of New Orleans, did not have a full complement of passengers, much less freight, and would not provide much pickings for a gambling man.

It was an inescapable truth: the waistcoat would have to go.

The boat had pulled away from the wharf at last. Upon the promenade deck what passengers there were stood waving at loved ones or spitting over the side in good riddance. It was moving sluggishly, turning as heavily as a matron at a ball. The passengers on deck numbered around thirty or so; doubtless there were more below, or on other parts of the deck. A wind was blowing, no pleasant zephyr, it was as bitter as the still brittle sunlight. I buttoned up my frock coat, as much to hide the waistcoat as against the cold. My eye perused the assembled passengers; choosing an expectorator rather than a waver, I accosted a squat fellow, whose stomach and florid cheeks betokened an acquaintance with the grape and grain. His moustaches were grandiose even by colonial standards; the hair on his head, if clean, might have been described as golden blond.

'Hullo,' I thrust out a hand and attempted the more robust manners of the indigenous population. 'Anson Northrup, pleased to meet you.'

'William Haycock, cain't say likewise. But if yuh'll stand me a drink, I'll try to oblige.'

We repaired to a saloon bar, which was superficially similar to that of the St Louis establishment where I had recently acquired my attire. It differed, in the main, on a question of scale and, it must be said, of quality and cleanliness. Naturally, Mr Haycock ordered for us both the national spirit – that is, something purporting to be whiskey. I sipped at mine, realising that it was quite as foul as Drummer's Sample Number 13, although it numbed the throat a little less. Equally naturally, he allowed me to pay, after instructing the man tending the bar to leave the bottle.

The clientele was entirely male, although aside from Mr Haycock and myself, these numbered only three: all standing as far from each other at the bar as space would allow. Each had a whiskey bottle and a small glass fit to contain only the product of a brief inversion of said bottle. I imagined that there might be more profit in Mr Northrup's alternative profession than the taste of Number 13 had led me to believe. These three solitary drinkers took only sufficient notice of us newcomers as perhaps we merited, certainly in comparison to the more serious business of ensuring their whiskey bottles were emptied, or going blind, whichever came first.

'Reckon we'll sit, Mr Northrup.'

Haycock smirked and gestured to a rough table. Though not of exquisite craftsmanship or any particular value, it had – perhaps wisely – been bolted to the deck. The chairs around it had not. We sat facing one another with the whole width of the round deal between us. Haycock's glass being empty he filled it and poured a lesser amount into mine, since it was yet half-full.

'First time upriver?' The irritating smile was still present.

'In point of fact it is, sir.'

'Call me Bill.' He let out a laugh, mayhap occasioned by the unbuttoning of my frock coat and the glimpse of the waistcoat it afforded.

'Anson, you may call me, if you like,' I retorted.

'Weeeeell, Anson, how 'bout a little Poker?' He produced a grimy, dog-eared pack of cards. 'Guess you know the English deck, huh?'

'Of course, I am recently returned from there.'

'Shore you are, Anson, shore you are,' Bill said.

Familiar as I might have been with the fifty-two-card pack, I knew nothing of Poker, save that it was the game of choice on the river. I had not thought to play myself before a chance to observe others first. Fortunately, I had experience of both drawing and gaming rooms in London and did not disgrace myself when he handed me the grubby pasteboard. A simple riffle, followed by a hindoo and I handed him his cards, which he accepted with a grunt. He dealt the cards in singleton fashion and then produced from his pocket a quantity of markers about the size of small coins, painted in various colours which had faded through time and handling. One of these he placed atop the stock.

'Got no markers, Anson?' His eyebrows lifted.

I shook my head, 'In the cabin.'

'You got cash, right?'

He swept all but the marker on the reserve cards into his hat and dropped the headgear to the floor beside him. Then he placed Half-Eagles, Quarter-Eagles, silver dollars and lesser coins, right down to a half-cent, on the table in front of him. I emptied my pockets in imitation though with less resultant noise on the wood of the table.

He picked up the cards, as did I. What I had appeared valueless, being of various suits and non-consecutive in number. I had not even a pair. Bill looked at me expectantly: I pushed a copper penny towards the centre of the table. Bill's laugh was hearty and his bet was twenty-five times the value of mine. I matched it.

'How many?' he picked up the stock, brushing the marker to the side.

I kept two, an Ace and pipped card of the same suit. Bill dealt three in quick succession.

'I'll take two,' he said and dealt himself the cards.

My situation had improved, I believed, basing my assumption on my experience of alehouse Brag in Cheapside. I laid another quarter on the table. Bill pushed a dollar forward. It became merely a contest of wills, in my view. My means being exhausted, my opponent appeared to take pity on me saying, 'Hell, I'd like to see those cards, Anson.'

I laid the black Aces and Eights on the table and the Jack of Diamonds beside them.

'Well don't that beat all!' He guffawed and I saw tears start to his eyes.

I reached for the pot, but he stayed my hand and revealed

his own: red Aces and Eights with the Jack of Clubs for company. He pointed a long index finger at my chest and said, 'Yessir, Anson Northrup, you are either the luckiest – or unluckiest – man alive.'

Rather foolishly, I thought, Haycock pushed half of the pile toward me, which meant I had, in fact, made a small profit on my first venture into the mysteries of Poker. Though but half the bottle had been consumed during our brief hand, my new friend made for the bar to purchase another. On his return, he took a seat facing away from the other customers and the bar and stationed himself at my right hand. He pushed the half-empty whiskey bottle toward me and de-corked his. Then he leaned toward me, wide-eyed.

'You a friend of the railroad?' he asked.

'To tell the truth, Haycock, of late my funds have not permitted me to travel so luxuriously. Besides, I prefer the river.'

He made a sound between a clearing of the throat and an exhalation, 'What I mean is, are you a shepherd?'

I choked a little on the whiskey, not entirely due to its particular charms.

'No, my talents have been employed in other fields.'

Haycock twirled the end of one of his prodigious moustaches, before saying, 'An agent? You understand?'

I did not, but after brief consideration, decided to attempt to descry what the loon was talking about.

'An agent, how did you guess, Haycock?'

The guffaw that greeted this query lifted the moustaches as a strong wind might lift a lady's skirt.

'Hellfire, Anson, ain't no riverboat gambler knowed as little about cards as you do! Who ya meetin'?'

'Surely you cannot expect me to reply?'

'Course not. But...' he broke off and looked to either side, 'my paw's a stationmaster, back home in Illinois.'

He gave a slow wink, which did not, as he perhaps supposed it might, enlighten me.

'The railroad? I see.'

'Cargo,' he said and gave two vigorous nods.

'Quite,' I replied.

'Yuh got ta be meetin' somebody, or else why the vest, huh?'

Why indeed? I thought, but merely nodded at the man.

'Reckon it's a stockholder,' he nodded again and laid a finger alongside his nose. 'Don't worry, Anson, my paw's been sellin' tickets on the Gospel Train as long as anybody. I'll git along now and you can look out fer yer meetin'. You need me, Bill Haycock'll come.'

With that he took his bottle and headed, rather unsteadily I thought, above decks.

4

The boat seemed to be making erratic progress upriver. The swilling of the whiskey in the bottle caused by this left me a little bilious. I had heard that navigating the river required the services of a pilot, which fellow was normally hired by the Captain of the vessel out of his own pocket. These pilots claimed knowledge of every shoal and bank of the river. I took myself forward to see this marvel of memory at work firsthand.

Not unexpectedly, the 'pilot-house' as it was termed, stood near the bow of the vessel. It was wooden framed, scarce better than a skillion superstructure, though half-glazed, doubtless to offer good all-round visibility. A stern-looking fellow stared forward as if intent on reading the river. A bluff and portly man hovered at his shoulder; his eyes darted hither and yon as if Tennyson's Kraken were about to emerge from the water at any moment. He caught sight of me and waved me in.

The space was surprisingly large, accommodating all three of us and still with room enough to invite half the passenger manifest in, had the Captain felt so inclined. At the windows – although I could envision no occasion for their use

– were garish curtains in gold and red. There was room for a well-padded sofa and a high-backed banquette. Above this seating was a double-doored hatch to the rear wall, between the two stern-facing windows. A pot-bellied stove stood on the floor, flue rising up and through the high ceiling, although evidently the hardy river-men felt its ignition unnecessary. For carpet there was oilcloth and I supposed that at New Orleans near the mouth of the river, estuarine conditions might make for a rough ride. The brass knobs for the bells were highly polished and the wheel, which stood as high as a man, was exquisitely carved. In general, the pilot house appeared to be the only part of the riverboat that received any kind of attention.

The Captain, portly though he was, was enveloped in a quasi-military coat festooned with braids and buttons, whose gilt was no more than a little tarnished. Atop his head he wore a battered cap with a peak and altogether too much ornamentation. The pilot by contrast was simply dressed in a long frock coat and a round shaped hat – also with a peak – in a dull, grey colour.

'Passenger, what's your name? You're welcome in here to settle an argument.'

The Captain's voice was as bluff as his manner.

'Anson Northrup, Captain. You have the advantage of me, sirs.'

I made no more than the sketch of a bow.

'Fancy manners, Pilot, huh? I'm Cap'n Holden Grey, this here is Pilot Ireland.'

He jerked an elbow into the Pilot's back, but he gave nary a flinch, nor any indication that his person had been assaulted. The river took all his attention. I wondered how any kind of argument could have been ongoing between them.

'See, it's this.'

Pausing, he took a pipe from his pocket and started to

puff at it, without recourse to lighting it. Perhaps he took sufficient comfort merely by having the stem between his lips.

'Pilot Ireland reckons,' he let out a laugh, 'a man cain't recognise as a gommint, one that's a slave's gommint too! Hell, what kinda talk is that?'

Before I could answer, the Pilot spat with delicate accuracy into a cuspidor at the Captain's feet and interjected, 'Majority don't make for justice, jus' cuz there's more of 'em. Cap'n.'

'Didja ever hear the like, Mr Northrup?'

Rather than confess that I hadn't, I replied that it was certainly a point of view.

The Captain spluttered a little, pipe-stem still clenched by some miracle between his teeth.

'Well, it just ain't...' Here his chest inflated to such a size as to almost fill the coat he was wearing before he let out, with a bellow, 'DEMOCRATIC!'

The Pilot seemed undisturbed by this outburst, merely striking the target of the cuspidor unerringly once more and adding, 'Man's only obliged to do what he thinks is right, Cap'n.'

The Captain seemed on the very point of bursting – his heart, if not the coat. At that moment there was a timid knock on the pilot house door.

'C'mon, Boy!' Captain Grey bellowed.

A young negro entered, his white apron providing a violent contrast with the black of the rest of his uniform. He looked like a butler or an employee of the most exclusive of hotels. He bobbed his head at each of us in turn and strode over to the double-hatch. Swinging the doors wide, he revealed that a dumb-waiter serviced those on duty, since a large tray held a glass decanter, a plate piled high with chops and the glasses and crockery to facilitate their consumption.

The Captain said, ' You'll join us for a little sump'm, Mr Northrup. I enjoy the company of a clear-thinkin' man.'

He shot a look at the Pilot as he said this, but the man's eyes remained fixed on the river.

The Captain informed me that the Texas Tender would remain until we had finished our repast. The latter nodded his head vigorously in affirmation. There was no table, so the man merely held the tray at chest height, whilst the Captain piled a quantity of roast pork chops upon a plate and gestured to me to take the remaining three on the serving dish. The Pilot reached behind him to the Captain's plate and snagged a chop without a backward glance.

Conversation was conducted, by the Master of the vessel for the most part, in between much smacking of lips and chewing of chops. He gave me the benefit of more of his political and philosophical insights. Most of these proved to be a contradictory mish-mash of half-remembered quotes and a peculiar idea of Bentham-ite theories, wherein the principle of the greatest good for the greatest number was somehow *not* undermined by a strong belief in the credo, 'Every man for himself'. The Pilot was not moved to interject, no doubt relieved that some other soul was present to bear the burden of the Captain's company.

Wiping his hands and his jowls on a swatch of cloth from his voluminous coat, he added as a coda, 'Mr Jefferson Davis, he done the right thing, 'at's a fact.'

The Pilot made his last contribution to the political debate with a further jet at the cuspidor.

'Welll, Mr Northrup, it shore has been a pleasure gittin' the benefit of yore 'pinion. Me and the Pilot's got a tricky tract a-comin' up, so if'n you'll allow the Texas Tender to escort yuh aft, I'd be much obliged.'

The Pilot grunted, 'T'ain't bad 'til Cairo, Cap'n.'

The Texas Tender and I made our way out. Surprisingly, the dumb-waiter's use was restricted to the conveyance of in-coming food, not out-going dishes, and he seemed more in need of my assistance than the reverse.

The young man jumped and the crockery rattled, when I addressed him directly. Merely having asked his name, I was a little taken aback by his reaction. He stood stock still, looked back at the pilot house, some yards behind us, looked to the larboard side and then stared for a few moments toward the stern.

'Thomas Jefferson, is ma given name. You heard what the Cap'n says. You 'on't need no name for me, suh.'

'Well, Tom, I should like to see every part of the vessel. In the interests of... curiosity.'

'Yuh mean the galley? Or whut?'

'Everything,' I said.

I had hooked my thumbs in the pockets of my waistcoat, as I had seen Haycock do, and attempted to look the young boy in the eye. This proved impossible, as his eye was drawn to the waistcoat, while his jaw drooped leaving him open-mouthed. He recovered himself a little and said the strangest thing:

'You Northrup? You him?'

Which utterance begged the only possible answer, 'Yes.'

My education at the feet – and sundry other parts – of a lunatic in an Edinburgh asylum had been, there was no gain-saying it, eclectic. The manner of its imparting was indeed rare, depending entirely on which historical figure he believed himself to be at the time. He had a great tendency toward Greek philosophers, but on reflection this may have been driven by a secret admiration toward their concept of the relation-ship between teacher and pupil. He was at great pains to instil in me a belief in Chryssipus's notion of causal necessity. My favourite aspect of this idea involved an assumption that 'every-thing that happens is preceded by something with which it is

causally connected'. After all, if he had not chosen to educate
the boy in the asylum, he – or rather I – would not have stolen
his identity. A man who reinvents himself once, will have no
hesitation in doing so again, and therefore, with that one word
of affirmation, so I did.

I followed Tom below decks. He did indeed lead me
toward the galley, but only to divest himself of the tray and its
contents. We passed through the galley, toward the stern. The
engine room, naturally enough, was in the waist of the vessel, so as to be located near the great paddles to the port and
starboard sides of the vessel. The way through was strait, and
hot. Four enormous black fellows shovelled coal into the steam
engine, whilst the shortest man in the engine room looked
on, swearing oaths and sweating more than any of the men
doing the work. He took off his peaked cap and stared at
me, not addressing me directly but merely continuing to blas-
pheme, whether at the heat or the stokers, I knew not. We
entered a very narrow passage along the side of a mountainous
heap of coal in the next compartment, my own raiment was
covered in smuts and soot moments afterward. Tom's apron
remained pristine white and his trousers a glossy black. This
compartment was necessarily long. At the end of it we came
upon a storeroom. It was filled with sacks and crates and Tom
informed me that it was the dry store for the galley. It might
have measured twelve feet by twelve, the roof was sufficiently
high to allow both of us to stand upright. On the far wall,
there was a... hatch, I suppose I must call it, although it was
a wooden door as would not have disgraced a farmer's out-
building. It had a padlock through a hasp arrangement, but a
determined child could have forced entry. Nonetheless, Tom
produced a key and unlocked the door.

This compartment was smaller still than the dry store, by
about a third. Cots stacked one atop the other in threes lined

the walls, there were eighteen in all. No grown man could have slept in them, except if they curled up like a dog.

'Who sleeps here, Tom?'

'We all do, Missuh Northrup. It's the Texas, leastways, our part of it.'

'All?'

'All the coloured people,' he said. 'They's our bunks.' He said it proudly.

'But...' I counted the bunks again.

Something moved on three of the uppermost bunks. A sleepy voice enquired, 'What the hell's the time? Ah ain't had my turn!'

'Tain't time yet, Grover, go back to sleep,' Tom said. 'Missuh Northrup, lookit,' he whispered, pointing to the deck in the centre of the room. An exasperated sigh came from one of the bunks.

I saw nothing, save that the deck was covered in sawdust. Tom pointed a toe and daintily described a square in the sawdust. Suddenly, he squatted and removed a section of the deck with his fingertips. Holding the square in one hand he pointed down into the dark.

'Lookit, Missuh Northrup!'

There was a cramped space, I could see water in the bottom. It was clearly a space between the Negro quarters and the keel of the riverboat.

'At what, Tom?'

'Missuh Northrup, ain't nowhere written the Gospel Train gotta travel on rails.'

It was the second time this peculiarly named mode of transport had been mentioned to me. Although not yet sure what it might be, I was sure that it did not involve an engine or any kind of rolling stock.

'You're a slave Tom, are you not?' I asked him.

'We all slaves, 'cept the barber, Missuh Northrup,' he replied.

'Do you not think of escape, of freedom?'

He looked at me as though he had never met a duller specimen.

'Ain't nobody free, less'n we all free, Missuh Northrup.'

'And what has this to do with me?' I asked.

Most definitely, I wished I hadn't, for a strong arm was around my neck and something sharp pressed into my ribs. Tom's face loomed close to mine, the large man behind me said nothing, but from the smell of him, it was one of the stokers. The waiter's eyes had slitted and he hissed at me. 'You shore you's Northrup?'

It was not the moment for panic, so I merely answered, 'You have seen the vest, who else would I be?'

The grip on my neck did not noticeably slacken – and Tom's face reflected both doubt and distrust in equal measure. If the moment was then more appropriate for panic, there was little I could do but rely on the best of lies, that is, a simulacrum of the truth.

'Don't be hasty,' I began. 'I have as yet received no instructions. I am aboard this tub merely by chance. There is a rendezvous I must attend in Hannibal, I am aboard the *Grand Turk* solely to effect my arrival in that place.'

The arm tightened and Tom's voice remained full of venom.

'Ron-day-voo? What's 'at?'

I felt that unless I could get him to address me once more as Northrup, all might conceivably be lost, and I could well make the rest of the trip upriver beneath the trap-door, in the depths of the hull. At least until my remains caused sufficient odour to occasion a clandestine jettison of them into the wide Mississippi river.

'A meeting. I'm to wait for someone to ask me for news of Levi Coffin.'

Tom's eyes widened at the mention of this name, and I was relieved to feel a little less pressure around my throat. I did not mention the packet I was to deliver.

'Might be alright, Washington, if'n he knows the President uv the Railroad.'

Tom looked past me at my captor, who though a little gentler in his treatment of my person, still afforded me no chance of escape. A deep and cultured voice caused my ears themselves to vibrate:

'It might indeed. But why should we take a chance?'

I was desperate to see the face of this man, but could no more turn in his grasp than dance a polka.

'Shore don't talk like an Illinois man, he fum Philadelphy, you think?'

The hearty laugh caused a great deal of pain to my tympanum.

'No, Thomas, he's not from Philadelphia, he's a Britisher.'

'Indeed I am not! I am recently returned from those shores after many years. I am as American as either of you.'

And was this not so? Since they were slaves, they were surely not American citizens.

The dark voice rumbled again, 'With whom is the supposed rendezvous, Mr Northrup?'

I felt that the sarcasm enveloping this appellation might well leave some physical mark on my ear. However, at least he had used it.

'Winona, Winona Shepherd.'

Thankfully his grip was released before his laugh filled the slaves' bunk room and deafened me. I turned to get a look at the face of the man with the educated tones. He was enormous, as befit a stoker of engines. Undoubtedly handsome, he looked at me with an intelligence in his gaze that he surely must have kept hidden in the company of Missouri white folks. He held out a hand.

'George Washington Irving, pleased to meet you, Mr Northrup, if that's who you be.'

I shook it and moved to take my own hand back, but he held it in a grip as strong as he had placed round my neck.

'Best you be him, too. Mr Northrup. The big river's a dangerous place. You get along topside, now, where you belong. Better take him back Thomas, I'm not convinced this fellow could find his posterior with both hands.'

Tom laughed, although I was unsure whether he understood the joke, or simply acknowledged that it had been made at my expense.

I resolved to check the contents of the package given me in the Yaller House at the earliest opportunity.

5

My cabin, of necessity, was no luxurious stateroom, rather a singular version, if a little better appointed, of the slaves' quarters below. The bunk, for it was too humble to aspire to being a bed, had apparently dictated the length of the cabin wall, rather than vice versa. A large chest served as the only furniture and there was, in fact, little room for more than the porcelain any traveller requires. I was not discontented, however. The alternative had been a barely plusher version of the slaves' quarters available above decks for the more impecunious passenger. The fellow I had purchased passage from on the quayside in St Louis had intimated that – between Agent's sales and ad hoc arrangements like my own – this often meant a top-and-tail arrangement for some legs of the journey. Having taken the carpetbag from the chest, I removed the Yaller House packet and sprawled on the bunk to examine my prize closely.

The packet was wrapped in oilskin and sealed with string and wax. These latter I removed with a knife, one of the few items – other than the watch – I had kept from my own possessions. On opening the oilskin the dusty smell of foxed pages and damp leather associated with old books met my nostrils, occasioning a fit of sneezing. I no longer enjoyed ancient tomes in the way I once had, having found – contrary to Mr Pope's belief – drinking deep of the Pierian Spring to be ill-advised, since a deal of learning had often proved to be far more dangerous than a little, at least to me. The book was about the size of a journal, but it was not any such thing. The binding was unmarked by any title or sign of ownership. Inside it seemed like a ledger or some kind of book of accounts in miniature.

The first page was filled in so:

Station	Station Master	Stockholders	Conductors	Pass. Max
NO	23	5	25	15-20 p.n.
NO-StL	17	3	20	20
BR	-"-	-"-	17	20
Na	2	1	4	10

There was more of the same until 'St L' appeared in the left-hand column on the following page and became the left-hand notation in the extreme right-hand column. The other notation of the pair read 'M-StP'. This state of affairs continued through four pages of the ledger. Subsequently came a list of digraphs, such as 'CL' or 'AN'. Each of these were annotated to the right hand of the page with any one of 'StaM', 'St', 'Sth' or 'Ab'. There were hundreds of these entries, taking up many pages. I could make neither head nor tail of it. My conversation with Bill Haycock did come to mind since he had been at pains to quiz me whether I was to meet a stockholder. However, since this made the ledger no less of a puzzle, I was about to throw the book to the ground in disgust when I caught sight of a drawing inside the back cover. A title of sorts appeared above and to the left. It read 'Miss R'. There was no delightful cartoon of a nude below it, however, but a representation of what I took to be the very river I was navigating. At the southerly end a tidy hand had placed in minuscule lettering 'NO'; at the other extreme the same hand had scribed 'MstP'. At the foot of the page, I read, 'M to Can, how?'

It seemed a most unlikely treasure map. Indeed, I felt that it perhaps held no value at all – save to the earlier incarnation of Anson Northrup. I clapped the book shut; it made a satisfying sound, but the dust which shot out of the binding brought on another fit of sneezing. When I had recovered myself, I looked down at the book still in my hand. Something was hidden in the spine, between the glued leaves and the binding. I pulled it out, with the aid of the point of my knife. It was yellowed rag-paper with a most indistinct watermark. Most likely this betokened much handling rather than any great antiquity. Unfolding it was a delicate matter, the creases caused by the folds so sharply deep as to have almost perished the paper.

It appeared to be some kind of official Warrant. It read as follows:

From the Office of the Governor of the State of South Carolina:

Be advised that the bearer of this Warrant John Mudsill has been engaged on State business in a plenipotentiary capacity within the United States.

It is requested that all Federal and State authorities render any and all assistance to the bearer on request without cavil or protest.

It was adorned with a complicated design at the foot of the page. This I assumed to be the State Seal or some such. Next to it was a signature with the name and title written more legibly beneath: 'James Henry Hammond, Gov. South Carolina'.

I wondered who John Mudsill was. It was a name I associated only with an inflammatory speech made several years before. I remembered my surprise at remarking a New York periodical's interest in an obscure politician from the South. That this was the very man who had signed the paper, was more intriguing still. Given what I remembered of the Governor of South Carolina's speech, I thought it not beyond belief that 'John Mudsill' was no more anyone's name than Anson Northrup was mine. None of this, however, gave any clue as to why Northrup had been charged with delivering this paper in such a bizarre manner.

Even carefully folded, the paper would not have survived concealment in its former place, therefore I sequestered it in the middle of the book and replaced the oilskin. I retied the string but took no pains whatever over the wax seal. Anyone who might expect someone to deliver a sealed package intact seemed to me a rare gull indeed.

Pausing only to remove the waistcoat, I resolved to repair to the saloon bar, in hope of some diversion. Of a sudden, I felt the cabin to be smaller yet and wished to be among company, in more spacious accommodations.

On deck, I noted that the *Grand Turk* was making its most dilatory way between two large sandbanks. I stopped to look at the flock of birds on the bank to the port side. An almost impenetrable accent coated the voice in my ear, as I stood at the rail. On bidding him repeat his words several times I gathered that I was looking at 'a gulp of double crested Cormorant, fine river birds as ever were'. The man was dressed in the outré style of the Southern Gentleman of Leisure, with a waistcoat – or vest – as offensive to the eye as the one I had lately discarded.

In the manner that I still found shocking, he thrust out a hand and barked his name:

'Beauregard Duchamp, late of New Orleans, pleased tuh make yuh 'quaintance.'

I sighed and shook his hand, fervently hoping that he was not obsessed with ornithology, a fault which I found difficult to forgive in any man.

There was something bird-like about Duchamp himself. Perhaps it was the incessant chatter that came from his pursed mouth – so like a beak as to make no difference. Or even the violent red of his waistcoat, made so prominent by his bantam chest as to make him seem an over-sized robin red-breast. I proposed making our way to the saloon bar, in the hope that more gregarious customers might be in attendance – and that I might successfully shake him off thereby.

Players were at cards around all of the tables. On the far side of the saloon, Haycock caught my eye and lifted a finger-tip to the brim of his hat. The same three solitary drinkers, or some fellows very like them, were at the front of the bar. The card playing appeared to be quite a boisterous affair, accompanied by a deal of shouting and on one occasion an outbreak of fisticuffs. The loser of this particular altercation left the game, nursing a bloodied nose. Duchamp and I stood at the bar and I bade the barkeeper furnish us with a whiskey each. It seemed a matter of honour among the Americans to demand that the bottle be left at one's disposal, for Duchamp, as Haycock had, did so.

'A vigorous pursuit, this Poker,' I opined.

'Yes, suh, it is that. T'aint po-lite tuh call a man a cheat.'

'Indeed not, even should you know it to be true.'

'A Southern Gentleman will always call a man on such an accusation, Northrup.'

Duchamp held open his ill-fitting coat and I saw a pistol

ensconced in some leather arrangement attached to a belt. The leather gleamed and I fancied it would creak loudly if he moved the hip underneath it suddenly.

'Ah find the Navy Revolver a great defender of a man's honour.'

In common with many of my acquaintance among the short of stature, there was something of the aggressive in everything he said. He espied me looking intently at the pouch containing his firearm and continued:

'Bought it in St Louis, Grimsley & Co. A fine company. Y'all go back to St Loo say Duchamp sent ya, might change the price.'

And there was no reason to believe it wouldn't, although I suspected that any adjustment might be upward.

'Reckon ah'll take that feller's seat in the game, excuse me and all. Ah'll stand y'all a drink, soon as ah take the pot.'

The card table appeared to be the only place where an immediate handshake and blunt introduction was deemed unsuitable, for Duchamp took a seat amid nods and grunts, and waited while the players played out their hands. The winner proved to be a very large man, with a lantern jaw that a great deal of black stubble did more to accentuate than hide. He was smoking a cigar, whose outer wrapping leaf was a violent shade of green rather than a more customary brown. The smell and fog – for it was far denser than smoke – was un-remarked by the other three players, or the newcomer Duchamp. I thought it might prove diverting to watch a hand or two.

The hand-guns belonging to Duchamp's playing partners lay alongside their markers on the table. He had merely undone the flap of his holster after taking his seat. Duchamp's markers seemed to be made of ivory; I noticed that some of the players referred to them as chips. The majority of these, as Haycock's rough-shaped discs had been, were made of wood.

I did note that several seemed to be made of clay; although, if so, these surely would have shattered under the treatment suffered at the table. The game – of course, it was Poker – continued through several hands. Duchamp's pile of chips diminished steadily to the benefit, for the most part, of the fellow smoking the cigar. One of the other two players was worthy of note in as much as he could have passed for Haycock without the grandiose moustaches. The other, however, was a giant of a man, or rather youth. New stubble flawed his creamy young skin. I doubted he had reached sixteen years. He appeared to be playing carefully, no callow enthusiasms betraying his fortune – good or bad – with the cards being dealt him. His wrists and a great deal of forearm were visible below the end of his sleeves, although his clothing appeared quite new. The gun before him on the table was an older, less well-polished version of Duchamp's Navy Colt.

The deal passed to Duchamp for a third time. He began to win, in spectacular fashion, the cards in his hands trumping the pairs and prials that were the best of the others', even after the deal passed to them once more. The cigar smoker let his tobacco go out; the smell remained, while he chewed the stub to a noisome pulp. The boy developed a tic in his cheek. The remaining player contented himself with a great deal of sighing and puffing. Finally the cheap wooden chips in front of the boy had diminished to one remaining disc. He looked across the table at Duchamp.

'Yore a damned cheat, Mistuh!' He drawled the words, as if they had been some kind of off-hand compliment.

Predictably, Duchamp's chair clattered to the floor behind him, his improbable chest thrust forward still more, if that were possible. A squeak of outrage emerged from his beak-like mouth:

'How dare you, boy? Call me a cheat and I'll shoot you like a dog.'

'Ah said yore a cheat and ah meant it.'

The boy had shot Duchamp through that chest before the defender of the fellow's reputation had cleared its holster. The man's red vest took on a darker hue as the blood stained the damask. Haycock appeared at the young man's shoulder, placing a hand on it, something he would have found difficult had the boy not still been seated.

'Aw hell, Dallas Stoudenmire, cain't ah leave you alone for a minnit?' Haycock said.

'Self dee-fence, ever'buddy saw it. He drawed on me.'

Haycock looked at me, nodding toward Duchamp's relict.

'You know this guy, Northrup? He travellin' with someone?'

'I doubt it Mr Haycock, the man was entirely too deficient in charm to have any willing companion.'

'Guess that means no. Don't reckon the Cap'n'll want a cadaver aboard all the way to Hannibal, somehow.'

Haycock nodded at the cigar smoker, and then spoke to the other card player.

'Oliver Otis, lend a hand with this sharper, let's get him on deck and see what he wants us to do.'

The man nodded at Haycock and said, 'Shore, Cuz. Let's check his pockets though, wanna cash in our markers first.'

Dallas Stoudenmire, Oliver Otis, Haycock and the cigar smoker crowded round the body, emptying pockets. Several playing cards fell to the floor as the sleeves of the man's coat were disturbed. I could think of no circumstance wherein a cheater at cards would require so many examples of the Queen of Spades, not even in so outlandish a game as Poker. A thick wad of bills in a money clip clattered onto the table, as did a purse, which clunked, metallic and satisfying beside it. A gold repeater watch on an extremely heavy chain joined them. It was picked up by the man with a fresh cigar at last at his lips.

'Guess I'll take this, you gents can have the money.'

Otis Oliver and his cousin transported the late Mr Duchamp out onto the deck and I wondered how many cheats had really been in the game.

6

I followed the corpse bearers on deck. They seemed on the point of heaving the body over the side, when Haycock caught sight of me.

'No point botherin' the Cap'n.' He cocked an eyebrow at me. 'Leastways, least said, soonest mended, don't they say?'

There was no great splash, as the riverboat was so low in the water. I gave the Cousins Haycock a nod and turned aft, crossing the decks at the rear of the superstructure.

This far upriver the banks were closer together, but not by any great deal. Where there were no sandbanks, a great many boats, large and small, could navigate in comparative safety. There were even a few skiffs, darting about like water-boatmen. Most likely they were as irritating for the trade and passenger ships along the river. I stood at the rail staring across the water. About a mile upriver, an enormous shape hove into view, even at that distance dwarfing anything else on the water. As if to advertise its presence, a loud blast of a steam-whistle played a chord of dubious harmony. Even so far down-river as the *Grand Turk*, the small skiffs began making for the safety of the bank, several taking great risks in front of the riverboat's bow. In ten minutes, the leviathan was alongside the

Grand Turk, and I calculated that the beast was travelling at a healthy six knots. The name on the prow was the *Natchez VI*; it was a huge thing out of Cincinnati and I found it hard to credit that both this giant and the somewhat less than *Grand Turk* went by the name of riverboat. A loud blast came from the steam-whistle, a three-pipe affair of quite unnecessary size. I felt that my ears might bleed if I had to hear it ever again.

We would not reach Hannibal for another seven days, by my calculation. So for several days and nights I took myself to my cell of a cabin to practise with the concealed derringer. I meant to become deadly in the use of it. It seemed to me more likely that I could master its use than become a proficient enough cheat at cards, in the time available to me.

There being only so much of his own company that a man might stand, I ventured once more onto the deck, thinking to complete a circumambulation of the *Grand Turk*, before trying my luck once again in the saloon bar. As I passed the pilot house on the port side, the pilot himself briefly took his eyes from the river, and allowed me a glance, before shaking his head. It was an insupportable insult from such a crude ruffian, but it was impractical to make him pay for it. I contented myself with the knowledge that the man had to contend with the Captain's company. The weather was fair: what clouds were visible were both very high and very white. It was cold, true enough, but it was yet early February. In truth, I was most fractious, having had no company of any sort since that of the unexpectedly talented Muskrat Jaw Jean. There had been damn few ladies aboard the riverboat at all, it seemed – and I found the charms of the men altogether too rough for my tastes.

Several deck hands, all black, were performing some incomprehensible task toward the bow of the vessel and it was necessary to request their co-operation in the matter of crossing to the starboard side. I was a little nervous of doing so, for there was no one in a position of responsibility present. However, they stepped aside with a tug of imaginary forelocks and to a man mumbled, 'Lord bless you, Missuh Northrup.'

It really was most peculiar.

Amidships, standing at the starboard rail, stood two ladies, dressed most fashionably for Missourians. Both figures' trim waists were accentuated by their bell-shaped skirts. Attractive though the sight was, I was reminded of how much was impractical for women, since these same skirts occupied most of the deck between the rail and the forward superstructure, through which I needed to pass to complete my constitutional. They appeared to be mother and daughter: the younger of the two looked to be about eighteen, with a fresh, unlined complexion, free of rouge or other artifice. Her mother, if that she were, wore no disguise that I could detect; what lines marked her face were attractive and pointed to a predisposition to laughter and enjoyment.

'Good afternoon, ladies.'

I swept off my hat; it was an imposing example, in grey. I had thought it quite the thing and had been unable to bear exchanging it for Northrup's on assuming the rest of his clothes. The younger woman merely looked at the hat and laughed. It was provocative and bold behaviour, but I laughed too.

'Britisher habits, ladies, I am recently returned from those islands.'

'Charmed, I'm sure,' the older of the two replied. 'Mrs Octavia Hatfield; may I present my niece, sir, Myra Maybelle Shirley.'

The girl dropped a little curtsey and I felt myself relieved that she was only Mrs Hatfield's niece, rather than her daughter, in which case a dalliance with both was not out of the question.

The saloon bar seemed an unsuitable place for the entertainment of ladies – even such as came from Missouri – so I invited them both to the restaurant. It was a short walk along the deck to the entrance. Forming the starboard half of the superstructure housing the saloon bar, it was therefore of similar size, and as sparsely populated. I surmised that the general run of passengers could not afford to eat in it. In contrast to the furniture of the saloon bar, the tables in the restaurant had the benefit of napery, albeit the colour of this bore only a distant relationship to white. The seating, of necessity, was not so delicate as might be found in a London house of quality, as I discovered when I drew one each backward to seat my guests. The table was bare of crockery and cutlery, I supposed to ensure that no irregular motion of the riverboat caused their precipitous departure therefrom.

We had hardly taken our places, when Tom, the Texas Tender, arrived at the side of the table, the white parts of his uniform shaming both the cloth on the table and the napkins in front of us.

'Missuh Northrup! Kin ah git y'all sump'n?'

Mrs Hatfield's eyebrows raised. 'You are known aboard, Mr Northrup?'

'More than you might guess, Mrs Hatfield.'

'Call me Octavia, Mr Northrup.'

The women in this country were indeed so bold that I felt a certain Miss Pardoner of old acquaintance would surely have passed for a native.

'Very well, Octavia, are you Missourians yourselves?'

'For myself, Mr Northrup, no more than you.' She sat a

little straighter in her chair and lifted a charmingly retroussé nose. 'I am of the Hatfields of Mingo County. Myra Maybelle—'

'May 'r Belle, one or 'tother, ah cain't stand both and as fer Myra—'

'Myra Maybelle is returning to Carthage, after we visit cousins in Hannibal,' the older woman continued.

'Hell, ah hate that name.' She gave a most attractive pout.

'That's enough, Myra Maybelle.'

The girl rolled her eyes, and Octavia Hatfield's diction slid a little as she informed her niece that she was not too far grown to 'git her a spankin''. I felt it best not to dwell on this not unpleasant image and turned to the waiter to enquire, 'Well, Tom, what can you recommend?'

'Not much, Missuh Northrup, 'at's a fac'.'

His honesty was to be admired, I supposed.

'What should we order then? Do tell.' I winked at the two women, who had not thus far acknowledged the presence of the servant. Both continued to look anywhere but at Tom, as if some contagion might afflict them should their gaze fall upon his skin.

Tom continued to address me, 'Allus best to have whut the Cap'n has, Missuh Northrup.'

'And what is the Captain's preference today?'

I could admit to no great shock when the waiter pronounced with some satisfaction, 'Pork chops!'

The ladies nodded at me, and I informed Tom that his recommendation was acceptable. The set of the older female's shoulders relaxed somewhat with his departure to the kitchen. Her niece remained quite stiff in the spine. Octavia Hatfield tilted her head.

'Did you see it?' she said, in a voice suddenly become quite breathy.

'Did I see what, madam?'

Her niece rolled her eyes, whether at her aunt's clumsy flirtatiousness or at my obtuseness, I was unsure. Mrs Hatfield gave a tut.

'Three days ago, the *Natchez VI*, did you see it?'

I found it quite mysterious that one more riverboat, however large, might excite such interest several days after its sighting. Still, in the interest of politeness – and the oldest pursuit – I replied, 'Indeed, quite remarkable, wasn't it?'

It appeared that Miss Shirley's contempt had been directed at me, for she interposed, 'Don't that beat all! Don't y'all know who was on the dang boat?'

'Well, as you know, I am but recently returned from England…'

It would have cost me dearer still to admit my ignorance, had not the younger specimen been diverted by the arrival of the chops in great quantity. Mrs Hatfield was not to be distracted by the viands and bellowed, with a degree of excitement tinged with, I could have sworn, lubricity, 'Jefferson Davis, President of the Confederacy!'

Miss Shirley having already set about the chops without benefit of cutlery, I employed a fork to apportion a pair of cutlets to her aunt and then served myself. Waving over at Tom, I bade him fetch the company some wine and some glasses.

'Yessuh, Missuh Northrup. Wine. What kine y'all want?'

'Might we have a Burgundy aboard, Tom?'

'We got red and white wine, Missuh Northrup, 'at's all I know.'

I gave a sigh and said that red would be fine. It proved to be anything but, of course.

Having noted Mrs Hatfield's excitement over either the Confederacy or its recently elected President, I enquired as to how this had come to pass.

'Secession, Mr Northrup. The right is on our side. Like Mr Davis says, the white race is superior in every respect.'

It was inconceivable to me that he had ever said any such thing. Even a Southern politician would not have risked outraging the sensitivities of the Yankees with such a bald statement. Nonetheless, I did not say so. But for harbouring thoughts of a little *divertissement* with the woman, I should have informed her that – whilst having no great knowledge of the black man – my experience of the white races had convinced me that a great many persons of my own race were in no way superior to the Barbary Ape, much less a man of a different colour.

The ladies' accommodations went by the name of stateroom, and although that was a little grand, they certainly put my own to shame. Whilst not so commodious as to permit the wielding of any feline with gusto, that was no handicap to the entertainment both ladies provided. Miss Shirley was most inventive in preserving her honour for any future husband and would have stood higher in my affections, had not her aunt surpassed all my expectations. From the moment she excoriated me for being 'uppity' until – at the appropriate moment – she began bellowing out a tune unknown to myself but whose lyrics included 'Brothers will you meet me', she seemed rapt in her own performance as a woman at the mercy of her own property. In spite of this, it seemed that if any such event might one day come to pass, the woman would gladly join the Abolitionist cause. I was reminded, not for the first time, that women were quite beyond my understanding.

It was dusk as I made once more for the saloon bar. A pair of birds circled above; although of no great size, they had a predatory look. Suddenly, both made a dive towards me, I swept off my hat and began flapping it at them in a most undignified manner.

'Guess they liked your hat, brother.'

I did not divert my attention from the task in hand, at least until the report of a firearm sounded altogether too close to my ear. The birds flew off, alarmed but unharmed.

'Mississippi Kites, dang pests.'

I turned toward the owner of the voice. On noting his attire, it was with a sinking feeling that I realised I was in the company of such a one as I would cross an ocean to avoid. Viz. a clergyman ornithologist.

The man was tall and gaunt, thin-lipped as a banker. His attire was as black as sin; his thin and angular limbs gave him the look of a crow or one whose function was to scare them. Inevitably his hand was out, and I took it, dropping it quickly, for it was as clammy as a toad.

'Reverend Elijah Truecross, Southern Baptist Church, Cairo, Missouri, pleased to meet a Christian man aboard this ship of shame.'

'Anson Northrup, at your service.'

The clergyman's eyes became slits.

'No, suh, not at mine, nor God's,' and he gave me his back, a prospect marginally more pleasing to the eye than his front.

The saloon bar was as busy as I had yet seen it. I had hoped to engage Haycock in conversation, in the hope of coming to some arrangement to our mutual benefit, but there was no sign of him, or his cousin. The overgrown youth was there, but I felt he would prove an unreliable confederate. The other party to Duchamp's departure of this life was the large fellow with his malodorous cigar. Thankfully he was not yet seated at a card table, merely dwarfing his fellow drinkers at the bar, who gave him plenty of elbowroom. Even so I watched him strike another drinker with that very joint, and the ensuing altercation gained the big man another bottle of whiskey to stand beside the quarter-full exemplar in front of him. This might be the very fellow, I thought and I clapped him on the shoulder, hand of greeting out, ready.

'Anson Northrup, I wonder if I might have a word?'

He turned round very sharp and if his handgun had been on the bar too, I thought I might have regretted disturbing him. He relaxed, 'The Britisher!' he said, then thrust his jaw toward me.

'Actually, nothing of the kind, an extended visit…'

'Sounds like a Britisher, hell if yuh don't look like one in that hat! Near as makes no difference to me. Caulfield McGraw, folks call me Cuffy.'

He took my hand at last and shook it hard. I jerked my head towards the entrance and we went out on deck.

A wind had risen, a head-wind as light as a zephyr, but as cold as an Edinburgh lawyer. I shivered a little. McGraw seemed not to notice. Before I could fashion any opening gambit concerning my plans. He hissed, 'What in hell you playin' at?'

'Wh-what do you mean, sir?' He loomed over me and I took a step backward.

'You ain't been at table onc't! Damn me if'n ye didn't get on this tub at St Loo!'

'I did indeed, what of it?' I attempted a step forward, but merely struck his significant paunch.

'What of…? Lissen up Mistuh Northrup, lucky we knowed you wuz on board. Where in hell's the vest?'

'I thought it a little conspicuous, myself,' I said.

'Conspik-you-us? We supposed tuh reckanize yuh! How in hell you gonna lose enough money 'tween here and Hanni-bal?'

It dawned on me at last that this ruffian, and others on the *Grand Turk*, had been expecting my arrival, or at least that of

Anson Northrup. My boarding of this particular riverboat had been serendipitous, surely? Or had a vast network of Negroes been on the look out for the fantastical design of the waistcoat?

'Lose money?' I wondered what money this might be, and whose.

'Ah course, lose money! Silver Dollars, Northrup. Or at least ones as is s'posed to look like 'em.'

I supposed it must be some fourrée coin that he meant, but the real Anson Northrup had had nothing else with him but what I had taken.

'Furry?'

McGraw's eyebrows lowered and his forehead was creased by a frown as deep as a knife-cut. Evidently, I had said the word aloud.

'Plated base metal, Mr McGraw,' I informed him.

'How yuh gonna lose enough now, huh?' he retorted.

'Enough?' The man was clearly a half-wit, unable to express himself in any intelligible manner.

'Y'all s'posed to lose 5000 Silver Dollars on the dang boat.'

'Well, the boat must sail down-river too, after all.'

'Are yuh some kinda half-wit? T'aint no good down-river, the junk money got to travel north!'

Plainly, Mr Northrup had been involved in some very strange affairs. Be that as it might, I wondered how I could placate the big man in front of me, despite having recourse to no more than ten dollars, legal tender or counterfeit. I began to speak, thinking to bamboozle McGraw with sufficient verbiage as to enable my departure from his company.

'There has been, you might say, an unforeseen, not to say, unlikely change in circumstances, necessitating the abandonment of this stratagem.'

I saw his eyes glaze over most satisfactorily. However, his hand hovered alarmingly close to the gun thrust into his belt.

'Someone else will bring the dollars, next trip upriver. Look for the waistcoat, as before.'

'Weskit?' He looked as puzzled as a dog watching a fly.

'Vest, I beg your pardon.'

I fled back to my cabin, thinking that my debarking at Hannibal could not come soon enough.

That hermit's cell remained small, despite a significant absence from it. I lifted the carpetbag onto the bunk. Removing all my clothes and the whiskey drummer's case, I ran my hands over all the cloth of the bag, inside and out. Turning the whole monstrosity outside to in, I reflected that the coarse lining was only marginally less objectionable than the busy pattern of the exterior. Having withdrawn my knife from the pocket of my frock coat, I ran the blade down the seams. My manual exploration of the bag had revealed nothing, at first, but just wielding the knife brought its own comfort.

However, the last parted seam revealed something hidden inside the bag, after all. Paper! Was ever anything of as little use to the world as paper? It was, however, paper of a most peculiar kind: preposterously thin, and its texture led one to believe that it was covered in a fine glaze. There were two sheets both of a particular and distinct size. Their dimensions were reminiscent of those pertaining to some financial instrument rather than any size such as pinched post or Royal, whether quarto or octavo of either. One sheet bore only a phrase or two in a familiar, but as yet un-confirmed hand: 'Bona Fides: Mudsill, January 1861: Facsimile.'

The second sheet of the strange paper appeared to be some kind of Government Bond, it was headed 'Confederate

States of America'; the date of issue was 1 April 1861. This was interesting indeed, not only because the date lay some weeks in the future, but also because I could not decide whether All Fools Day was an appropriate day to launch a government-backed bond. Really, I felt in need of an archivist, so many documents had I accumulated, thanks to the late Mr Northrup.

Fortified, if that were the word, by some of Northrup's samples, I laid out the papers and the journal-sized ledger on the cot. I gave the ledger no more than a brief look, before deciding there was no sense to be made of it. I looked once again at the hand-drawn map that had been hidden inside it. At first, I noted no more than earlier, a crude representation of the Mississippi, with initial letters marked alongside. Evidently the major towns on the river were annotated, for some reason. However, something I had missed before struck me. Underneath a spidery 'H', which I supposed to refer to Hannibal – although my geography regarding the river was hazy – in the most minuscule of glyphs, was written 'WS M's B'. WS had surely to be Winona Shepherd, with whom I had been charged with making a rendezvous. M's B remained a facer, for a moment or so, until I glanced at the Warrant from the Governor of the State of Carolina. The bearer of this and the exceedingly premature bond were one and the same.

I chose not to waste time in attempting to fathom what these connections – or coincidences – meant, if indeed they meant anything. It seemed to me far more preferable instead to replace everything in the carpetbag, save the playing-card waistcoat – and then look for comfort in the blessed sleep of the less-than-innocent.

7

Which sleep, though deep, did not last long – being interrupted by a forced entry to my cabin on the part of Cuffy McGraw. He was quite drunk, his eyes achieving the difficult feat of rolling each in different directions. Nevertheless, his physical presence was enough to put a gentleman recently woken at a considerable disadvantage. Certainly, if one took the pistol being pointed in one's direction into account.

'Werrrzamoney, No-nor-nth... Mistuh!'

The prospect of the firearm being inadvertently discharged seemed imminent.

'Mr McGraw, I told...'

The ruffian let out a bellow whose concomitant exhalation would have rivalled the fire-power of the weapon wavering at my chest.

'Shaaddddduppp!'

I kept my counsel and waited for some more intelligible discourse.

He closed one eye and this had the beneficial effect of halting the rolling of its mate.

'Yuh gotta have it. We wuz tole!'

'Very well, very well. If you would just allow me to get dressed, Mr McGraw.'

Like many of the New-Worlders, the man proved to be somewhat prudish, and turned away. Perhaps he would not have done so, had he not been so inebriated. No matter, my knife travelled upwards through the nape of his neck, under the cranium and thereby solved the immediate problem. His pockets revealed little of interest to me, save a quantity of genuine silver dollars and a fine lace kerchief as might be carried by a lady. Naturally, it had become grubby in the hands of such a fellow, whilst the remains of an embroidered monogram were insufficient as to allow any conjecture regarding the initial it had represented. It had a faint, musky smell, as though a lady had used it in a more intimate fashion than customary, and for that reason I secreted it in a pocket of my clothes.

Dressed, with the waistcoat about my torso, I realised that it was strange that the poor fit of this garment had excited so little attention, although for the most part the other clothes that I had purloined from Mr Northrup were more than passable. With some effort, I laid Cuffy McGraw's corpse on the bunk. The adjustments to his posture to enable this meant that few would mistake him for a sleeping drunk. Besides, the floorboards of the cabin still told a tale in spite of my efforts with McGraw's jacket.

It was my belief that the *Grand Turk* was to draw alongside in Hannibal during the early evening of the current day, so I resolved to enquire of the man on board most likely to have the right of it. At the pilot house I was struck once more by the relative elegance of its appointments. There seemed altogether more fresh paint and shined brass than one might have expected. I gave a firm knock at the entrance, although both the Captain and Pilot had seen me approach, I was sure.

'C'mawn in, Northrup, ain't it?' the Captain bellowed.

The Pilot gave no more than the slightest flinch, although the Captain's mouth had been scarce inches from his ear.

The pilot house was so warm as to be uncomfortable: indeed beads of sweat decorated the low forehead of Captain Holden Grey. No such concession to the heat was being made by the pilot's mortal vessel. I imagined he would be as little affected by the icebergs of the frozen north as the fires of Hades itself.

'Quite correct, Captain,' I said. ' I wonder if I might enquire as to our arrival in Hannibal. I mean to say, sir, at what time can we expect to come alongside.'

The Captain exhaled noisily, causing a flapping of lips like that of an exasperated horse.

'We-ell, cain't rightly say. We's s'posed tuh git there t'day, shore. But who knows, the Mississip' is as capreeshee-us as a un-marrit woman.'

I refrained from remarking that – in my experience – the boon of a husband was in no way a restraint on the capriciousness of women. In any event, the captain – as I suspected he was in many things – was gainsaid by the Pilot.

'You'll be on dry land at a quarter after five this evenin', Mistuh.' And his expectoration struck the cuspidor with a sound between a slap and a clang, which punctuation put an end to any discussion of the matter.

The Captain gave a sound between a clearing of the throat and a snort and turned to me.

'Guess I can leave Pilot Ireland in charge o' the *Turk* fer now.'

His eyes darted sideways at the stolid figure, before he added, 'Would y'all take a livener in my cabin, Mr Northrup? Ah find yore comp'ny preferable to some.'

I gave my consent and I followed the captain aft. Forward of the superstructure housing the saloon bar and restaurant was the part of the ship that contained my own bunk. This was a twin-decked affair. . I was pleased to note all of the accommodation – like my own – in this rearmost part of the ship had no water-view, since there were no portholes – or indeed any orifices, which might have permitted natural light to enter. The Captain, however, led me up an external stairway, which led to a door at the forward end of the structure. This arrangement was mirrored at the aft end, and I saw a line of passengers descending very slowly, the stair being too narrow to effect any more rapid progress. Captain Grey produced a heavy ring with a respectable number of keys attached. He selected a rusted affair with multiple projections and cuts – the simple keyhole in the door must have provided access to the most complex of warded locks.

It afforded him no difficulty in the matter of opening however, despite the appearance of the key itself. The Captain's cabin was, naturally enough, a deal larger than my own. And if it were extravagance to give over such a large proportion of the limited space on board to the comfort of one man, then I for one did not begrudge him it. I had felt claustrophobic aboard the *Iowa*, crossing the Atlantic, even whilst on deck facing the open seas. An endless succession of navigations of the same river would have had much the same effect, I believed. Still, it was a most peculiar lair. The whole of one wall was covered in an enormous flag. It belonged to no country that I knew, being a blue Latin cross on a red field. There were 15 white stars on the cross and, on the red field, palmetto and crescent symbols. An enormous bed failed to dominate the space, since there was room enough to dance a quadrille between it and sundry other furnishings.

'Drink, Mr Northrup?' the Captain enquired.

'Might you have a brandy, sir?'

'Hell yes. All the way from Paree, France.'

I sincerely hoped such was not the case. He strode across to a sideboard to pour whatever it was we were about to drink.

The first sensation on the tongue was a burning: not the smooth heat engendered by a cognac, by any means. The next was a numbness and, it seemed, a swelling of the tongue itself. This was soon forgotten in the acid corrosion, which began to assail the gullet. I gasped and said, 'Capital, Captain Grey, simply capital!'

He tipped his own glass to his lips and swigged as though it were a mint cordial and replied, 'Ain't it though, Mr Northrup? Ain't it though?'

Captain Grey appeared to descend into a brown study at this point. Even had I wished to initiate some conversation then, I could not have done so, since, rather unwisely perhaps, I had attempted another swallow of my host's 'Brandy from Paree'. I took the opportunity to look more closely at the contents of the cabin, now that I had recovered from the shock of the unknown flag and the enormously sized bed. There were two portholes each in three of the walls of the cabin, and for all I knew the giant flag covered another two. These were all mere affectation surely, since the cabin was high above the main deck, not to speak of the waterline and therefore any kind of glaziery would have been appropriate. In one corner stood a hideous brass object: the ubiquitous cuspidor. It seemed that any space with pretensions to the entertainment of guests – paying or otherwise – must needs be blessed with some or other exemplar of a spittoon. This alloyed urn was claimed as the property of 'The Yaller House, St Louis' by dint of an ill-engraved plaque affixed uncertainly to its exterior. I turned to the Captain with a view to engaging him in some trifling raillery concerning his acquisition of the receptacle.

However, it seemed that I had been quite mistaken as to

the man's meditatory habits, for he was – to all appearances – in the grip of the Grand Mal. His earlier introspection had been either Petit Mal, or some other event precursory to his fit. The Captain fell to the ground, jerking like the subject of one of Signor Galvani's experiments on amphibians. Briefly, I pondered allowing his seizure to take its course, but decided that perhaps the death of the riverboat's Captain might inconvenience my departure from it. The Captain was most fortunate in his toppling, his head having missed the heavy wooden frame of the bed. The only cloth I had available was the musky kerchief purloined from McGraw's corpse, so I held this to my nose against the results of the Captain's fit-induced incontinence and fashioned a serviceable gag from a corner of the bed's coverlet.

The fit lasted no more than a minute or so, but resulted in a faint at the end of it. I thought that the banging of his head against the deck would no doubt occasion a considerable headache on his recovering consciousness. Removing the bloody end of the bed covering, I noted that I had not entirely saved the Captain's tongue from being bitten. The rifling of his trunk yielded nothing but an unlikely number of female undergarments and no pecuniary advantage at all. Under the bed was the curious leather item the Americans are wont to call a saddlebag. It was empty. I had a mind to kick the Captain while he was down, but contented myself with adjusting his position on the deck with a gentle application of the toe of my boot.

The noise the Captain made, on waking from his stupor, would more likely have been heard on a whaler rather than a run-down riverboat like the *Grand Turk*. Slowly he came to himself – I found it quite amusing to see the sniff of disgust at his realisation that he had befouled himself.

'Northrup?' he croaked. 'Did y'all... were y'all...'

On seeing my smile, he turned his head away. His voice if anything was more feeble still when he said, 'Go on over to the bell-board.'

I looked about, scanning the walls of the cabin.

'It's at the bed head.'

It was a cheap deal board affixed to the cabin wall, within easy reach of anyone lying abed. There were six brass bell-pulls. Crude poker work lettering was visible beneath each one. Most were marked as one might have expected, 'Pilot', 'Engineer', 'Galley' and the like. It was quite clear that I was to operate the last bell-pull, since it was marked 'Bilhah'. The Captain remained supine on the cabin floor, groaning from time to time. Presently there was a knock at the door. Upon opening it, I was greeted with the sight of the most beautiful woman I had seen in many years. She bore a large ewer of water, evidently heated judging by the steam rising from it, and in the other hand a large ceramic bowl piled high with white towels.

'Who in hell're you?' she said. I stumbled over any reply, but it mattered not.

'Huh! Northrup,' she went on. 'Well, you don't look the biggest toad in the puddle, mistuh! An' that seven-by-nine vest don't fit at all.'

She shouldered me aside, calling over her shoulder, 'Shut the door, why doncha?' I thought I had never seen a better refutation of the argument for the inferiority of her race.

Bilhah knelt at the side of the Captain, inspected the bumps on his cranium and peered at the damage to his tongue. The groans subsided to a contented purr. The woman began removing the Captain's outer garments. She turned to me.

'Mistuh Northrup, ah need some clean clothin' heah.'

I went over to the chest, selecting a pair of trousers, a shirt and a coat at random. Bilhah gave me a look she might have given a particularly dull infant.

'Underclothin' too.'

A look down at the Captain revealed that his handmaiden was in the midst of removing a rather prettily ribboned – if soiled – pair of lady's bloomers from his person. On returning to the chest, I selected the least frivolous garment I could find.

A glance out of one of the portholes revealed nothing but a darkening sky. The accumulation of clouds was rapid and their motion across the sky itself equally so. I turned to look at the flag on the wall more closely, but it was of as little interest to me as the flag of Wallachia. I heard the clearing of a throat and turned toward the others.

'Ah, Mistuh Northrup, ah trust there is such a thing as a confidence between friends?'

Bilhah held my gaze with her own.

'Of course, Captain Grey. Might I call you Holden? In fact there may be a little difficulty you could help me overcome.'

He cleared his throat again, 'Guess so.'

'I'm sure the young lady has the laundry to see to, Holden.'

Which young lady let out a sound resembling nothing so much as the hiss of a disturbed snake and departed, hesitating only to grapple with the door, rather than beg my assistance.

'Well, Captain,' I said, 'the little difficulty is the corpse in my cabin.'

I derived great pleasure from the look of shock that appeared but fleetingly on his face before he replied, "Zactly so, Mistuh Northrup: one hand washes the other, don't they say?'

'Indeed,' I said, denying myself the opportunity to observe that somewhat more than his hands had but recently been washed by another's.

The Captain, perhaps still exhausted from his fit, lay on the bed and, reaching back behind him to the bell board, pulled a bell-pull marked 'Deck-Hands'. It was not long before a knock came at the door, and the invalid feebly begged me open it. I should not have been surprised quite so much as I was by the appearance of George Washington Irving and two other strapping fellows, once I had done so. Perhaps less surprising was the absence of the cultured tones and immaculate diction in which that same man's warning had been delivered in the slave quarters.

'Cap'n, suh, we's heah, Cap'n, suh!' This was accompanied by a rolling of eyes which would have disgraced a performer in a minstrel show. I could have sworn that Irving winked at me at one point.

Captain Grey said in a voice that did not inspire confidence, 'They's a package fo' disposal in Mistuh Nothrup's cabin, it's to go over immediate. To the mid-river side.'

'Yassuh, we'm gonna do dat by'm'by,' Irving said.

It was all I could do not to laugh. I walked over to the Captain and leaned over, so that I might look him in the eye, as I said, 'I shall supervise the operation, Holden. I trust you do not assume yourself discharged of any obligation to me?'

For answer he gave a vigorous shake of the head and he shrank away, almost far enough to fall out of the enormous bed.

'Holden is beholden to me,' I laughed. The Captain, however, seemed not to care for the pun, since he turned over onto his side, the better to look away from me.

In my own cabin, Irving began by sending his fellow crewmen outside, or at least not allowing them to complete their ingress, since the cabin did not allow all four persons to stand in it. The door safely closed, he took a step toward me. Not wishing to fall on McGraw's relict, I did not recoil.

'Why on earth did you kill this man? You must make your rendezvous, you must!'

He seemed most agitated for someone yet to be convinced that I was Northrup. I put the question most apposite to his remark, 'Why?'

'You need to take care, Mr Northrup,' he replied. Then he shouldered McGraw as though he were a half-bale of cotton and strode out of the cabin.

8

I was waiting at the rail, carpetbag in hand, as the *Grand Turk* hove to at the jetty in Hannibal. It looked a busy little town: horses and carriages bustled about the streets beyond the riverbank, in numbers sufficient to befoul the streets more than was pleasant. The architecture was a mixture of clapboard dwellings and false-fronted pretenders to grandeur; I failed to see why the Brothers Clemens had been so inordinately proud of it. A look at my watch confirmed that the Pilot had been over-confident in his own abilities concerning an estimate of my arrival. It was inconceivable that I might make my way down the gangplank and onto the wharf in the two minutes before the quarter-hour struck.

At closer quarters, Hannibal was no more prepossessing. Oh, it was busy enough: grain and hemp being loaded in no small amount from jetties and wharves. Boats and barges from the north disgorged lumber onto other landing places. The noise was cacophonous in the extreme; there was no music in the shouts and cries, as one might have found in the East India Docks. Foremen exhorted longshoremen to greater efforts with bale and pulley. Occasionally, a loud crash would advertise the dropping of some cargo – and a louder scream the loss of another livelihood.

I turned my back on the jetty onto which I had disembarked and began to make my way toward the clapboard and brick of the town proper. A hand grasped my elbow, I turned rapidly. The derringer shot into my palm but I failed to grasp it: the damned contraption had failed me. A finely dressed figure was bending down in front of me. She handed me the pistol. One corner of her mouth lifted, 'Yaws, ah b'lieve.'

'It is indeed mine, one should be careful approaching someone from behind in such a stealthy manner.'

'Indeed, is it? Ah think yore a humbug, mistah,' she seemed about to flounce off, which would have been a pity.

Her eyes narrowed, 'Thet vest yores?'

'Am I not wearing it?'

'Don't fit too good, do it?' She looked me up and down once and then square in the eye.

'Well…?' she said expectantly.

'I do not cut the figure I once did, since returning from England my constitution has been… delicate.'

She stamped her foot.

'That all yuh got to say to me?'

'I should be delighted to engage you in conversation at some more suitable venue…'

A most penetrating screech emerged from this not unattractive young woman:

'Ah'm Winona Shepherd, yuh danged ninny!'

Clearing my throat, I said, 'Ah. And how is my old friend Levi Coffin?'

She grabbed my elbow and dragged me toward the town, muttering something about 'danged fools' and a long tirade which I interpreted as her questioning as to what extent such 'danged fools' should be free to roam on their own cognisance.

The woman finally let go of my arm after two or three blocks. It was all I could do to match her pace. Clearly, she was in need of some relaxation; in my experience a surfeit of vigour in a woman had ever betokened a deficit in the meeting of certain needs. She led me down a street called Center after the peculiar fashion of the Americas. At the 'corner of Center and Eighth', as she termed it, we stopped in front of a false-fronted clapboard building. A tiny cross stood atop the false front meant to foster the illusion of a second storey. The front itself put one in mind of a triptych, and the three stained glass windows in each of the three lobes did nothing to detract from this. The windows offered no depiction of the suffering of Christ, or any Old Testament fratricide, infanticide or any of the other –cides, which fill the good book's pages. My face must have betrayed a little of the contempt I felt for the humble church. Miss Shepherd, in an accent considerably less flavoured with the corn so beloved of the South, said, 'We'll have a brick-built church one day. Good things are done here, Mr Northrup. Many good deeds.'

I replied something to the effect that I didn't doubt it, and worried inordinately that it might be true.

We entered via a plain door. No key was required. The church was silent, but not empty; or rather, I should say, it fell silent the moment I crossed the threshold behind Miss Winona Shepherd. Aside from our own there was but one white face in the building. It belonged to a soberly dressed man at the front of the congregation. The pulpit stood central to the rear of the large auditorium. Banked empty seats flanked it, forming an arrowhead pointing to the stained glass window in the rear wall. This feat of glaziery *did* show a representational composition. In a crude, almost child-like style, the pieces of glass depicted a tall and stately looking man. He wore a set of rags in remarkably clean condition and had a skin-colour unlikely to have been seen at all on a native of Colossae, which location was conveniently if inexplicably inscribed on a signpost in English rather than Greek. The slave was being returned to one Philemon, whose name was conveniently inscribed below his figure. In the background an older fellow in a green mantle with a red robe sat astride a horse attempting to juggle a book and a scroll whilst struggling with the reins. But for the long and pointed beard, it would have been the very image of the shepherd of the church's flock.

As he caught sight of Miss Shepherd and myself, he gave out a bellow worthy of a buck-shot buffalo, as Mr Clemens might have put it.

'Welll-cooome! Sissssterrr Shepherd and Brrrroootherrr Norrrthruuuppp!'

This long, drawn-out greeting was greeted by cheering and whooping from the congregation. I looked at Miss Shepherd, who appeared a little uncomfortable. This may well have been occasioned by the enthusiasm of the welcome, but – though it might have been vanity – I thought her discomfort more on my account than any other.

'You will join my brrootherrs and ssissterrs in worship?'

The preacher appeared to be addressing me, but it was a purely rhetorical question, as he put a pitch pipe to his lips. The congregation broke into a song I'd heard once before, and I recognised immediately the endless round of exhortations to some fellow's brothers to meet him. The tune was rousing enough and might have gone well in a comic song at the Canterbury in far-off London. Thankfully there appeared to be no more than thirteen choruses in the version performed by the assembled voices, several of which were almost as tuneful as a crow's.

The hymn being over, the preacher began a rambling prayer, which mentioned Philemon, St Paul, our 'Negro' brothers, servitude and manumission, several times more than strictly necessary. At last he performed a manumission of his own and released his congregation to the street, save for three ragged fellows who edged to the wall end of the pews on which they sat.

'So, Brrootherr Northrup, art come to save the Canaanites?' he asked.

Being quite tired of the manner in which the fellow rolled the word around his mouth as though it were a particularly hot and delicious sweetmeat, I replied, 'I am not your brother, sir and am quite tired of being at a disadvantage in the matter of names.'

The preacher looked at Miss Shepherd open-mouthed.

'Pay him no mind, Reverend, he always talks like that, says he's been twenty years in England.'

'The Lord moves in mysterious ways indeed, sir. I am the Reverend Erastus Newberry, shepherd to these sheep who take refuge in the House of God.'

He spread his arms wide as if the church were yet full, but he did fix his eyes on the Negroes seated at the side of the auditorium.

It took a modicum of self-control not to smite the fellow then and there. The humbug of the clergy had ever been a source of provocation to me.

I held out a hand and lied, 'Anson Northrup, pleased to make your acquaintance, Reverend.'

His grip was strong, the hand calloused, his eyes showed white all around the mahogany irises: I didn't doubt that he considered himself as muscular a Christian as ever attempted 'the advancement of righteous causes'. It was yet another reason to despise him. He ushered Miss Shepherd and myself toward the banked tiers of seating behind the pulpit. It seemed strange to have such an arrangement for a choir, when the whole congregation had proved itself entirely capable of great volume if not harmony. We sat, Reverend Erastus Newberry stood, as if unwilling to meet such mortals as we on level terms.

He addressed Miss Shepherd, the over-wide eyes unblinking.

'Does he have it?'

'I don't know Reverend, I brought him here directly.' I heard a tremor in her voice.

The Reverends lips tightened, I doubted that a hair could have passed between them. Then he exhaled and exclaimed at one and the same time, 'PAH!'

The peculiar fellow then held out his hand to me.

I fumbled with the leather buckle on the carpetbag and brought out the oilskin packet. The man of God snatched it in a most un-Christian manner.

'You have opened it, man!'

The Reverend clearly found it difficult to moderate the volume of his voice to lower than that sufficient to address a deaf dowager at the rear of a concert hall.

He took out the ledger and removed the crudely drawn map. The warrant in the name of Mudsill and the strange bond were yet in a pocket of my frock coat. The near-empty church was filled with the sound of riffling pages and what seemed most inappropriate language from a man of God.

'What's wrong, Reverend?' Miss Shepherd's voice had begun to sound more tremulous still.

'It's not here!'

'W-what isn't?' the young woman seemed quite beside herself.

'The necessary!' The Reverend bellowed once more and began to kick the plain wooden pews and the pulpit. He seemed on the point of running over to kick the three church members, when he fell to the ground writhing and began to speak in what I believed to be known as tongues. I stifled a guffaw as the congregation, including Miss Shepherd, offered choruses of 'Praise the Lord' and 'Tell it, Brother' at intervals in what I considered to be little more than an unusual tantrum.

When all five of them had recovered sufficiently for conversation, the Reverend despatched the few parishioners to the front of the church to keep 'cave', although I suspected he required them to be unable to hear what passed. It proved a vain hope regarding his contributions to the conversation that followed, but I supposed that they were unable to glean much from them. Miss Shepherd, who had studied the book rather more carefully meanwhile, spoke low and with more composure.

'The route is safe, with guides – shepherds, I mean: there is sufficient financial support. It is, however incomplete. From Minneapolis to Canada, there are no arrangements. But the river is safe, or at least the towns along it are.'

'So!' Needless to say, this was a somewhat loud interjection from Erastus Newberry.

'You intend to use the boats to smuggle, then?'

'Of course we do!' Miss Shepherd nodded over at the ragged fellows by the door. 'Our poor brothers deserve their ride on the Freedom Railroad.'

At that point, I would have left, except for two things: the first being that the lunatic preacher managed to say something in what was almost a whisper, and the second – what he said:

'And the silver, don't forget the silver.'

Miss Winona Shepherd, complexion a most fetching scarlet, covered her mouth with a dainty hand. The Reverend's mouth slid sharply closed as though not operated by the hinge of a jaw at all.

'Silver?' There was no point in using a dozen words where a solitary one would suffice, after all.

'Of course! The Underground Railroad does not run on fresh air, you dolt!' The preacher said, spittle spotting his own black shirtfront.

The gleam in his eye indicated that, most likely, he himself was a large part of the Railroad's expenses. There was nothing, I believed, to provide greater opportunity for a man of intelligence to turn a profit than the greed of others. With this in mind, I asked, 'What silver?'

It was a mistake.

'Don't you know?' The Reverend, as noted before, seemed a particularly muscular Christian and I doubted I could best him in a brawl. Furthermore, it would indeed have been a breach of good manners to knife or shoot him in his own church, I felt. Therefore, when he took a threatening step toward me, I took a prudent step backward.

'How should I know, sir? Are there not eager ears to overhear the most clandestine plans? My trip here has been both a dry run and a most necessary rendezvous, has it not?'

The angry Christian looked unconvinced, as his clenched fists betokened. Clearly, he thought me some black spy, employed by his real or imagined adversaries. Miss Winona Shepherd interposed, 'It is natural. Suppose he had been in possession of the plan? They are not above torture!'

Again, some distress or excitement caused her to warble a little. The identity of the mysterious 'they' held my interest rather more than Miss Shepherd's emotional whirligig.

Erastus Newberry let out a loud, 'Harrumph!", which ejaculation I had never before heard pronounced as though it had been a word. The preacher then shouted to his parishioners, 'Stay here, we'll be back 'ere long.'

We departed the Church of St Onesimus. Newberry made sure to lock the door behind us with a shining brass key.

The Reverend escorted us to yet another clapboard building, this time several genuine storeys high. He turned to Winona Shepherd and despatched her on some errand whispered into her ear with an intimacy un-befitting a clergyman. The woman skipped daintily off in the direction of a building marked with the sign 'Clemens General Store', before going in. I made a mental note to avoid visiting this emporium myself, if at all possible. The building before which we stood looked like a poor quality bawdy-house: the windows were heavily curtained though it was yet daylight, the door was more imposing than the building itself and the only thing of real note about it was the large painted sign stationed centrally above the entrance bearing the letters, 'YMCA'. A scruffily painted banner was draped lopsidedly below: it read 'New Opinned, Orl Welcum'.

9

It did indeed appear newly opened, in as much as it was entirely deserted, save for a bent and gnarled old fellow whose snoring at least proved he was, as yet, still living. The floorboards were in need of a vigorous application of lye and a brush. The reception desk, behind which the old man remained steeped in oblivion, took up half of the vestibule. There were numerous doors, which may have led to rooms, and a staircase leading to the upper floors. We took the staircase, after the Reverend had removed a large key from one of a quantity of hooks on a board behind the sleeping sentinel's head.

Newberry stopped at a room with ill-aligned numerals indicating that we were about to enter a room numbered 101. To the rear of the building, the room could have been less comfortable, perhaps: the mean cot was ideal for a man inclined to the more self-denying aspects of his religion, there was no crockery in which to wash or perform any necessity. There were no drapes at the many-paned window, which was deficient of its full complement by a single piece of glass. There was no wardrobe, chest or indeed anywhere to store clothes or anything at all. There was a mound of discarded trousers, shirts and underclothing over by the window.

Erastus Newberry un-stiffened his spine a little and his lips spread in something one might have thought a smile, if ever a jackal might wear one.

'So, Northrup. The silver: shall I tell you? Or are you merely a spy?'

I was so taken aback by the civilised volume at which he spoke, that I could not immediately reply. The churchman's gaze remained fixed on me. He had eyes so brown as to appear black, as though some freak of nature had deprived his eyes of any iris at all, and the enormous pupils were windows darkened by the soul beyond them.

'I am no spy, sir.'

'Perhaps not, sir, no matter. The escaping slaves are not my concern. There are enough holy fools to help them on their way.'

I felt myself warm a little to Erastus Newberry, since I was beginning to suspect that he was no more a reverend than I.

'Go on,' I said.

'There is one such holy fool – such idiots can be useful – he worked in the New Orleans Mint.'

'So? He no longer works there, what good is that?'

'There are plans afoot. He is still there. He will still be there in March, when Louisiana joins the Confederacy and it reopens as the Confederacy's Mint.'

I laughed, 'Confederacy? My friend even a neophyte like myself knows that it's just a pipe dream. A nonsense concocted by a few politically ineffectual blowhards.'

The black eyes gleamed, 'How wrong you are, Mr Northrup.'

'In any event, how is profit to be made from events occurring so far away?' I asked.

'The mint is striking no coins at the moment. Jacob Holzbein is well-placed to ensure the silver store does not overflow.'

'I'm afraid, I remain none the wiser.'

'There are slaves working at the mint, Northrup, and Holzbein is a fierce abolitionist.'

'The silver?'

'It comes with escaped slaves, they will surely be caught if they take the Freedom Train overland, but that's why we want them on the *Grand Turk*. We'll relieve them of the silver at St Paul.'

'And the Master of the Riverboat, Grey?' I asked.

'Where better to hide slaves than aboard the vessel of a dyed-in-the-wool secessionist?'

I had to admit it was a bold plan, and I heartily wished I had spent at least a little more time in the cramped slave-quarters aboard the *Grand Turk*. I was struck too, by the generosity of soul evinced by a man who would put the welfare of his fellow man above bullion for the sake of a philosophical stance.

It seemed appropriate to ask the man what he required from me.

'Is it possible? You have seen the riverboat. You saw the slaves.'

'I not only saw them, they seemed to know who I was.'

'Did they? Did they really?'

And, of course, they did not. They had made assumptions because of a ridiculous, if memorable, article of clothing and the rumours that abound on a vessel of any size, be it at sea or navigating a river. I wondered why the Negroes had seemed so in awe of Northrup. No matter, I could turn that fact to advantage, if I were to find myself on board the *Grand Turk* on another occasion. Unfortunately for me, at least one of their number had not been convinced, and I did not relish the prospect of running into George Washington Irving again. Such thoughts lasted but an instant and I replied to the Reverend's initial question, 'Of course it's possible, everything is possible.' And I felt myself coming round to Professor Pangloss's view in a burst of optimism that had long been deficient in my moods.

'Then you must return to New Orleans with the utmost despatch.'

This time the disturbing eyes glittered with greed and excitement, the thin lips flattening wide in the smile of Satan contemplating the arrival of the blackest sinner. However, I was convinced that surely there had been more reason to meet Miss Shepherd than the delivery of the package, for that had seemed to be only of interest to the Reverend. The eponymous chatelaine of the Yaller House had been most insistent on Northrup's meeting with Miss Winona Shepherd. Besides she was an attractive woman, if religious. I informed the Reverend that I would be spending at least a few days in Hannibal, as I had to address the matter of my finances. For a few moments, he seemed in the grip of an inner struggle, before he said, 'Ah... well, I'm afraid I couldn't possibly... you understand. The money... for the cause.'

I did not doubt that any moneys that came his way were entirely diverted to that cause to which he was most dedicated, namely the enrichment of the Reverend Erastus Newberry. I bade the Reverend farewell, and left him in his tiny room with his pile of clothing and avaricious dreams.

Miss Shepherd was outside the building, standing on the raised wooden walkway that passed for a safe place for those navigating the town on foot. She carried nothing that she might have purchased in the Clemens' general store that I could see. Her chin was tilted upward and she gave me a steady stare, until I greeted her.

'Well met again, Miss Shepherd. Will you take a walk with me? I should like dinner, might you know of a suitable place?'

The chin remained high, but she deigned to reply, 'Suitable for whom?'

I was truly glad she had abandoned the affectation of a Southern accent.

'Why, for a lady such as yourself,' I said.

She gave a most unlady-like snort.

'In that case I do not know such a place, but we'll have to make do.'

She turned on her heel and I had but little choice than to follow her.

We arrived in South Main Street after a brisk walk; the young woman was sure-footed although the sun was long down and the few lights in the streets were clustered round the more expensive residential properties. We stopped in front of an unmarked 'store-front', as Miss Shepherd referred to the building. The young lady rang the bell, gave a rhythmic knock and pulled the bell again. The door opened and we passed inside. It was an eating establishment, although of no great quality, judging by the poor ratio of cuspidors to tables. Many of these tables were occupied, although the hour was late. I could scarce credit that there were so many free persons of colour in the township of Hannibal. Service was provided by a crude imitation of the *Grand Turk*'s Texas Tender, this personage lacking any footwear, polished or no. His shirt and apron might once have been white but were now an uncertain colour between grey and beige. The trousers almost made claim to smartness, although the effect was spoiled by the gingham patch on one of the knees.

Miss Shepherd's arrival drew nods of greeting from the waiter and from many of the diners themselves. It was uncommonly dim in the dining room: candles were ensconced at rare intervals on the walls and each of the four windows to the front aspect was obscured by hessian or a horse-hair blanket. We took a table in a particularly dark corner, next to the ever-swinging door leading to the kitchen. The smell was uncommonly strange, if by no means unappetising. The waiter approached our table, a grubby towel over one arm.

'Evenin' Miz Winona.' His smile seemed genuine enough.

'Good evening, George. What do you have for us this evening?'

'Well we got pork, thass pig's feet or chitlins, o' course, and they's eggplant, okra, black-eyed peas an' rice. And they's melon too, Miz.'

Miss Shepherd turned to me and said, 'Well, Mr Northrup, the choice is not great, the feet or the guts: which is it to be?'

I was on the point of answering, when George dropped the grubby towel and received quite a blow from the rough edge of the table in his attempt to recover it. The pig's trotters seemed the lesser of two evils and so the choice was made, just as soon as the waiter had recovered himself.

He returned with a large porcelain jug and two pottery tumblers. Miss Shepherd poured a cloudy liquid whose colour was uncertain in the gloom. To my dismay it contained no alcohol, although the taste was not unpleasant. My companion informed me that it was lemonade, and I found it uncommon sweet. The food arrived and it was hot and surprisingly tasty. However, I must confess that I was quite starving by that time. Miss Shepherd ate efficiently if not daintily, and without too much noise. Thankfully the meat fell from the pig-trotters, since they were tender enough to have been cut with a spoon, of which implement I was put in mind by the sharpness of my knife.

We forwent the melon: this was a source of some disappointment to me; I should have enjoyed the watching of Miss Shepherd's consumption of such a thing.

'Well, who are you then?' she asked. 'It's plain you are not Mr Northrup, any more than you are an American, Yankee or, indeed, a Southron.'

She gave a low laugh, which quite distracted me from any consideration of any answer I might have given her.

'A simple question, with a most complicated answer. One I might be prepared to give in more... intimate surroundings.'

She laughed again, 'I don't think so, sir. I don't at all.'

The café was still empty save for ourselves, a grizzled old man asleep face down in a dirty plate and George. My companion motioned with her head toward the exit. I stood and drew back her chair, earning myself a splinter in the process. At no time did money change hands, which was the most pleasing aspect of our repast, for me. Afront the restaurant, Miss Shepherd bade me accompany her, at least, to the main thoroughfare. I assured her that I would accompany her to the very side of her bed. She, in turn, informed me that no such thing would be necessary – or indeed desirable on her part.

Nonetheless, we took ourselves off in a direction that she informed me was 'Downtown', although a large proportion of the route appeared to be in an upward direction. We stopped before a large townhouse, which would not have looked out of place in fashionable parts of Paris. It did look somewhat incongruous in Hannibal: a single file of stone-built, several-storey residences dwarfing the less pretentious clapboard houses in its vicinity.

'Well, Mr Northrup, I thank you.'

She was atop the steps, hand already on the bell-pull.

'You might invite me in, I might tell you something of myself,' I said.

'I might, but I am certain that you would not.' She offered the encouragement of a smile.

'Surely this grand edifice–' She gave a snort as the last word escaped my lips, 'has a drawing room? Would you not be entirely safe in the company of your parents?'

'What makes you think that my parents live here?' she asked.

'Oh, please don't tell me you are the orphaned ward of a rich and philanthropic couple!'

She smiled, 'Not everything is what it seems, Mr Northrup.'

This observation was not something to be denied by me.

'Come, Miss Shepherd, I give you my word. I shall tell you all you might wish to know.'

I did not enjoy the tone of supplication in my own voice. Still less, the bell-like laugh she gave in answer.

'Surely you would take a gentleman at his word?' The words came rapid and hot, it was true.

'I would if there were any such present,' she said, as she gave the bell-pull a masculine jerk.

The door opened wide. It was opened by a white man of middle years, who raised his eyebrows. Whether this was in greeting in honour of Miss Shepherd's return, or in surprise at the company in which she had arrived was, of course, open to argument. The eyebrows had almost descended to a customary level by the time he sputtered, 'Good evening, Miss Shepherd, ah... were we expecting a guest?'

'Don't worry, Fitzwilliam, Mr Northrup will take a drink and be gone within the hour.'

I was unsure whether to feel flattered or insulted at the

relief visible in the retainer's face. He ushered us along a wide vestibule, lighting our way with a candelabra, which sported a familiar number of branches. We passed into a withdrawing room in the English style. Fitzwilliam lit candles in sconces, of which there were many. He stopped short of finding the long taper required to light those in the chandelier, but the light was comfortable, if unsuitable for reading. A long-case clock in the corner chimed eleven. Fitzwilliam backed out of the room and Miss Shepherd gestured me toward an upholstered chair in the style of Chippendale, while she sat primly and – to my eye – uncomfortably on a chaise longue whose pattern matched the chair.

'Fitzwilliam will see to some wine in a moment,' she said. 'You may begin.'

Tempted though I was to begin *in medias res*, I began as many had, in my experience, at a beginning. Had it been mine, I should have been very proud of it, and yet I was so, despite its fictive nature. I confessed to Scottish birth and some interest in writing, wherefore I had come to the Americas incognito, in search of inspiration and raw material. Owning to the name Edward Waverly, I recounted a tale of encounter and intrigue to account for my appearance as Anson Northrup. That man, I said, had accosted me in St Louis. He gave me a woeful history about gamblers, gambling and moneys owed to less savoury fellows than those with whom he was accustomed to treat. To lend this preposterous tale a sheen of veracity, I revealed that he had given me such funds as he had, save for a few dollars he placed in the pockets of my own clothes, after we had exchanged them in an upstairs room in a St Louis saloon. Taking a sip of the reasonable *vin ordinaire,* which Fitzwilliam had delivered in silence, I finished my account so:

'So you see, Miss Shepherd, I am no more than the dupe of a talented liar.'

'As, perhaps, you would have me be, whatever your true name.' She laughed, and I suspected that she might at last confide some intelligence that had been saved for the Northrup she had been expecting.

'Clearly you are an enterprising man, but you are an imposter. It would take only a word in the Café, here in Hannibal, or on one of the riverboats to see you dead at the hand of one or many of our black brethren. Northrup has – how shall I phrase it – resonance and meaning along the Underground Railroad. Imagine the disappointment if a fraud were revealed. Whatever might such disappointed people do?'

She waited, although clearly I was not expected to answer, merely digest her words. She placed her own glass, barely sipped from, on a spindly-legged table that stood between her seat and mine.

'So, my Ship of Theseus, I do not care if you are Plato's carriage or Socrates', step you again into Heraclitus's river, or at least ride the riverboat down it. The silver is on your charge, I expect you to ensure its use by and for the Freedom Ride.'

Being quite disgruntled by her mixed philosophical metaphors, I contented myself with thoughts of a non-allegorical use for my grandfather's axe.

'Well?' Her chin came up and she looked at me expectantly. The golden butter tone of her skin under the candlelight caught my attention, and I was reminded of someone I could not quite place.

'What is it that you expect me to do?' I asked.

'You'll go to New Orleans and you will make sure that the silver boards the *Grand Turk* when it docks in The Crescent City.'

The woman was quite above herself, but I restricted myself to the enquiry, 'How?'

'Most boats are faster than the *Turk*, sir. I have booked you passage on the *Enterprise*. She leaves in the morning.'

The woman stood, Fitzwilliam appeared, and I was escorted to the street.

10

If I had been harbouring hopes that the *Grand Turk* had been the least impressive exemplar of a riverboat possible, I was sorely disappointed on arrival at the wharves. In superficial degree, the *Enterprise* was similar to the *Turk* in many respects: there were no masts or rigging or any tackle at all. Just two large and indifferently housed paddles on either side of a long, barge-like hull, sitting low and flat in the water like a whale in wait, if ever such beasts lie in wait for anything. Two improbably tall stacks were a little forward of amidships and – though the vessel was at anchor and seemed fastened alongside by the only hemp in evidence aboard – these sooty tubes belched forth a black and acrid smoke at frequent intervals. The pilot house had at some (long distant) time been fully-glazed. Now however, such glass as remained was a danger to all in terms of sharp edges. The view to the larboard side of this edifice was obscured by two highly contrasting pairs of pantaloons, which had been fastened – one hoped in a temporary arrangement – to provide either privacy or shelter. I doubted their efficacy in the latter case. Toward the stern, a miniature terrace of wooden-shackery in sharply contrasting styles evinced the availability of staterooms, although clearly the state of which one was reminded most was Mr Swift's imaginary isle of homunculi. Immediately aft of these infinite varieties of accommodation was a long, low structure, boasting only one entrance. Outwith this stood a man in clothes of uncertain provenance, in as much as it was difficult to tell whether they had originally been of cloth or leather. I approached him to ask the whereabouts of the Ship's Agent's office. He replied with some immediacy if not with great clarity, 'F'yer fixin' tuh travel, I'm your man. Ain't no Agent's Office. Leastways not now.'

'Well, I have passage booked,' I began, and the fellow continued as though I had not.

'Stateroom fer the show-folks, least the durn manager. Hell, ah usetuh sleep in that office!'

'Passage booked in the name of Northrup,' I hardened my voice a little.

'Why'n'cha say?' He stepped aside.

The hall-like superstructure was filled with tables placed end-to-end in the manner of a refectory, although the hubbub did not put one in mind of any religious or scholarly institution. Given the hour – a little after eight – the agglomeration of tea, coffee, bread, butter, salmon, shad, liver, steak, potatoes, pickles, ham, chops, black puddings and sausages could only have been breakfast. I could scarcely squeeze into a chair between a rapidly moving and un-matched pair of elbows. Each of these was attached to a figure of some corpulence. Both in their turn were intent on maintaining or improving on this state of affairs, judging by the debris before them. No sooner had I made myself comfortable than two black men ran the length of the table several times in quick succession removing every dish and plate. This collection they piled upon a large sheet or tablecloth of which they each took hold by two corners and then bore the whole away as though it were some bat-tle-slain unfortunate on a litter.

The two fellows at my side, having cleaned their forks and knives with diligent tongues, stood up and began, with the help of the fellows opposite, to fold away the table at which we had been sitting. This action was repeated the length of the long refectory. A quantity of the tables, numbering about half of the total, were stockpiled at one end of the long room, to one side of a noxious and extremely noisy stove. The remaining tables, save one, were used as battering rams to force passengers, both those bearing their own tables and those without, aside from the plum positions, that is to say, in the vicinity of the stove. Toward the other end of the hall, two passengers erected a table quite close to the wall of the long room. A chest stood padlocked, hard against the wall just behind the table. The ship's agent entered, brandishing a large and tarnished key. He removed bottles in some number from the chest and I resolved to breakfast on some alcoholic tincture, thinking that the journey ahead might require more fortitude than I presently felt.

The ship's agent-cum-barman gestured at the few bottles of whiskey he had placed on the table.

'Take yore pick, Mistuh.'

I grasped the nearest bottle to hand, as the man sneered, 'Dime a glass, quarter a bottle.'

Being undecided as to which choice would inconvenience the fellow most, I threw the first coin encountered in my pocket upon the deal surface. It was a dollar.

One of the owners of the discommoding elbows approached that end of the long room bearing a chair before him; this ensured safe passage through the crowd of those who had recently broken their fast. All seemed disinclined to leave for the decks: perhaps because there was limited space thereon, so far as I had been able to tell. The man placed his chair determinedly in the only thoroughfare that the multitude had allowed from the entrance to the stove. Thereupon he sat down in it and promptly fell to snoring. I caught the barman's eye: he threw his head back, raised his eyebrows and managed the feat of appearing to look down a prodigiously long nose at myself, though he was the smaller by a foot.

'Peculiar fellow,' I said, motioning towards the sleeping brute.

'Feller's jest makin' shore,' the man behind the table grunted.

'Sure of what?'

'Gittin' a shave afore the razor's blunt.' He began a fit of laughter, which soon deteriorated into raucous and phlegmy coughing, to which he put an end with a hideous jet of tobacco juice fired to the left of my own right boot. As if this were some kind of signal, the entire company of passengers in the long saloon – excluding rather fewer of the women than might have been imagined – began a symphony of expectoration which made me quite glad that I had missed breaking my fast. How I longed for the presence of a single spittoon; I thought with fond nostalgia of the *Grand Turk*, which for all its faults was possessed of a cuspidor even in the pilot house.

The barber arrived. He was not black , as I had expected, but a white man of extremely tall stature. Long and thin of shank, he had a cadaverous look belied by the still bleeding cuts caused by his own barbering. He carried a copper bowl and a mug with a grimy brush-handle peeping above the rim. I stood aside to let him approach his customer. Rather than disturb his slumbers, he began applying soap dexterously during the shortest of pauses between the inhalations and exhalations of the snorer. No cloth was draped around the slumberer's neck, but not a stain appeared on the man's clothes. I watched, fascinated. The barman stifled a yawn, the conversation continued all around, punctuated only by the slap of sputum on the wooden floorboards. The barber stepped back at last to leave a skin on view that was quite as unblemished and smooth as a cherub's and the customer immediately awoke and paid his fee.

I waited to see the miracle repeated twice more and was on the point of taking the chair, when a man with particularly bristle-darkened jowls shoved me aside. The man behind the bar gave a great sigh. Choosing to make nothing of the affront, I resolved to wait my turn. I decided against a shave at all, shortly after the first of the yelps and curses emanated from the chair.

'Blunt now, ain't it?' the barman said.

I shook my head, but certainly not in disagreement.

A few moments later, a hunched figure lurched in. The improbable dentition looked familiar. He looked no older than he had in his guise of itinerant puppet-master near St Paul's, or indeed the frock-coated figure in the Coble Inn in far-off Northumbria, though both guises had been left some years behind. He was dressed in a garish frock coat of the brightest blue. His waistcoat was a darker blue with white stars. His pantaloons were striped in red and white. There could be no doubt that I knew the fellow, for had his voice – with its grace-note accents of the gypsy or Bohemian – not convinced me, his words could not but do so.

'Still ahead of the Nimmers, sir?'

The barman looked on, yawning.

'I fear you are mistaken in me, sir. Northrup. Northrup's the name.'

'Of course, it is, sir, of course it is.'

He smiled and the gleaming teeth slid a little forward, but not at the alarming rate I recalled from our last encounter, in as much as they remained confined by the limits of his mouth.

'And your name, sir, what might that be?' I asked, truly the abrupt manners of the Americans were affecting my own.

'Why, it might be anything you like!' This time he laughed and the teeth strained once more to escape.

It took quite some self-restraint not to grasp the man by the throat and dash his forehead against the deal surface until his teeth finally did come out. Perhaps a little of my ire showed in my face, for he gave a less confident laugh and went on, 'But I go by Shiloh Copland.' He gestured with a sweep of the arm at his own attire. 'A *nom de théâtre*, of course.'

The man, who by my calculation must have seen many more than seventy summers in whichever lands he had spent them, could hardly have looked less like an actor to my eye, even taking in to account his clothing.

'Shakespeare, is it?' I enquired.

His mouth made as much of a pout as his unfortunate dental arrangement would allow.

'Sir Garrick Cattermole gives a little of his Lear, depending on the audience. And my own moment centre stage is a reading from *The Posthumous Papers of the Pickwick Club*.'

'You must be hard put to make more than a quarter of an hour's entertainment out of that,' I told him, thinking to myself that should the fifth part of such a quarter-hour's entertainment consist of anything from the pen of Mr Dickens, it might well make the whole seem ten times as long.

'Ah… the majority of the entertainment consists in a very fine minstrel show.'

Which accounted for his bizarre raiment, if not his presence on that side of the Atlantic Ocean, on the very steamboat on which I had taken passage. There must have been some motive for his appearance, if not, it struck me as a ludicrous coincidence worthy of the sentimentalist hack himself.

Thankfully, the bizarrely dressed man had business at

the other end of the long room and took himself off there to arrange several of the tables as some sort of large, raised dais. I do not mean to infer that he himself laid a hand on any part of the furnishings, merely that he directed operations in a loud if repetitive fashion. It was indeed surprising that those passengers, mainly gruff and menacing males, made no great cavil at being directed in this feat of construction by the strangely dressed crouch-back. Truth to tell, they went about it with an enthusiasm surprising in such glowering brutes. I turned to the fellow behind the makeshift bar.

'I am somewhat astounded that such a one found so many willing to do his bidding,' I remarked.

The fellow let out a steaming jet of tobacco juice only slightly deflected away from my coat by the surface of the whiskey bottle before me.

'Gotta have a stage, if ya wanna have a show,' he shrugged.

'Show?'

I was dimly aware that the fellow was in danger of thinking himself in conversation with an imbecile. He did, however, manage a near-civilised reply: 'Mat'nees an' Evenin's. Minstrel Show. Best show on the river. That Shiloh, he make me laugh fit ta bust a gut.'

Having – momentarily – considered busting the man's gut for him with the aid of a blunt knife, I bade him good day and went out on deck. The barman called after me, 'Mat'nee at 12, Mistuh!'

The moment I set foot outside the long room, I felt a juddering, which shook my bones from toe to cranium. This was accompanied by a screeching and crunching in combination, which suggested – at the very least – a minor earth tremor, and possibly some more catastrophic seismological event. To my relief, the noise was reduced in sufficient time to preclude any bleeding from my eardrums and followed by an almost imperceptible movement of the steam-powered boat astern. By-and-by, the vessel made a desultory drifting movement to the centre of the Mississippi and I discerned that the *Enterprise* was underway.

It was a dull day; the sky as drab as the water of the river, to the point where it was uncertain which of them reflected the other. Ahead of me, toward the bow, a snake-like procession of passengers seemed in the grip of the same desire to circumambulate the entire vessel as though claustrophobia had set in the moment the *Enterprise* had cast off. I toyed briefly with the idea of turning about and walking widdershins against the tide of travellers, but caught sight of the slim figure of a woman a few yards to my front. The protests from the corpulent couple I pushed aside were drowned out by the shocked shrieks, when they fell into the stateroom of two swishes who doubtless wished they had had the foresight to bar the door against any intrusion. I caught the woman by the elbow; she turned to face me. I noted that the clothes seemed patched and shabby, although clean. There was something strange about her, although I recognised Miss Winona Shepherd straightway.

'Yessuh, wha' kin ah do foh yuh?'

She gave a smile, and I was for all the world convinced that she did not know me. I began to stutter an apology, so astounded was I. To tell the truth the skin on her face was several shades darker: but when she narrowed her eyes, I knew her for Miss Shepherd truly.

'Do not speak to me,' she hissed.

I dropped my hold on her arm and watched her progress around the boat's bow, my jaw as low as any bumpkin's at a London market.

My mood was set no fairer than the weather. It seemed that it might rain, but that would have made little difference to the drab quality of the light. The *Enterprise* itself seemed affected by the turgidity of the conditions, I estimated that it was labouring to travel above one-and-a-half knots and that downstream. Any thoughts of calculating the number of days until disembarkation in New Orleans were discouraged by this. My perambulations of the vessel took no longer than twenty minutes: this despite the throngs of passengers in the thoroughfares, which, by dint of the space occupied on the deck by the pilot house, funnels, the Texas, passenger accommodations, the saloon bar and sundry other structures of indeterminate purpose, were strait indeed. Finding myself once more at the door of the long saloon, I was on the point of entering when the strangely dressed crook-back cartwheeled out of it. Judging from the look on his face, he seemed to have received some assistance in achieving this unusual manner of egress. An instinct for the contrary provoked me to catch him by the tails of his coat as he flew past, or he would have bathed for ever in the muddy Mississippi, save that he were prodigiously gifted in the sport of natation. When he had recovered a little, he crouched, hands on his knees and gasped, 'M-mo-mo-Moff...'

I clamped a hand over his mouth and hissed, 'Northrup!'

It scarce seemed possible that his eyes might bulge still further, but by pinching his nostrils between my thumb and the palm covering his mouth, I proved that it was. His papery skin had taken on a lapis-lazuli hue before I removed my hand and this time the gasping was not accompanied by any attempt at discourse. Finally, he drew himself as upright as a man of his age with his affliction could do so.

'So,' I smiled, 'Shiloh, it shall be. *Quid pro quo.* The past is gone for ever, is it not? Only a fool would travel back to such a far country.'

'Quite so, let the past be history.' He had mustered a dignified grace, though he was yet a little hard of breathing.

'Why not?' I replied. 'As the Corsican said, it is only a version of the past that people have decided to agree on. A drink?'

He shivered a little then licked his lips and I surmised that if such had not recently been the cause of his ejection, it would on some future occasion be so.

Inside the saloon, the bartender-cum-ship's agent glowered at my companion, but retreated under my gaze, pausing only to leave a full bottle of the dreadful whiskey on the table in front of us.

'So, a matinee, a show,' I said.

He gave a sigh, 'It is not the Fantoccini. Nor even Signor Bologna's Punchinello, but what is there for a broken old traveller, but to travel in company?'

'Who is this Cattermole? An actor? English?' I took pride in uttering the latter with only a modicum of contempt.

The hunchback cackled, 'As you or I, Mr Northrup, as you or I.'

My fist was clenched and half-raised before he added, 'You'll see for yourself, soon enough. Most of us need a little something before we take the stage.'

Perhaps he had the right of it, although I suspected it might be the audience who were more in need of the stimulatory effects of any strong spirits.

Of course, though I had silenced the man the moment he attempted to utter the name by which, however briefly, he had known me, that did not mean that my own curiosity about Shiloh Copland Esquire had abated in any way. When last encountered, the others in my company were convinced beyond persuasion that the man before them was one Septimus Coble, a man whose fortune I had not quite inherited and whose gravestone we subsequently visited. Whoever he might – or might not – have been, he remained the man I had first encountered as owner of a Fantoccini entertainment, which he was in the habit of pushing on a handcart through London streets with the aid of a hurdy-gurdy man. There remained still in the man's cadences and consonants something of the Central-European; although I could not say – no more than previously – whether he was a Prussian or Romany or Magyar thief. However, this did not matter, save that, perhaps, in frontier towns or among rude mechanicals, he might have had to answer to the name 'Dutch'.

On the point of broaching the subject of any past meetings, I was thwarted by the entrance to the long room being thrown uncommon wide, and a bellow coming through it in simultaneous fashion with a bizarre figure, clothed in attire fashionable at some point in society. Whether this point was identifiably geographical or temporal, I was hard put to say.

'Hi, halloo! Barkeep, whiskey, now if you will,' were the words thrown so forcibly into the air that Copland had flinched.

I took a moment to take in this phenomenon. From the waist down he appeared to have dressed in approximation of one of Dumas Père's Musketeers. The trouser legs bunched heavily over boots whose tops were turned down most haphazardly over the calves. His upper part owed little more to the modes of the day, being a once-white shirt with no manner of collar in evidence, covered by a top-coat which may once have been in possession of a bifurcated tail, but which now could only offer one long swatch to the rear, alongside its crudely truncated companion.

He fixed me with a shining eye which suggested that he maintained a supply of medicinal spirits in whatever part of the ship he lodged, and enquired, 'Join me, sir? I feel even on these inland waters, every sailor deserves his wine of height? Don't you?'

The peculiar combinatory spectacle of his dress was as nothing to the auditory surprise effected by the commingling of accents from the Liffey and the Thames that infused his words. I found it most bizarre: as though a parrot had been taught the vocabulary of a gentleman, but not the diction. He did cut a handsome figure, topping my own stature by an inch or two. I could imagine a certain kind of shallow female considering his looks appealing – for a man of fifty or so. He held out his hand, 'Sir Garrick Cattermole, theatrical manager and actor!'

His words made the long trip from Temple Bar to Cheapside in the course of this short sentence and I would have wagered the man was no more a Knight Baronet than a Chinese Mandarin. Nonetheless, I grasped his hand and shook it, offered him the name of Anson Northrup and pushed my own bottle of whiskey towards him.

'Action is eloquence, sir.'

It was not in him merely to speak; he could not help but declaim. He saw me flinch at the volume at which he did so, and I wondered if he knew he put me in mind of other words from the Swan of Avon, wherein one might 'dote on his very absence.'

Sir Garrick Cattermole reached for the bottle, raised it half-way to his lips before he caught my eye and roared at the man behind the bar, 'A vessel, a glass, a cup, a tumbler, a goblet, you buffoon! Do I wear feathers and buckskin?'

A smeared and dusty tumbler appeared. Cattermole slopped a goodly measure into the glass and onto the surface of the table serving as the bar. The colour leached from the wood in several moments more than the taste of the spirit might have led one to believe. The actor took a long draught from the glass and replenished it with a little more accuracy than before.

'That it should come to this,' he said.

This seemed to require no answer, and therefore I gave him none, merely taking a sip from my own glass.

He fixed me with a fearsome glare; the noble brow above it darkened and I could see that perhaps he would find ideal roles in certain of Sweet William's creations. The fool on the heath perhaps, or Caliban: his lighter range might even have included poor maligned Malvolio. At length, he spoke again, 'I have trod the boards in Drury Lane, sir, Kean himself told me that I should be as great as he one day.'

By my own estimate, unless the man was much older than he appeared, he could not have been more than twenty-three years old at the time of Edmund Kean's disastrous last appearance on the stage. The manner of Cattermole's speech indicated that if he had ever encountered the late actor at all, his own role had much more likely been that of hansom driver to Kean's customer, than any theatrical part.

'Well,' I began, 'you are, sir, an Actor–Manager, no doubt with charge of a sizeable troupe. I do not see that it has come to so very little.'

The actor's chest puffed up to a size he could not maintain for too long and his next utterance came with an exhalation, which put me in mind of the rotting corpse of a pye-dog.

'You are kind to say so, Mr Northrup, but it is a poor substitute for London Theatre.'

His smile would have had to stretch beyond the flesh of his face to have reached any wider extent. I could see that he was no more immune to the effects of flattery than any actor of my acquaintance. Indeed, in my view, a follower of Thespis was only conquered in the matter of vanity by that empty-headed and strident creature, the politician. Reckoning that there must be at least one member of the actors' company who might prove diverting on the long voyage to New Orleans, I brought myself to compliment the fool further.

'We shall see, I look forward to the matinee with some fascination and expect to be, if not royally, at least nobly entertained.'

The improbable smile wavered not a jot, although I confess my own slipped a little when the door swung wide once more and the remaining members of the troupe entered. These five seemed more suited to employment in the circus than any theatre.

The five entered in grand commotion: identical – and extremely short – twins rolled arsey-varsey in the midst of an altercation blessedly bereft of any weaponry. The tallest, not to say ugliest, woman I had ever seen in my life followed them in, dressed in patched gingham and a ludicrous mobcap which flopped around her jowls as though it were melting. She preceded a man of vast girth, who had apparently been quite unable to acquire any apparel that might enclose his improbable dimensions. Pallid and suety flesh emerged from every ill-met hem and fastening. At the last came a man of middling height but extreme thinness, dressed in the black serge and ribbons of the professional mourner, so that I half-expected the feathered horses of a hearse to come in behind him. Each and every one of the five wore the expressionist, and purportedly comical, theatrical make-up that I had learned was called 'black-face'. Turning to Cattermole, I saw him give a shudder and take a mighty draught of the dreadful spirit. Behind him, Shiloh Copland's crouch-back shoulders shook in silent and malicious laughter.

Cattermole directed Copland to usher the troupe to the ad-hoc stage at the far end of the salon. The dwarves somersaulted away as though a pair of Siamese United Twins, though conjoined topsy-turvy. I wondered if this whirling battle was some long dispute or merely their accustomed mode of perambulation. I thought – almost fondly – of Mrs Gonderthwaite's

twin boys, perished over a decade since in Gibbous House. Sir
Garrick Cattermole looked after them, his eyes glistening. I
turned away to leave him to his sentiment.

Whiskey in hand I made shift to a crooked row of chairs
set before the jury-rigged stage. One heavy-jowled fellow was
slumped, legs stretched out before him, mouth open and emit-
ting noises of which a rutting Wessex Saddleback would have
been justly proud. Next but one to this lump sat a familiar figure. I did not address her for fear of provoking the disproportionate reaction she had earlier evinced. Besides, this time she
was not alone. A matronly figure of some fifty years sat beside
her, hands clasping a voluminous bag. She was speaking at Miss
Shepherd, rather than to or with her, and the young woman's
gaze was held downward in a most submissive manner, her
very occasional replies restricted to 'Yes'm' or 'No'm' and in all
probability 'Three bags full'm'. I took a seat, leaving one free
between myself and Miss Shepherd and her mistress.

At one side of the stage, Shiloh Copland sat before an
instrument of keyboard type, so small as to seem designed for a
child. It looked to encompass no more than an octave or two in
range. Copland sat most cramped before it, pumping fiercely at
some bellows with his knees scarcely escaping painful barking
against the underside of the keyboard itself. Presently, he lifted
an arm with a flourish and attempted to coax a noise from the
keys. Had it been the lost chord that he found, I could not have
been more surprised by the noise that emerged from its half-
perished reeds. It might have been an unusually diminished
fifth, or perhaps an unexpectedly augmented fourth. Then
again, it was not impossible that the depression of the keys had
resulted in the strangling of a pair of cockerels confined within
the shell of the instrument. Copland seemed satisfied with the
outcome. In any event, he refrained from any further exercise

or rehearsal. Never was an instrument less aptly named the har-monium, in my opinion.

To my rear, a clattering and scraping announced the tak-ing of seats for the performance. I turned to look over my shoulder: the seats were arranged in rows for the most part, although here and there a group of four chairs clustered around a card table. These seats' incumbents intended to hear the show at the very least. I watched at least one bearded fellow with one good eye making most fantastical contortions to look back-ward at the stage every few moments. It yet remained bare, save for the harmonium and a solitary oil-lamp burning down-stage centre. Presently, their footwear clumping on the table-tops serving as the stage, the entire troupe entered and formed a circle on it. The two midgets had ceased hostilities, at least to the extent of placing the giant woman between them and reaching up to join hands with her. The circle formed by the actors resulted in a view of what was perhaps Cattermole's best side. I noted the inexpert patching on the xanthous material of the coat into which he had changed for the performance.

Cattermole nodded his head, the midgets bellowed, in a voice quite disproportionate to their size, 'Mucha Mierda!'

The cadaverous fellow, still in his mourning weeds, gave a timid, 'M-Merde!'

The giant woman sang a coloratura,'Mi-er-da!' and I feared for the glass in my hand.

This was followed by the obese fellow's, 'Dreck!', Cat-termole and Copland chorused, 'Break a leg!' whereupon the actor manager clapped his hands and said, 'Places please!'

As might have been expected, Copland, the crook-back, re-took his seat at the harmonium, and, with great flourishing of his bony arms, coaxed forth still more sounds reminiscent of the visit of a fox to a hen-house. The twins sat cross-legged at the tall woman's knee as she made a comfortable settle out of the enormously fat fellows back, just as soon as he had lowered his bulk to its hands and knees. The solemn faced mourner stood behind the tall woman, placing a hand upon her shoulder, though he had to reach upward a little to do so. The whole presented some gross parody of a familial tableau. Cattermole stood centre stage and addressed the audience as follows, although this gives no flavour of the peculiarity of his numerous accents.

'Ladies and Gentlemen, I superbiate at this unwonted and irreproducible opportunity, nay salivate at the prospect of the serendipitous good fortune that you our blessed audience are about to enjoy, namely, viz., to wit, that is to say, *The Sir Garrick Cattermole Minstrel Show and Compendium*. Please lay palm to palm in a cacophony of manual approbation as we offer for your delight and delectation, with scientific applications to the banjo and occasional help from the harmonium, an old favourite made famous by the Virginia Minstrels...'

The assembled crowd, including the one-eyed Jack playing Poker, let out a roar of approval that seemed quite unnecessary in view of what followed. The mournful bone-rack fingered a banjo dextrously, if less than tunefully, whilst the remaining members of the tableau bellowed a jaunty ditty, exhorting the excited audience to steer well clear of a somewhat boisterous party by the name of 'Old Dan Tucker'.

In truth, for the most part, the minstrel show minded me of nothing other than a penny gaff, save that there seemed to be no constraint of time. Cattermole's role as master of ceremonies – unlike that of such a fellow presiding over any show in the rear of a Chiswick public house – did not include random termination of the acts in an effort to generate more income. In spite of this, the whole of the show was of so poor a standard to require a fee paid to the owner of the riverboat to perform it, rather than a transfer of moneys in the opposite direction.

The songs thankfully persisted through no more than two or three examples of lively, if crude, ditties. At this point, the Actor–Manager took centre-stage once more and gave forth thus:

'And NOW Lay-dees and Gennulmen! I lay before you the finest example of its kind, an exemplar of the art of stumpular oratory, please make more welcome for… Caractacus Monroe, with a monologue entitled "De Jews In Egypt".' This last word was accompanied by yet another of the harmonium player's approximations of a chord and this was the finest representation of the sounds of poultry-cide made to that point. Cattermole made way centre stage and the mournful-looking beanpole took position. The monologue was unintelligible to me, while the crowd laughed loud and long from the very beginning. To my ear the man appeared to be speaking in an exaggerated version of slave dialect, though I doubted any bondservant ever spoke so incoherently. After fifteen minutes I could make out more than the occasional word, happily this period coincided with that allotted to the purported entertainment. Monroe's final words were, 'Let My People Go'. I looked over at Miss Shepherd, who whispered to herself, 'Go down, Moses'.

At that very moment, a ruffian stumbled before me and landed, as if by chance, in the empty seat between Miss Shepherd and myself. If the man was not drunk, he had chosen to bathe in a vat of whiskey, perhaps in an effort to ward off some infection. He surely was unlikely to be infected by any unwanted company, though any efficacy against infirmity remained in doubt. He fixed me with one blear and bloodshot eye and amid much expectoration opined that, 'It wash a gud schow, scho far.'

If I could not agree with this entirely, there was no doubt that the show at that point became exceedingly worse. Cattermole, with accustomed prolixity and proximity to good usage informed us all that he was about to give us something from the Scottish Play. Sadly, it was not the scene where Macduff returned triumphant with the head of the protagonist. Most unfortunately, the head of the troupe chose to murder the tyrant somewhat early by committing grave injury to his speech on the occasion of seeing the dagger. The crimes committed by this miserable creature against the Bard of Avon began as follows:

'Is THIS a dag-GER which I behold before ME,
    The 'an-DULL two -ORD moy 'AND? Cumlemme clutch 'EE.
    I 'AVE 'ee not, yet I see 'EE STILL!
    Art vou NOT, fey-TALL vision, sensi-BULL
    to feelin' as ter SIGHT?'

The spirited fellow next to me jumped to his feet, suddenly more sober, at least in as much as he did not immediately fall over. He bellowed sufficiently to overpower the mighty projections of Cattermole:

'Ain't 'at Macbeth feller s'pose to be a Scotchman?'

The actor Cattermole gave a theatrical stagger, although the blanching of his face seemed genuine enough. He threw up his hands and jerked his head towards the fat and mournful members of his company, 'Get him out! Get him out!'

I was doubtful of the pair's ability to carry out this task, but I was much mistaken. The blubberous individual moved the quicker of the two, much to my surprise, but the majority of the man-handling fell to the black-garbed skeleton and it in no way over-faced him. The rest of the audience seemed to treat the ejection of the erstwhile critic as part of the general entertainment, roaring encouragement as he passed their row, his booted feet barely troubling the bare boards of the deck.

Was it fancy that the faintest splash preceded the longest and most deafening applause of the afternoon? I resolved to keep my opinions of the show to myself, at least within earshot of the actors.

The final part of the farrago appeared to be an approximation of a short play: Cattermole played the owner of a cotton plantation, one Simon Legree, whilst the rest of the players played various enslaved unfortunates. One of these was named Uncle Tom and was played with such pathos by the lugubrious Caractacus Monroe, that I was very hard put not to laugh aloud at his demise. For some reason, this death signalled the end of the play and 'Uncle Tom' was resurrected in the Lord just in time to take part in an altogether superfluous reprise of 'Old Dan Tucker'. The audience rose to grant this last a rousing ovation, Miss Winona Shepherd took the opportunity to slip a folded sheet of paper into my hand, whilst holding a finger to her lips and shaking her head. I made my way on deck leaving the fools to their applause.

11

The breeze was cold and brought the smell of sulphur and steam into my face. The day was as grey as any in London in the springtime. There were fewer passengers strolling the decks, there being so little to reward their attention save the wide river and the cacophony of birdsong. I unfolded the paper Miss Winona Shepherd had slipped into my hand. It was much creased from folding, but it was by no means a palimpsest. The sheet was blank, save where a neat, feminine hand had written,

'Come not near me, 'til I may pass again.'

The note was unsigned, but it was reasonable to assume she had penned it herself. As to meaning, I could afford it none and placed the paper in a hidden pocket behind a Queen of Hearts.

A man stood perilously close to the rail, hidden behind a newspaper that must have been more than a day old, since the riverboat had not docked in that time. The newspaper was the *Hannibal Journal*. The paper was yellowed and a few rips and tears embellished both the front and back pages.

'Good day, sir,' I said. 'Anything interesting in the news?'

The newspaper remained shielding the fellow's face, but shook a little, before the reply came,

'Ain't much in the news, that's why I'm readin' the olds.'

The newspaper shook again.

I stepped closer to peer at the date by the masthead; the paper was dated some seven years previously.

The paper jerked down and I found myself looking into a familiar face. It began speaking.

'Course, this paper hasn't been of any account since the Clemens Brothers moved on.'

The familiar laugh confirmed the man's identity, my heart had truly sunk to my boots as I realised Mr Clemens Junior had moved on as far as the *Enterprise*.

'You were Nevada bound unless I'm much mistaken?' I said.

'I still am, Mr…'

'Northrup.'

It was strange that he was travelling in the wrong direction. He gave me a quizzical look.

'Northrup, hmm?'

'Incognito, Mr Clemens, I'm collecting material for a book.'

'Is that a fact? Reckon it'd be easier to *publish* under another name, myself.'

'It's a book for a London house, the perils of the riverboats. I felt a gambler might gather more material.'

He laughed, 'Reckon he might if he didn't sound like the Fifth Dook of Dorset.'

'I have recently returned from London, where I have acquired some reputation.'

He smirked, and I was sure he was about to ask me as what, but he merely enquired, 'Writing books, easy work for a man, is it?'

'For some, I'm sure.'

'So, your book, 'bout riverboats. People like to read other people's travelling? Why not go yourself?'

He really was a most tiresome ninny, but I forbore from pitching him over the side and replied, 'Evidently they do, perhaps it is a question of pecuniary assets and the vicarious voyage is better than none at all.'

I turned on my heel; Clemens had folded the *Hannibal Journal* and was rubbing his chin, staring into nothing. It was to be fervently hoped I had not unleashed his unsophisticated humour on the world.

The days congealed into weeks devoid of events or interest. Perhaps the boredom suffered by passengers accounted for the rapturous reception accorded by them to the dire theatricals. For myself, I could not countenance suffering yet more choruses of the profoundly irritating 'Old Dan Tucker' and chose to be absent from the long refectory at such times as it might be heard. On occasion, I would encounter the crouchback, Shiloh Copland, who would offer me a slow wink as he left the vicinity of the makeshift bar. He did not attempt to engage me in conversation, however, and I was mightily glad of it. Of Miss Shepherd there was not a sign, as though she had departed the ship in the black of night, clambering over the side into an itinerant lighter, somewhere between Hannibal and Vicksburg. Mr Clemens was often to be seen scribbling in a notebook with a rather grimy looking pencil, the end of which he placed between his teeth from time to time as though it were a fine cigar.

One evening, shortly before our scheduled arrival at Natchez, I was standing at the refectory bar, meeting the former-ship's-agent-cum-bartender's conversational gambits with monosyllables and the occasional request for further libations, when Sir

Garrick Cattermole made an entrance better than any he had made on any stage. The door swung wide, and he struck a most noble pose, with one arm outstretched and his chest thrust forward like a latter-day Demosthenes. This effect was only slightly marred by his toppling like a felled cedar moments later. I sincerely hoped the lack of cuspidors did not inconvenience him too much, for his face had surely made close connection with the consequences thereof.

It was boredom that induced me to prod delicately at the fallen theatrical genius's ribs with toe of my boot. This produced no discernible effect. A gentle tap returned nothing but a prodigious snore and a few mumbled words. I took the only recourse remaining, that is, I gave him a hefty kick to the thoracic region. The outcome was far more satisfactory: Cattermole sat bolt upright and bellowed, 'Ah mother, would y'ever leave a poor boy alone wit' his dreams.'

This was something I felt had never been uttered by any Greek orator. I offered the dazed fellow an arm to assist his rising and called for another bottle of whiskey. To my surprise he refused the drink. At least for the polite period of several moments. I lifted my glass, 'To Dublin, city of dreams!'

He ran a finger round the inside of his collar and then rubbed a hand over his face.

''Twas no dream of mine, Mr Northrup.'

The look of disgust might have been prompted by the sight of what his hand had removed from his face, but the glassy stare was taking no account of what he saw on the palm of his hand.

'And why not, *Sir Garrick*?'

Perhaps he heard the contempt in my voice, for he fixed me with the gaze of a whipped hound, before giving a bitter laugh.

'Well, wouldn't an actor have a stage name, now?'

'So, a protégé of Kean?' I enquired, but he was not to be needled, I saw only trembling of his lips and surmised that the glassy look in his eyes might be lachrymose in origin. After a moment or two he gave answer, 'I did meet him once, or at least he left a copper coin in my hat.'

'Was that in Dublin?'

Cattermole hawked, spat fiercely to the side and stared at the resultant gobbet as though such a thing as phlegmamancy might exist.

'No,' he said, 'that wasn't Dublin.'

The man seemed quite unlike his usual bombastic self. As I was so unconscionably bored, and considered this an improvement, I asked him if he was, or had ever been, a native of Dublin.

'My family were from West Clare. The Mahons levelled our house and ate lobster in their own. I ran away to Dublin, I begged in the streets and, when I could stand it no more, I killed a man for the ferry fare to Liverpool. I went to London and I begged in the streets there.'

He heaved a great sigh, before continuing, 'One day, a woman stopped. She kicked my hat over, the few coins rolled into the gutter. I leapt to my feet, I swear I would have hit her, though she could have been of an age with my departed mother. But she gripped my arm and hissed, "You'll do." I was much surprised, and, of course, quite weak with hunger and I let her take me where she wished.

'It was a large house in Holborn. The woman fed me well. So well that I was quite ill for days. When I recovered, the woman – Peggy, she said her name was – brought me downstairs to a large room, like a salon in a bordello, save that there was not a woman in sight, Peggy apart. Many of the men were young, affecting powder and the fashions of a century ago. The woman told me that I was for special customers and that

I would be well rewarded "for treating them kindly". Many of the men that I treated kindly were actors, some were lawyers and some politicians. They often asked me to call them Jack or John, but some I recognised thanks to the gossip of the boys of the house. With the food and comfortable living, I grew quite large and cut the figure you see before you.'

He swept an arm out as if to show himself at his best. I stifled a laugh.

'In any event, Peggy let me go with a generous sum and I bought passage to the New World.'

'Why?' I asked.

'Did you know the Choctaw Indians sent money to the Irish poor?' he said, as a tear rolled down his cheek.

'Money? Not beads?'

Cattermole lifted a meaty fist and I held up both hands in surrender, 'How so, then? It seems rather unlikely to me.'

'Ye'll have heard o'the famine.'

Who had not? Though I'd had more pressing concerns in that particular decade.

'An unfortunate lack of potatoes, so I believe.'

Cattermole's glass shattered in his hand. I called for a replacement.

'One hundred and seventy dollars. From the red man to the black Irish. Poverty does not care a whit for the colour of a man's skin, Northrup. Ye'll drink to that, won't ye?

I confess it. That evening I became quite drunk. It would not have ended in Cattermole's bed else. However, it seemed that the former ship's agent's office had been transformed into a stateroom of almost adequate proportions and comfort. There-fore it was with some regret that I departed it the next day to the accompaniment of Cattermole's snores.

The *Enterprise* lumbered downriver, ugly as a manatee, docking at Natchez and sundry small towns by the side of the great river. I felt no inclination to stretch my legs in any of these provincial places. Even from the ship's deck one could see that they were utterly, interchangeably dull. Nevertheless, by the time the riverboat drew up in Baton Rouge, I knew that I must debark the vessel or commit murder. Scarcely had I left the gangplank, when I caught sight of a familiar figure leaving the dockside and heading into the town proper. The clothes were expensive, or looked so, from such a distance as separated us. The woman's carriage and purposeful stride convinced me that it was Miss Winona Shepherd, although since I could only see her back, I could not tell whether she was 'passing' or no.

It was not mere boredom that caused me to follow the woman. She was, after all, involved in both the Underground Railroad and the convoluted scheme in which I – or at least Northrup – was embroiled.

I kept my distance, occasionally turning to look backward the way I had come or stepping into an alley. There were fewer opportunities to hide, however, as the buildings became grander.

After an hour, Miss Shepherd led me to some parkland, magnolia trees abounded on and around the rolling hillocks, the centrepiece of this Arcadian setting was most unexpected. It was a white-washed approximation of a castle. It was a fussy and impractical agglomeration of crenulations and turrets that no more belonged in Louisiana than I.

By this time, I was struggling not to catch up with the still unwitting – as I supposed – Miss Shepherd.

The day was relatively pleasant: the sky visible between the clouds being an approximation of blue rather than the customary grey. I decided to take a turn around the grounds of the grotesque building. Miss Shepherd appeared to have the same intention. My patience ran out before too long and I shouted 'Halloo!' whilst waving my hat at the young woman. Several other people turned to look. Miss Shepherd looked to her left and right, shrugged and covered the ground between us instanter. The change was remarkable, since the last time I had seen her, but the fine clothes and the white powder I discerned on her skin could not deceive me. It *was* Winona Shepherd, if indeed that were her true name. However, I was no closer to knowing if she were a lady or a lady's maid. In either event, I found the prospect of her company most stimulating.

She drew me away from any who might overhear. 'You great fool! Why are you following me?'

'Put the case that I have, though I do not admit it, been following you, why does it bother you so?'

'Because I have work to do. And I do not need distraction from it.'

'Perhaps I can help.' It was a measure of my earlier *ennui* that I uttered these foolish words.

'Perhaps you should. Thanks to you we require a convincer for the mint.'

At first, I was unsure to what she referred. Could it be the Governor's Warrant made out to Mudsill? Though I had kept it out of contrariness alone, my misgivings over Northrop's carrying of a paper with the name 'Mudsill' had led me to ponder whether there was a Benedict Arnold among the conspirators. Which person, of course, might conceivably turn out to be me, or at least Northrop.

Miss Shepherd looked over my shoulder into the distance.

'They're leaving now.'

On asking 'Who?' I received for answer a finger pointing at the building in the distance.

From our vantage point at the edge of an arcade of trees

in the northeastern quarter of the grounds people snaked from the entrance to the building. The majority of people were men; stout, be-whiskered fellows in the prime of life. Some were dressed in dark frock coats and affected stovepipe hats. Far more were in braided uniforms or in flamboyant cutaways and waistcoats of noisy pattern, as easily remarked as my own would have been at such a distance. There were few women. These seemed at most half the age of their male companions.

'Step away now, sir, and do not follow.' With that she disappeared into the trees.

A man was approaching, intent on something, for he made no acknowledgement other than a nod of the head of my greeting. The countenance between the suspiciously black hair and the strikingly white beard was unremarkable. He affected a military style of dress, but I did not consider him a soldier, for there was something quite slovenly about his bearing. I watched him continue to trail Miss Shepherd, he strode through the arcade, entered the spinney at the end of it and was lost to view.

In due course, the gentleman, a little flushed about the jowls, made his way back toward the Capitol building. In passing he managed a curt, 'Good day, sir.' I grunted a reply.

One would have thought that the interval between the man's departure and the putative Miss Shepherd's appearance would have afforded her sufficient time to ensure that her bonnet was quite straight. Nonetheless I felt the jaunty angle an improvement. The young woman's cheeks bore no trace of flushes, but perhaps the whiteness of the powder kept this colour at bay also.

Her intimation that she felt hungry did not surprise me.

12

Miss Shepherd led me quickly out of the park. Her quick short steps devoured the ground at a surprising rate. My breath came short as a consequence and from time to time she looked back at me with a most provocative smirk. Therefore, we made rapid progress down the road away from the State Capitol, until we arrived on River Road: a wide street with chandlers, bars and rooming houses meant for the flotsam and jetsam of the Mississippi trade. Clearly Miss Shepherd had some destination in mind, but she did not deign to enlighten me as to what it might be. We had almost reached the Public Dock when she took us on a sharp left onto a street, which was somewhat misleadingly named North Boulevard. It may well have stretched in a northerly direction but the few scrawny trees that ran alongside its ungenerous width gave the second part of its name the lie in no small degree.

The young lady brought me up short in front of a clapboard fronted building, which bore a painted sign advertising that the establishment was a 'Miss Porter's Rooms'. We did not enter by the front entrance, but took a walkway barely wide enough for my shoulders to pass through to the rear of the building. In light of the establishment's name, I half expected a bordello of some sort, but it was in fact a reasonable facsimile of a tearoom. It was, of course, no Twinings of the Strand, however it seemed pleasant enough and a lady of advanced years led us to one of the many empty tables. We took our seats and the woman, I assumed her to be Miss Porter, asked, in a voice as dry as a snapping twig, 'What kin I getcha?'

I was spared any reply to this on my own behalf, by Miss Shepherd's long litany, which began with the word tea and finished with English muffins, having passed through every manner of sweetmeat, from strudel to pirozhki via 'old-fashioned American pancakes' as she so quaintly put it. She had been most circumspect in her description of the extent of her hunger in the park, in my opinion. She thought me a most tremendous glutton, else.

In any event, such was not the case. After the tea arrived, a grand succession of dishes, heaped high with sugary confections of the baker's art began making their appearance. Miss Shepherd scooped the topmost exemplar from each before the bottom of the plate touched the white tablecloth. I watched in fascination as she crammed pastries, éclairs, scones and all manner of delicacies that oozed creams, custards and preserves, which covered the lower part of her face. Having removed her gloves by this time, she made good use of a talented tongue, so that she might not lose any morsel of these sweet delights. Finally, she sat back in her seat in a most unfeminine manner and belched behind a hand. Her ministrations had removed the powder from her face and a light caramel brown was visible from under her nose to her chin, giving her face a peculiar piebald look. She lifted her light tan chin and said, 'I am a free woman of colour, but it is better to pass as the poorest white woman, Mr Northrup, and that is something I wish to change, although I know that I cannot.'

'Such things are nothing to me, Miss Shepherd,' I gave

the answer she seemed to expect, for she thanked me and excused herself. I admired her slim figure and wondered at her capacity for patisserie. She returned from the powder room, having used it for that very purpose since she no longer sported a parti-coloured visage. There was a faintly sour smell about her and she proceeded to drink draught after draught of the strong black tea, nodding occasionally at me over the rim of her cup.

I had eaten but little, not for lack of opportunity, rather by reason of disinclination. Miss Shepherd had enjoyed the food more than sufficiently for both of us. It was the moment to ask her what she wanted of me, since I assumed that she had wanted more than an audience for her feats of consumption. However, she thwarted me in this and said, 'The Reverend must not get his hands on the silver. You must prevent it. You must see that the first consignment reaches St Paul, if not Canada.'

I raised an eyebrow, 'That rather presupposes that any silver can be spirited away from the mint, does it not?'

The powdered face was anything but a mask and I read there a look of bitter amusement as though I had uttered some risqué drollery at the expense of her nearest relatives.

'Mr Northrup.' She showed her teeth on pronouncing the name. 'You seem to me a man who might accomplish anything, just so long as some benefit might accrue to yourself.'

'That's as may be, but I have no introduction to your accomplice in the mint, nor any means of acquiring any.'

She gave a laugh, as dull and unmusical as tapping on a cracked glass.

'Here, Mr Northrup, here is your introduction. I am not so sure of our accomplice as some.'

The folded paper in her hand was a little damp from its hiding place next to her breast. I inhaled the musky scent. Miss

Shepherd gave a shudder and placed her hand over mine, 'Take care, friend, that paper was hard come by.'

I opened it, it was a paper entitling the bearer to all co-operation necessary within the confines of the New Orleans Mint and it was signed by the Governor of the State of Louisiana.

We sat silent for a time. Finally, I asked Miss Shepherd if she were returning to the *Enterprise*, for it was due to leave within the hour. She shook her head.

'I must go upriver. Erastus Newberry is not a man to leave alone with any of the Railroad's assets for too long.'

'There is money in that old church?' I coughed.

'There is a modicum of silver hidden under one of the pews, but he will never find it.' She smiled.

'What then?'

'I do not trust him with our passengers. He does not value his black brethren as he should.'

I laughed, 'Why is he involved with the railroad at all?'

'God moves, Mr Northrup, God moves.'

It was true that if any such being existed, his actions were certainly mysterious. I was reminded of a Yiddish proverb my late wife had taught me: 'Man plans, God laughs.'

We took our leave of the tearoom. I made as if to settle the account, but was waved away by the ancient crone, Miss Porter, 'Anythin' for the Freedom Train, sir.'

At that moment, it occurred to me that there might be some small advantage to involving myself with the Underground Railroad after all.

It was a short walk to the dockside. Miss Shepherd took her leave of me at the blue riband berth where a leviathan of a riverboat was moored. It seemed quite as large as the *Natchez*.

Naturally, the *Enterprise* was not in a prime position, rather it was berthed at the extreme end of the riverside dock, whence it was approached by means of a long and precarious jetty. Once on board, I repaired to my cabin. I was in need of some relief, and the *Enterprise*'s manifest appeared not to offer much opportunity of such. A further dalliance with Cattermole was not be countenanced. Besides, there was nothing so attractive as the unknown and new. However, a turn around the deck provided no prospect of sport of any kind. There was little alternative but to return to my cabin and make provision for my own entertainment. I resolved that when the *Enterprise* finally reached New Orleans, my first port of call would not be the mint, but an altogether more lively establishment.

My solitude was interrupted by a fierce knocking at the door of my stateroom.

A male voice, over-modulated with excitement, and betraying the accents of the riverside communities, bellowed, 'Northrup! Northrup! Quickly!'

This put paid to my pleasant, if solitary, diversions. I rearranged my attire and opened the door.

A man of low stature and mean clothing stood without, fist raised in the act of renewing its assault on the cheap deal of my door.

'Northrup?' His voice had settled into an even if dull pitch.

'That would depend,' I said.

'This here is Northrup's cabin! If you ain't Northrup then what in tarnation are you doin' in it?'

I made as if to shut the door, but the fellow had insinuated his foot between it and the jamb, thereby thwarting me at some pain to himself, judging by the yelp he gave. Boredom and caprice had ever provoked unwise impulses on my part, and perhaps the decision to admit to the name of Northrup at that point was one of them.

I followed the man to the pilot house of the *Enterprise*, whereupon he left me with a grunt and a jerk of the head towards it. On guard was a man of less than military bearing. His attire might indeed have consisted of uniform clothing, but from several different armies at least. Atop his head he wore a once-smart cap like the French kepi. Since it had clearly once belonged to either a child or a pinhead, this adornment perched on his balding head, as prone to shifting as a pea on a drum. His jacket resembled that of a Prussian Hussar, save that such frogging and loops as remained were incorrectly fastened, as though he had been dressed by a drunk. For his lower limbs he had chosen to wear a pair of faded and patched riding breeches whose cuffs came woefully short of the top of his boots. I presumed this harlequin figure to be the pilot engaged for the navigation of the shoals of the Mississippi. The man lifted a hand to the tiny cap as if to doff it in welcome, but he merely affected its retention on his bald pate.

He spat a gelatinous gout towards a chamber-pot that clearly had been doing double duty for some time judging by the smell and the splash. The man had but the one eye, the other being sewn shut by a most inexpert seamstress. His solitary orb was the azure blue of tropical skies.

'Captain Jubal Kincaid,' he said extending a hand as grimy as a tanner's.

I took the hand: its grip was firm for an instant and then resembled a stranded fish.

'Northrup, at your service,' I said.

'Guess'd ye might be, since I sent for ye and all.'

'Indeed you did,' I looked at the man. He was quite short, and so finding riding breeches too deficient in the leg for even his small stature must have been quite a feat. He merely returned my stare, for what seemed an unconscionable time, before nodding his head slowly, several times.

'If'n I said "Mudsill", Mr Northrup, you'd know what I meant, I reckon,' he spat once again, by way of punctuation.

'I might,' I replied.

He fished in the pockets of his bizarre clothing and placed a copper penny in my hand.

'Mudsill has the Copperheads at his disposal, if you get my drift.' He winked with his one blue eye and the effect was quite macabre. He turned his attention to the steering of his vessel and I left him to it, none the wiser as to why I had been summoned, save to inform me that someone named Mudsill had some snakes. I looked at the coin still in my hand; it was no more than a copper cent.

The name had sounded familiar. I searched my memory for the context in which I had come across it. On returning to my cabin, I felt disinclined to continue with my solitary entertainment. Pulling out the hideous carpetbag that comprised my only luggage from under my cramped cot, I removed the book I had acquired on becoming Anson Northrup. I opened it and the onion skin warrant from the Governor of South Carolina fell to the floor, John Mudsill's name was clearly visible, and I remembered that he could expect all assistance on production of this instrument of law. Still, I had given no thought before as to who this person might have been and, though I gave it some now, nothing occurred to me. I resolved to enquire of someone as to the exact nature of a 'Copperhead'. The problem was finding someone who might know, someone I might ask without endangering myself. On replacing the paper within the pages of the book, I lay back on my cot and stared at cracks in the wood of the ceiling.

13

The riverboat having arrived in New Orleans at last, I realised it was the fiftieth birthday of someone I had once been. I wondered how old I was now that I was Anson Northrup. The last few days on the *Enterprise* had been torture indeed. My passions were such that I pitied any soul who caught my eye before I found some or other release. The *Enterprise* had docked at one of the less salubrious points in the port area of the city. Naturally, I took the time to explore the lively, unlovely streets nearest the riverside. For there was plenty of life to be found, even though the *Enterprise* had disgorged its passengers at the dark hour of five, long before the dawn. The north bank of the Mississippi river, the Front Levee, curled round forming the lower edge of a city of grid-like streets with the occasional diagonal. The unhappy and the hopeless came together in desperate clinches in doorways or on deserted jetties. An occasional stumbling figure would indulge in the futile oratory of the hallucinatory drunk. I saw several fights, only one of which involved a knife. A heavily tattooed sailor cut off the ear of his vanquished foe and attempted to eat it, chewing with great concentration, despite the distraction of the screams.

Dawn came grey, with a milky sun. The night people

disappeared as though they had been wraiths, to be replaced by the working population of the riverside. I resolved to turn into the next street that led away from the Levee. This proved to be a grand if shabby avenue going by the name of Canal Street. I confess that, by looking up at the sign, I had failed to see the dark-haired figure in front of me. His arms were outstretched and he was singing a sustained note that I could not identify, in a loud, if tremulous, tenor. He was quick to apologise, which saved his life. Dressed in a long coat and with a high-crowned top hat, he sported a bushy moustache very dark in colour. I should have said he had reached his thirties but recently.

'Begging your pardon, sir. It just does a son of New Orleans such good to return home.'

He shook my hand as if he were in need of several gallons of water and I the village pump. He gave a deafening 'Laaaaaaaaaaaa!' before introducing himself.

'Louis Moreau Gottschalk, composer, musician and true New Orleanian, at your service.'

His enthusiasm was so disarming that I released the handle of the knife concealed in my pocket.

'Anson Northrup, recently returned from Europe,' I offered.

'Ah, Europe. How I miss it! I studied music in Paris, you know!' He gushed.

'The Conservatoire?'

He reddened and ran a finger round his collar, which did seem a little grubby.

'Not exactly. And you? How did Europe hold you captive?' he asked.

'As long as she could, Mr Gottschalk, as long as she could.'

My new friend and I decided on a drink to celebrate our respective returns. We did not call into every bar and saloon on

Canal Street, for some were not open so early in the morning, but we enjoyed the comforts of more than half. Gottschalk's predilection for spontaneous attempts at notes not quite in his range served as sufficient motive to effect our removal from one or two of the more comfortable establishments. We had sampled both the spirit of the grain and a sufficiency of beer, therefore, the composer was quite discommoded by the time Canal Street ran out at North Rampart Street around noon. For myself, I felt a little crapulous, but more than capable of remaining upright without assistance. My offer to escort Gottschalk to his place of residence was rebuffed.

'S'alrigh',' he slurred. 'M'fine, m'friend. Le's go Congo Square.'

Enquiring as to where that place might be resulted in his throwing an arm to full stretch with finger extended, which same caused his person to fall prone, leading me to believe that either our prospective destination lay in a puddle, or that he was too drunk to go anywhere unaided. I sat him up, by chance causing his posterior to alight in the aforementioned puddle. This seemed to sharpen his faculties somewhat.

'Congo Square. Come, it will be a marvellous spectacle.'

My doubts about the matter were entirely disproven on arrival at the square. It was a Sunday. There must have been five hundred people in the square, almost all black. A market lined the outer edges of the plaza, although many of the customers and stall-holders must surely have been slaves. The hand-made artefacts and materials were bright in colour, numerous and varied. There was an expectation in the air, as if the purpose of coming were anything but the market. Gottschalk seemed animated by this same feeling and certainly less drunk than he had been only minutes earlier.

'What? What is it?' I said, some of the restrained excitement had infected even me.

'Wait,' he replied. 'You'll see!' The composer's eyes glittered and he shuffled from foot to foot as if dancing to a rhythm only he could hear. The women were, without exception, dressed in fine fashions or extremely colourful imitations thereof. The men, however, wore only swatches of bright material as sashes, necklaces of shells and beads, but nothing else. Suddenly, there was a beating of drums, as if Gottschalk had anticipated or provoked it with his own dancing. The sun burst the overcast sky at the very moment the music began. I saw violins, triangles and flutes alongside marimbas, gourds, two stringed banjo-like instruments, quill-pipes and, of course, the insistent drums.

The composer-musician cut a strange figure capering on the periphery of the throng. However, we were not the only spectators, across the square I could see groups of white folk pointing and clapping. Gottschalk spoke, 'Hausa, see. Look at the colours on the men.'

Quite what this meant, I had no clue. This group of dancers and musicians – they might have numbered as many as forty – danced for a quarter hour by my reckoning. Then they gave ground in the centre of the square to another group of similar size. Gottschalk whispered, 'Mandinka.'

I was somewhat surprised that the Africans' tribal heritage could be so publicly celebrated anywhere in the South, and I said as much to Gottschalk, who replied, 'Yes, we have slavery, we have the Code Noir, too. I imagine they have been careful to present these dances as folkloric rather than religious, to those who matter.'

'Still, such an assembly and for such a purpose as dancing! How so?'

'It is unlikely to be seen again, sir. That is why we came.'

And glad I was that we had.

I took my pleasure in watching the evident joy that the

women took in their dancing alongside, in front of, behind and almost touching the men. It was indeed a most stirring sight, and the more so for the lack of entertainment I had endured on the *Enterprise*. My companion watched the two hours of dancing with an expression of blissful rapture on his face, which I could not entirely assign to the alcohol we had earlier consumed.

'Bamboula, Mr Northrup. Bamboula! If not my finest hour, then surely theirs,' Gottschalk said. At this point I finally realised I had been in the company – if not of Liszt or Offenbach – at least of New Orleans' premier composer.

The musician waved an expansive arm towards the dancers and traders, who were packing up the stalls and retreating once more to 'the back of town', with which euphemism Gottschalk had referred to the black district, long before mentioning Congo Square.

As the dancers, musicians and market traders left, the previously hidden white spectators appeared, in coveys of three, four, five or six persons: male and female, young and old. One would have thought that they would have congregated like-with-like to watch the spectacle, but perhaps the shamefaced looks exchanged on catching sight of cousins or neighbours accounted for that. A tall woman in European-style dress and a towering, parti-coloured headscarf was stopping at every group of embarrassed spectators. To a man or woman, everyone took a step backward at the approach of this figure. Her headdress clearly achieved its aim, as even the tallest of men perforce had to look upward to take it in. As the woman worked her way around the crowd, it became clear that she affected greatly each person she encountered. Some men puffed out their chests, many women visibly shrank; among the last group she addressed, before approaching Gottschalk and myself, two men turned so white that I thought they might swoon. One of their much younger female companions did indeed fall to the ground in a faint. The colourfully dressed woman laughed before bending down to minister to the younger woman with a censer of smelling salts. I was most frustrated that the exchange that passed between the woman and the others took place at too great a distance for me to over-hear a single word.

Gottschalk looked a little pale himself by the time she arrived to speak with us. I doubted very much whether I would hear his quavering tenor for a while. There seemed little to fear – or admire – in the woman. The height of her headdress was successful in creating an imposing figure from a woman of only middling height, after all. She was plain enough, although her eyes were striking, the whites as bright and shiny as mother of pearl, the irises so dark as to show no demarcation of the pupil within. However, her voice was deep, as deep as many a man's. Slow as treacle, it was a hypnotic sound. Even so I could find no reason to fear even this. As to what she said, I could not say. She addressed Gottschalk alone in something that was not quite French, and which I took to be Creole. The musician seemed blessedly dumbstruck by the woman, merely nodding his head with a ferocity that denoted a slavish compliance with anything his interlocutor might require.

Finally, she turned to me. Her gaze proved that it was not her voice alone that had mesmeric qualities. 'Y'all come, too. At seven o'clock, 1020 St Ann Street,' she said, whereupon she passed a reptilian tongue across her lips. It was either the most repulsive or lascivious thing I had ever seen, or even, perhaps, both. She departed, leaving a musky, heady scent of menses and female ardour and I knew I would go to the address she had mentioned.

I looked at Gottschalk, who was now merely yellow, rather than alabaster white.

'Who was she?'

He stumbled over his answer, 'L-laveau, M-Márie Laveau.'

Gottschalk could scarcely be persuaded into the nearest tavern and refused all libations and tinctures once we finally did enter The Moon and Two Feathers. We drew the attention of all the clientele, both black and white. Gottschalk's enervation could have been the only explanation for it. Quite why he chose to consume such quantities of coffee was a mystery to me, since it made him no more lively – rather it increased the trembling of his hands acquired on encountering Miss Laveau. My attempts at drawing conversation from him produced nothing more than the occasional sigh. Behind the bar stood a man nearing the status of giant, his physique was impressive and in proportion to his height. His head however was not, being tiny in the extreme, at least in relation to the size of his body. Nor was this the only peculiarity regarding the caput. He was quite twice as wide in the jaw as the cranium. There was truly no possibility of any meaningful quantity of grey matter within it. Yet he stood, moved and dispensed alcoholic drink with remarkable competence. Speech came not so easily to this behemoth. His utterances did not extend beyond single words and those for the most part denominations of coinage, such as 'Dime!', 'Quarter!', or even 'Dollar!'. No quantity or combination of cordials provoked him into 'Fifty cents', and perhaps that was one more word than he could muster at any one time. I was put in mind of the giant of The Coble Inn in faraway Seahouses.

In any event, I was forced to engage a fellow customer to enquire as to the origins of the name of the saloon. It seemed more appropriate to a Wiltshire tavern, in my opinion. Besides, the man had been eyeing me in a most peculiar manner since his entrance into The Moon and Two Feathers. In the American manner, I thrust out a hand and barked, 'Anson Northrup.'

The man, sporting a stovepipe hat and a sparse effort at a Lincoln beard, spat elegantly to his left.

'Danged if y'are!' He said.

'I beg your pardon, sir!'

The man tugged at his left ear and gave a half-smile, the left corner of his mouth rising by the equivalent amount to which the right descended.

'Oh, I reckon, y'all could fool an acquaintance, Mister. But there ain't no foolin' a bosom-friend from childhood, is there?'

It was a coincidence at which even Dickens might have baulked.

'I can explain…' I began.

'Mebbe you could, if'n I let y'all.' His eyes crossed a little as he said this and I realised that the man was quite, quite drunk.

'Well, now, why not allow me to enlighten you over a drink?'

I looked over at Gottschalk, but he was staring glassy-eyed at the floor.

'A whiskey, then,' I said, receiving a grunt in answer from the 'bosom-friend' and a basso-profundo 'Quarter!' from the ogre tending the bar.

The man was at that stage of inebriation where the association of ideas, whilst not impossible, required a great deal more concentration than when sober. In fact, it appeared that two ideas could not even be entertained at one and the same time, for the promise of a drink proved sufficient to distract him from musing upon my imposture. I informed him he had the advantage of me, in the matter of names. His uncertain gaze fell on my hideous playing card waistcoat and his jaw worked as his brow furrowed. Evidently, whatever he could not bring forth from his memory was forgotten by the time he held out a slightly unsteady hand and said, 'Effingham T. Wallace,' whilst peering at me.

I took the trouble not to laugh, although I was sure he would not have divined the reason as being his ludicrous appellation.

'A pleasure, sir!' I said, raising my glass in his face, which caused his eyes to cross still further.

We consumed several glasses, under the unseeing eye of Gottschalk, who seemed lost in a reverie, which continued to prevent any trilling in his unsteady tenor. It was only a matter of time before Wallace began to salivate in prodigious volume, a known precursor to the drunkard's vomit. To Wallace's credit, I was forced to purchase half a dozen whiskeys to bring him to that pass.

'Gottschalk, I shall help our mutual friend to some revivifying fresh air.'

This information had quite as well been delivered to the cranially deficient goliath behind the bar, for all the reaction it provoked. My arm was solidly linked with Wallace's, though he did not resist, much less protest, as we left The Moon and Two Feathers for the dark cut-through to the side of the building. I would dearly have liked to prise valuable information from Wallace about the identity I had assumed. It was not possible, the man did not cease from vomiting from the moment we encountered the chilly evening breeze – not even when my knife slipped under his ribs. He had surely been drinking throughout the day for his pockets yielded only a dollar and a piece of animal gut, doubtless a French letter, both of which I pocketed against the day of need.

Quite why Gottschalk had chosen this particular moment

to shake off his brown study and quit the bar, I could not imagine. He peered at me from the mouth of the alley.

'That feller alright?' He looked from me to the crumpled form lying in the shadows.

'Of course, Gottschalk, just too much to drink.'

I took him by the arm and said, 'Come, we've an appointment in St Anne Street.'

Gottschalk craned his neck behind him no more than twice as we left Effingham T. Wallace to the final reward for his dissipation.

14

1020 St Ann Street was a less than imposing building. In common with other houses in the street it was clapboard. The paint was stained and peeling. There was, however, something that set number 1020 apart. It was not merely the air of gloom caused by the street lamp outside the house being unlit. Nor was it that – despite the lack of drapery – no light escaped from any window. Each glazed pane was as filthy as a tinker's shirt, but neither was this the cause of the house's apartness. Standing before the house, I discerned an odour – or, rather, the hint of such: it reminded me of the earthy scent Márie Laveau herself had exuded, when I had encountered her in Congo Square. But a few strides to the left and no such olfactory phenomenon was discernible, when standing a-front number 1018. Nor did 1022 St Anne Street pique the nostrils in this way. I enquired of Gottschalk as to what he thought the aroma might be. He mumbled something, but it was surely nonsense, for I heard only, 'Boo Doone.'

A tarnished brass bell-pull was mounted on the clapboard beside an imposing if slightly rotten-looking door. The handle of the bell-pull was in the shape of a snake's head: a snake that had recently been in receipt of some provocation, it seemed to me. I allowed Gottschalk to pull it, and we waited. Gottschalk shuffled from one foot to the other, which made the wait before the door opened irksome, if not insufferable. I was moved to stamp hard on his left instep to put a stop to it. The door opened as Gottschalk was still hopping and inhaling noisily.

A very tall black man opened the door to us and gave a bow, which would have been most courtly had he not been so cramped by the narrowness of the vestibule and his own enormous size.

'Mistuh God's Chalk,' he intoned, in a voice as deep as a well.

Gottschalk sketched a bow, 'M-m-miz Laveau invited us.'

The man bowed again and walked backwards as if in the presence of royalty, although it was simply that he could neither turn around, nor let us pass. The vestibule was not long however, and we passed through a beaded curtain into an extremely large room which might, or might not, once have been a dining room. Whatever it had been, it seemed too large for the house that contained it. Drapery hung on rails on the walls, between the windows. These curtains were drawn; the majority of them were in dark red damask. The effect struck me as quite bizarre, and I wondered what was concealed behind them. There were some thirty persons in the room, excluding ourselves, the man who had admitted us and Márie Laveau. The majority were white, their eyes darting around as if looking for – and dreading finding – someone they knew. The room was rectangular; Márie Laveau sat in a peacock chair in front of a bookcase, which covered the length, breadth and height of one of the shorter walls. My eyes watered. Incense fumes emanated from a censer standing near the entrance to the room. Perhaps that was why it took me several moments to notice the large snake Miss Laveau sported like a stole around her elegant neck.

There was not a drum in sight, but there was an intense low beat passing through our bones, as though an orchestra of percussion was performing in an adjacent room. I looked at Gottschalk in the gloom. He seemed barely able to keep still. Catching my eye, he mouthed something. I shook my head. He leaned close to my ear and whispered, 'Ashiko!' It was either a sneeze or he referred to the drums. The audience looked on; no others whispered between themselves as Gottschalk and I had done. Márie Laveau held them captive: up to that moment, by doing nothing more than sitting in a chair, wearing a snake as a necklace. She began to chant, counterpointing the insistent drums.

'Papa Lemba!
  Li Grand Zombi!
  Grant a wish
  For your Márie
  Voudoun magic,
  gris-gris, cries:
  make your Márie
  woman-wise.'

Miss Laveau followed this inane doggerel by throwing out an arm, whereupon the room was filled with light so bright as to blind all those present. There were shrieks as all became aware that the light had faded, but they still could not see. The drums continued. Thankfully, the chanting from Miss Laveau did not. The smell of Márie Laveau became noticeable once more, although it was different in some subtle way. Not some grace note of perfume, rather something old and knowing, and perhaps decayed. I chose to consider it a fancy caused by being temporarily blind.

After several minutes, I could discern shapes in the darkness and a clear outline of Gottschalk, whose face was close to mine.

'Isn't she magnificent?' Gottschalk whispered.

It was not the word that occurred to me. I preferred mountebank – or perhaps Magnesium – by far, and wondered how Robert-Houdin's principles of misdirection had been so thoroughly learned by the New Orleans woman. After five minutes it was possible to see more clearly, although not so well as before Miss Laveau's pyrotechnical ruse. Judging by the gasps from my fellow onlookers, they had recovered sufficient vision to see that an old, old woman sat in the peacock chair, her arthritic hands clutching at the snake around her neck. The voice was similar, of course, with the added croak and warble of the aged.

'Qui veut quelqu'-chose de Li Grand Zombi, demandez-vous à moi, Márie Laveau!'

The gullible stepped forward with their petitions for 'Li Grand Zombi'. My French was sufficient to discern that these consisted mostly of requests for success in business, in love or in sundry other ventures where luck – but not hocus-pocus – might play a part. One attractive matron bade the crone and her snake to ensure her some pleasure in the bedroom if she should meet a man to her taste. I resolved to make her acquaintance when we departed the ridiculous charade. After the last petitioner at the court of the Witch Queen had backed away in deference, the drums became gradually louder and I prepared myself once more for chanted verses of dubious quality.

'Papa Lemba!
  Li Grand Zombi!
  Grant a wish
  For your Márie.

Voudoun magic,
Cock-brained hen;
make your Márie
young again.'

My eyes were tight-shut by the time the croaking voice reached 'Cock-brained hen' and my hands had covered them before the verse had ended. Nonetheless, it was possible to detect the moment the flash occurred. I waited a long minute and opened my eyes. Two confederates were pushing at one edge of the book-lined wall and the whole edifice was rotating on central pivot. The aged crone on her peacock chair disappeared from view to be replaced by the younger woman once more. Perhaps I should not have laughed aloud, for my arms were grasped by two hulking fellows who had crept up behind me, whilst Gottschalk smiled in blind ignorance of my situation.

It was the work of moments for the men to manhandle me toward one of the peculiarly placed drapes hanging between the window frames. They pushed me through the curtain and into a passage, which bore sharply round to our left, before opening into a room devoid of windows. There was, however, a wall entirely lined with books. Of course, there was also an aged crone seated in a peacock chair before it. The woman croaked, 'Ça va!', my arms were released, and I felt the men move away to the rear. She crooked an already crooked finger and I stepped a little closer. Her scent was as distinctive as any animal's. She laughed, displaying more teeth than one might have expected.

'You are vair' 'andsome. Are you stupide, also?' She cackled again.

I declined to answer; any attempt at refutation might well have done no more than confirm her belief.

'Northrup, on dit, you are très important, no? For the rail-ro'?'

I should have preferred her to persist with her New Orleans French, since I barely understood her English.

'Perhaps,' I answered.

This time she gave a giggle, wriggled like a tickled child and said, 'Ah, not so stupide!' She looked down at a small deal table, which she could reach from her chair if she stretched her arm to full extent. She was fingering a playing card, one of several laid out before her in a cruciform arrangement. The card was quite old, depicting a horned devil atop a shallow-walled well, flanked by two child-imps chained to a ring at the front of the well. It appeared to be a trionfo from the Visconti-Sforza deck. Several years ago, I had encountered such a pack of cards in Northumberland, as part of a collection of similar bizarre – and even more improbable – curios. The woman grasped the card between two arthritic fingers and flicked it toward me with remarkable dexterity. I showed scarcely less in catching it with barely a stumble.

'Take it, M'sieu Northrup. Per'aps it will bring you luck!'

My arms were seized once more from behind and I was marched through a different passage to the rear exterior of the house. By the time I turned, the door had slammed and I was in the darkness of an alley that ran the entire length of the block. Having circumnavigated the entirety of said block, I took post in the shadows on the opposite side of the thoroughfare to number 1020 St Ann Street. No more than five minutes passed before the door opened and the audience began to file out onto the street, talking in excited whispers. Gottschalk emerged last of all, in the company of the woman who had been seeking satisfaction in her bed. I doubted that he could provide her with such, and so accosted the pair in mid-whisper.

'A fine show, Gottschalk!' I said, making a bow to his companion.

'Ah, Northrup, this is Miss Ginever.' The woman made an elegant courtesy, only slightly marred by the smirk that accompanied it.

'Delighted, Miss Ginever, what did you think of the show?' I enquired.

'Show, suh? It was voudoun.' Her smirk faded a little.

I raised an eyebrow at Gottschalk. 'Is that what it's called?'

Gottschalk made no reply and Miss Ginever detached her arm from his. We left him in the street in front of Márie Laveau's house of entertainment, no doubt pondering Virgil's observations on the fickle nature of women.

My new companion and I repaired to a place of entertainment somewhat more refined than The Moon and Two Feathers, although there appeared to have been no need to do so for Miss Ginever's sake. From the enthusiasm she evinced that night in the Hotel DuPont, I had no doubt she would have flourished in any Cheapside tavern.

Miss Elspeth Ginever, although poorer by the twenty silver dollars she had been carrying about her person, was left the richer for her experiences in my company. It was ten in the morning of a crisp day in late spring. A low fellow, in a topcoat made for a man several hands taller at the shoulder than himself, was muttering whilst scraping mud from a pair of clearly stolen boots. Since – to all appearances – the preceding night had been as dry as that fine morning, I stopped to observe him. There were few others in the street outside the hotel and they seemed too preoccupied with the business of the day to wonder at this incongruity. The man was unleashing a most colourful collection of oaths and curses: he did not have the look of a sailor, however, although under the voluminous topcoat he might have sported any number of exemplars of the tattooist's art. On my asking him the whereabouts of the New Orleans Mint, the man leapt as though bitten by the rattling snake of the prairies.

'Whassat there? Mint ye say? Who wants to know?'

It was the snarl of a Dandy Dinmont terrier, which is to say that it might have been more threatening had it emerged from a creature of somewhat more impressive aspect.

'Why I do, sir,' I laughed, at least until he sprang at me brandishing a rusty blade.

The removal of this weapon from his grubby hand I effected without incurring the slightest scratch. Indeed, the smell of spirits on his breath might well have done more damage. Grasping his throat with sufficient force to hold him on tiptoe whilst allowing him to answer me, I asked him his name.

'Ishmael, they call me Ishmael, though I only asked but once.' He hawked up a bolus from the tips of those very toes and spat to the side. For a moment I felt there was something familiar about him, but this feeling vanished when his eyes rolled and he began singing 'Hourra les filles a Cinq deniers', a song of quite remarkable antiquity, as such a sum would not have bought a woman in Marseilles, much less in New Orleans, for many a long year. Still, I found him entertaining, not least for his singing, so I brought his face close to mine and hissed, 'I need an ally, an associate, a… confederate. You'll do for me, Ishmael. A full-witted fellow would never do.'

He seemed to understand and followed me down the street like a dog.

Several women I importuned to ask directions to the mint recoiled when Ishmael did something indecorous, whether it was another verse about fifty-cent whores or urinating in the street. However, he managed to restrain himself long enough in the presence of a matron of redoubtable size to enable me to ascertain that we ought to be heading for the Vieux Carré. To be exact, the mint was on the northeastern extreme of the French Quarter. My companion and I strode briskly through the fresh vernal air, Ishmael reiterating his peculiar shanty from time to time, while I whistled a descant for luck.

15

The New Orleans Mint was a magnificent reminder of the demeaning effect red brick might have even on the most beautiful of architecture. The mint had the benefit of no such advantage, being of a hackneyed and uninspired design. It was in the Greek Revival style, which meant a superfluity of columns with capitals various at the front entrance. These achieved nothing save an air of incongruity, or perhaps a forbidding aspect, designed to discourage the hoi-polloi, although I doubted the most adventurous of Greek sailors would stray so far from the port of New Orleans. The brick was a plebeian red, like that of a Lancastrian mill; its only redemption lay in the fact that no sooty patina had dulled the colour to a satanic black. The grounds before it were green enough, but seemed on the point of going to seed, as though some weeks had passed since any horticultural ministration.

Ishmael looked from the building to me, and back again.

'Ass the mint, Mistuh. Wouldn't reckon much to it, masself.' He spat after this last.

'Indeed?' I found this statement gnomic, to say the least.

'I's a schoolmaster onc't!' he said.

Which served as confirmation that he was as mad as first I had thought him.

The building looked unoccupied: the entrance behind the grand portico of the ionic columns appeared barred and locked. I pulled at an enormous bell-pull, which creaked and groaned as though it had summoned no one since the construction of the building was finished. Ishmael sang something different although I suspected it was a song known to seamen even so, since it seemed mainly to consist of an exhortation to 'Blow the man down'. It was unclear who the man might have been, and, frankly, I did not care. I cuffed him to silence and awaited some response to the doorbell's summons.

It took an age and I raised my fist more than once to prevent a choral assault upon my ears by the cringing Ishmael. At last the sound of chains, padlocks and heavy bars preceded the opening of a door cut into the huge leaf at the right-hand side of the arched portal. A hunched figure peered around the edge of said door.

'Watcha want?'

The voice was querulous, an old man's voice. The face around the pinched mouth appeared to belong to a man of no more than forty, save that there was not a hair upon his head and his chin-whiskers were snow-white.

'Jacob Holzbein,' I said.

Before the man could answer, Ishmael threw himself to the ground in a fit of laughter; through his tears I could make out only the words, 'Wooden Leg, Wooden Leg!'

My amazement at the hilarity this provoked in the man was only surpassed by my surprise that the drunken sailor knew even these two words of German. A judicious application of the toe of my boot to Ishmael's torso brought about the happy outcome of restoring him to relative calm. He got gingerly to his feet and mercifully declined to sing. The shiny-pated ostiary revealed himself to be Jacob Holzbein, and I asked him if he would help the Railroad. His face was lit by a most unexpected and incongruous smile, wherein the teeth were as white as one who had neither drunk coffee nor wine in his life, not even in the most infinitesimal amounts. He put a warty finger to his lips and beckoned with his other hand that we might follow him inside. We entered a high-ceilinged, cavernous vestibule. It was empty of furniture and people. Holzbein's footsteps echoed in trochaic meter for he had indeed a deficiency of limb compensated for by a ligneous substitute. We followed him down a spur of corridor that led off to the east of the vestibule. The walls were half-panelled in walnut, the parquet of the floor was as dusty as a coffin in a crypt: I shivered, unable to ascertain the reason for my disquiet.

Holzbein turned to look at us, showed the gleaming teeth, and observed, 'It's the noise, suh. Ain't none, I mean. The smelters and the Uhlhorns wuz switched off by me personally on January 26th.'

He seemed inordinately proud of this fact, but I made no comment, merely followed the hunch of his back down the long passage. He stopped short; I managed to evade colliding with him, but Ishmael was not so careful, so I cuffed him away after he had careered into my rear. Holzbein cocked his head on one side, as if listening for something. There was not a sound to be heard, but the old man nodded his head as though convincing himself he had heard the music of the spheres.

'Do you want to see the presses, or...?' he asked me, a wistful note in his cracking voice.

'You know why I'm here, Holzbein.' He scurried on, and we followed.

At the end of what seemed an exceedingly long passageway, we were greeted by the head of some stairs, down which the coiner scuttled with only a brief backward glance. The stairs were of sandstone, and much worn as though the feet that had trodden them belonged to bearers of heavy burdens. At the foot of the stairs, which numbered some twenty-three, was a huge metal door. Holzbein withdrew a large key from somewhere about his person and proceeded to open the door.

'Wouldn't keep out an Injun,' Ishmael declared, before falling silent under my eye.

'It don't have to,' said Holzbein.

The door would not have swung wide had all three of us put our shoulders to it. As it was it creaked and groaned its way ajar as if in sympathy with Holzbein's panting and grunting. We entered a huge vault, and the mint's man picked up a candle from a table to the side. He lit it after striking a vesta match at the third attempt. The feeble flame lit the gleam of silver bars piled two men high, for all the world as though awaiting the Spanish Silver Train from Peru to Panama.

Ishmael was staring slack-mouthed at the argent towers of bars filling the vault. For myself I wondered how many escaped slaves I could persuade onto the *Grand Turk*, and how many ingots I might prevail upon them to carry. Of course, I had no clue as to how – or indeed where – I was to gather up the passengers for the Freedom Train. A figure stepped out from behind a stack of the silver bullion and I heard a familiar voice long unheard: 'Well, well, the redoubtable Mr M— no, I shan't say it. It's no more likely your name now than ever it was, I'm sure.'

It was a woman: to all appearances she was aged no more than thirty, although she must have passed at least ten more on her God's green earth. She was still not-quite-beautiful, being possessed of the same nose, slightly out of true, the over-handsome jaw and dark eyes inherited, not from a shipwrecked Armada sailor as once I had thought, but from her own Sephardic forebears. However, it was the curl of her lip that I recognised, and the bold stare that no woman of quality – no matter what her age – should ever bring to bear on a gentleman. I wondered what had brought Ellen Pardoner, spy and off-shoot of the House of Jedermann, to the New Orleans Mint.

Sketching a bow, I introduced myself as 'Anson Northrup', which provoked the most unladylike guffaws, to the point where her gloved hands were forced to hold her sides. From time to time she managed to utter but one word: 'Priceless!'

Ishmael had the look of a besotted spaniel and I was forced to admit his faculties extended to an appreciation of women, if nothing else. Holzbein was shuffling his feet, as though he could not decide between offering assistance to the helpless woman or running to the upper floors to escape her lunacy. She recovered herself moments before I entirely lost my patience and held out a hand to me. 'Very well, Anson Northrup. Eileen Fitzpatrick.'

She dropped an inelegant courtesy and seemed on the brink of another inappropriate fit of hilarity.

I raised an eyebrow and informed her of my pleasure at making her acquaintance.

'Ah well, it's a new world, after all,' she answered.

'Indeed, it is,' I admitted.

Her back straightened and she gave me the look I remembered so very well, that of a duchess at a dustman.

'So, Northrup? What plans have you made? There isn't much time.'

My heart sank as I realised that some responsibility had fallen to me.

'Why must we hurry? Surely we are reliant only on the vagaries of the *Grand Turk*'s time of departure upriver?'

'The Confederacy intends to reopen the mint, to produce its own currency.'

Her smirk was almost a smile and I was sure she knew me for a fraud, who was no more interested than Jefferson Davis himself in assisting the Underground Railroad.

'Let us depart then for a restaurant, Miss Fitzpatrick, and I will enlighten you in more salubrious surroundings,' I said.

At least the walk to the city itself would allow some time to ponder what indeed such plans should be, I reflected.

It was truly unfortunate that 'Miss Fitzpatrick' and I had Ishmael in tow. His behaviour doubtless seemed to himself to be the epitome of gallantry. My lady companion seemed less sure. Scarcely minutes into our journey, he stood in the way of a hansom cab, in an effort to halt its progress, that our lady-friend might cross Royal Street in safety. On recovering from his daze, he caught us up all too quickly. Later, in the manner of a New World Raleigh, he placed his topcoat over a large puddle in the mud of a narrow side street. Having neglected to remove it beforehand, he gave only the briefest of grunts as the object of his affection strode over his person.

16

In time, we came upon a low-fronted building in a grubby
alley off Bourbon Street. There was a discreet sign above the
door, 'Johns'. I remarked to Eileen that the lack of an apos-
trophe might be a guide to the quality of the fare. She merely
raised an eyebrow and Ishmael cackled, averring that there had
been no mistake.

'S'jes' a hoorhouse joke, ya rube!' he added.

I gave him a kick to the rump and indicated that he
should wait outside. We had scarce entered the narrow, deal
door when an imposing woman barred any further ingress.
Her arms were folded across an enormous bosom, which was
clad in over-decorated linen. This did nothing to divert one's
attention from her prow, which would have graced any ocean-
going vessel.

'Cain't come in. Sign's a joke, ever'one knows that.'

I looked at 'Eileen Fitzpatrick', somewhat mystified. She
addressed the behemoth in a most familiar tone.

'Come, Lucasta, he's no John, and I, though not a working girl, ask that we may eat here.'

'Miz Fitz? Is that you?'

'Miz Fitz' replied in the affirmative, her voice muffled in the expanse of her acquaintance's bust.

'Cain't letcha, though, Miz Fitz. House rules, you knows 'em.'

'Lucasta, there's the room in the back and this is Railroad business.'

I looked around the room; most of the tables were full. Women, mostly of middle age, were delivering plates with efficiency and speed. Not one male, save myself, was in the restaurant. The female clientele ranged from the nymph-like to the crone and all bore the paint best suited to nocturnal negotiations. We followed in the wake of Lucasta's considerable stern to the aforementioned back room. It was dark, snug to the point of confinement. A place for deals and compacts, illicit payments and threats. We sat in rustically carved and somewhat unsteady chairs across a baize-covered table. I made an effort to grasp her hand, which she avoided with skill.

'We are alone, Eileen... no, Ellen. Shall we not dispense with artifice?'

'I doubt that you can, Moffat, I doubt that you can.'

I felt this unfair, still, since, most likely, neither of us had ever given the other their birth name, though we had first met over a decade ago.

'Very well, Eileen it is.'

'Why thank you, Mr Northrup.' She smiled, her teeth gleaming in the crepuscular light.

She waited a few moments: her steady gaze, I confess, provoked both ire and interest in equal measure.

'You have not the slightest inkling of any plan, Mr Northrup, have you?'

She laughed, harsh and brittle. I shrugged and joined her in jocular effusion.

Moments later, two bent crones shuffled in bearing

wooden platters heaped high with rice and the torn flesh of some unidentifiable fowl. I hoped they would return with some bottled liquid capable of stunning my palate before I was obliged to begin eating. My dining companion caught my eye, 'Why Mister Northrup, I had thought such simple fare would have passed your lips shortly after your arrival in the Americas.'

Though her knowing smile annoyed me greatly, I allowed that at least it made a change from chops.

One of the ancient women returned with a bottle of some age – though perhaps not quality. The mere placing of it on the table between us caused a cloud of dust to fly from the glass. I sneezed in great volume and mass more than once. From across the table, there came only a light sniff. The old woman departed with the cackle of an agitated brood hen. In the dim light, Eileen's complexion was smoothed to that of the young woman she had been. On the point of asking what had become of Jedediah Maccabi, I declined to do so. It was not that the man's fate mattered a whit to me, I wished merely for some of the spark that had seemed eternal, when the woman and I had explored the secrets of Gibbous House. 'What's in a name?' What indeed! I wondered which doors would be open in Louisiana to a woman named Jedermann and doubted they would be those open to either a Fitzpatrick or a Pardoner. For a moment, I considered telling her I had no inkling of the kind of cabal in which I had become involved. Clearing my throat, I asked her, 'You might tell me, then, what you would do, since I am clearly the game's cod.'

She gave a laugh full of gravel and phlegm. 'Muggins, Moffat, Northrup, so many names and not one your own!'

I took a spoonful of the rice and bird-flesh. We had not been provided with such sophistications as a knife and fork. It has been my experience that silence in the presence of a woman can be most productive. They simply cannot bear the absence of conversation and will fill it with any discourse, however ill-advised. She had barely touched the mound on her plate, this woman whom I recalled had had the appetite of a navvy, when she said, 'In fact, Northrup, we have arranged everything. You merely have to be in place at the appropriate time.'

Again, I took refuge in silence, certain that any failure to enquire as to the identity of those she referred to as 'we' would provoke her into far more revelation than any show of curiosity. Laying down my spoon, for the food really was fit only for the meanest dog, I gave her a smile and waited.

The dishes had been cleared by Lucasta herself, her bulk seeming to absorb all the light in the already gloomy room. My dining companion cocked an eyebrow at me and instructed the woman to bring us two cigars. Once indifferent to the pleasures of smoking, there had been times in the Americas when it seemed the only pleasure left to me. I was expecting the arrival of what were vulgarly called 'cheroots' in the Americas. Properly called the Tuscanian, this cigar was near ubiquitous amongst the less discerning. However, to my surprise, two fat figurados lay on a silver salver alongside matches and a cutter. The wrapping was as dark as rich loam, the curved sides sensual. Eileen cut both cigars before handing me the first. She struck a match with a flourish on the floor and lit my cigar. She smirked, and I wondered if she had any care at all for convention or decorum.

It was a truly fine cigar. I felt as contented as ever I had been since arriving in the Americas.

'Cuban, then?' I asked.

'Oh yes, Mr Northrup, they surely are.' She laughed and plucked a dark brown strand of tobacco from her lower lip.

I had waited long enough; there comes a moment when patience's reward will not suffice.

'So,' I paused, savouring the smoke and odour. 'In what place? And what might be the appropriate time?'

A stream of the heavy smoke blew directly into my face, her words followed behind. 'There is a plantation no more than four miles from the mint. Campion Garroway's fief. His grandfather named it Molasses.'

'Sugar cane?' I coughed a little smoke. Eileen laid her cigar down on the table.

'Not at all, the slaves pick cotton and the owner grows fat. I have no idea why it is named so.'

'And when might the appropriate time be, my sweet?'

She pulled a pepper-pot pistol from her skirts and said, 'No time like the present, Mr Northrup.'

The firearm did not, in fact, look particularly fearsome, but I doubted that woman would carry anything which would not perform its task with an efficiency to match her own. I ground the stub of my cigar on the salver on which it had arrived and leaned back in the chair.

'Perhaps not, I had hardly thought to go anywhere at gunpoint.'

'You have some papers, Mr Northrup. I need to see them.'

The hideously patterned carpetbag was yet outside with Ishmael, if he had not disappeared in search of alcoholic libations.

'I have no papers with me.' At least this last was not a lie.

She raised the ridiculous pistol, 'You are expendable, Mr Northrup, we can find another cat's paw at very short notice and at very little cost.'

'My good woman,' I could not resist the urge to provoke her, 'I was expecting no remuneration.'

'The papers.' She waved the diminutive handgun and I told her that Ishmael had them in the carpetbag.

'Well then, let's go.' She stood and linked her left arm with mine, using it to cover the pistol barrel, which was placed snugly against one of my ribs. I was sure we made a handsome couple as we left the whores' canteen.

Daylight came as a shock as we stepped outside, even though it was still only four in the afternoon. The uninspiring repast had seemed long in the eating indeed. Ishmael lay prone on the sidewalk afront 'Johns'. His legs were crossed at the ankle and his head lay on the carpetbag. Snores quite incompatible with his diminutive stature issued from a mouth deficient in teeth to an alarming degree. Around his torso lay almost all of the miniature bottles from the whiskey-drummer's sample case that had been in the carpetbag ever since I had acquired it. The tiny corks all over his chest rose and fell in time with his breathing. One rolled down his rib cage and stopped at the toe of my boot. The remaining bottle was still clenched in a fist as though he had passed out before he could open it.

I roused him with a swift kick to his ribs.

'S'matter? T'aint time fer the dog-watch alreddy?'

Another kick persuaded him that it most certainly was time to be up and about. I picked up the bag and withdrew the notebook. Eileen allowed me to draw away from her, but she was not disposed to conceal the handgun in the street. I held up the oilskin package containing the book.

'Is this what you want?'

The woman gave a sigh and waved her pistol airily, 'No.'

As I shook the book from its crude wrapping, John Mudsill's warrant floated to the ground.

'This then, surely?'

'You damned fool!'

Her snarl made her all the more attractive, although I kept a weather eye on her ridiculous weapon. As a last resort I handed her a flimsy onionskin: the facsimile government bond, purportedly found on the mysterious John Mudsill, whoever he had been. It was less easy to extract from its hiding place in the book than Mudsill's warrant had been.

Her pistol did not waver as she cast an eye over the thin paper, 'I knew it,' she spat. 'Damn him!'

'Knew what?' I asked.

This time the pistol's barrel-mouth jerked crazily as she exhibited a display of temper as fearsome as it was attractive.

'The turncoat! That renegade, that traitor! The miserable apostate.'

The combination of foot-stamping and brandishing of the pistol by turns at myself, Ishmael and the sky was most diverting. I chose that moment to enquire about whom she spoke.

'Northrop, you double-damned fool.'

It was clear to me at last that there had been so much more to the late Mr Northrop than I could ever have imagined. I almost regretted my taking of his life, in more senses than one.

However, all lives are too short for such regrets, particularly since there was some prospect that my own might prove shorter still, if I could not wrest the tiny pistol from the incandescent Miss Pardoner, as was. Picking up the carpetbag, I forced the hideous material against the pistol barrel with my one hand, whilst seizing the woman's wrist in a firm grip with the other. The gun was discharged with a meagre sound and no shot or pellet penetrated the bag.

'Ellen, Ellen, let us stop this dissembling, call me Moffat. I am sick of this Northrop fellow. Why, he is such a will o'the wisp, he might be anyone at all!'

The woman laughed bitterly, 'Even you. Moffat, even you.'

But I thought he might equally have been Mudsill, and

realised that stealing Northrop's life and clothes might prove more complicated than first I had presumed.

Ishmael, looking fascinated and puzzled in equal measure, lay yet prone on the mud. The threat of a kick proved sufficient to bring him to his feet and I gave him a dollar to find the three of us some means of transport out of the city. Miss Pardoner asked where we were bound.

'Molasses, my dear one, Molasses.'

Her look of surprise was worth any amount of boredom awaiting me at the plantation of the preposterously named Campion Garroway.

Ishmael returned in the driving seat of something which might well have been called a Stanhope, had there been any coachwork at all resembling seating for the comfort of the traveller. In fact, there appeared to be nothing more to the vehicle than four wheels, a bench seat for the driver and a flat arrangement of planks to the rear, presumably for the transportation of freight. The wood, including the spokes of the crude wheels, of which there were four, was devoid of paint or varnish. Ishmael's face fell as I ordered him to the rear of the cart. I handed Miss Pardoner up to the bench seat and took my place next to her. The lady showed great fortitude, for I was moved to leap up immediately on sitting, due to a particularly vicious splinter. I had recovered the carpetbag from the muddy street and placed it under my rump. Since I took on the duties of driver, I felt I deserved such comfort as could be found and clearly my lady companion was in agreement, for she said nothing, merely sniffed, but perhaps this was a consequence of her recent loss of equilibrium.

It was a fresh evening. We rode for about an hour at Miss Pardoner's direction, ever deeper into a crepuscular gloom. It was peaceful, the only sound the insistent cries of whip-poor-wills and the grunts as Ishmael bore the buffeting meted out to him in just punishment for his dire choice of transportation. For the most part we followed the levee, passing dark green swampland and nothing that looked as though it might be tilled or cultivated to grow the meanest of crops of any kind. Presently, we left this wilderness and skirted one particularly rank-smelling area, foetid with the corruption and rot brought about by rainfall and flooding. Gradually the thoroughfare began to rise and we cleared the swamps, gaining an area that at least looked more home to the mammalian than the amphibian. At last we came upon some poorly tended cotton fields, which seemed to stretch for a great many acres. In the far distance was the outline of the plantation house, the home of the master of Molasses. Even at this great remove, the dilapidation of the building was visible. For design, the best which could be said was that it had an elegant simplicity, a single two-storeyed building for the main house with several long, barn-like buildings at some distance from it. Several furlongs from the plantation house, it became clear that one of the barn-like buildings was, in fact, a stables, and that it was the only building on Molasses with any pretension to a good state of repair.

There were few slaves in view. All were crouching around a sort of campfire, although none of the wood had been gathered from any copse. Inlays and fine marquetry could be seen as the varnish bubbled on what had once been fine furniture. Several nursing women had babes of lighter complexion than their own in their arms. One blind, grizzle-headed old man leaned on a hoe, although there was no vegetable patch in the vicinity.

A squat little man led a quite magnificent horse from the stables. It was black and its coat shone like polished jet. The man was as unprepossessing as the horse was magnificent. A bald patch was surrounded by a fringe of hair in a most unfortunate red colour. His effeminate Cupid's-bow mouth appeared to have been painted. His shirt and pantaloons were once white, but now boasted all manner of stains, doubtless caused by prolonged ministrations to the magnificent stallion. He looked to be about thirty-five years of age, so long as each and every one had been spent in very hard living. His piping voice was as irritating a sound as ever I had heard.

'Whatchall want heah? Prah-vit property. Ah'll run y'all off!'

My lady companion spoke up, 'The Governor asked us to call.'

This last was news to me, but at least it called forth a grudging welcome from Campion Garroway.

It was plain to see that luxuries were in short supply. I had never seen the like of what Mr Garroway wore on his feet. The upper was a complicated woven arrangement of leather, the sole appeared to be a dirtier version of the very same. No garment of cotton, silk or wool, intermediated between the leather and his rather grimy feet.

The little man seemed to remember his manners and offered a curt bow to Miss Pardoner and requested some proof of her bona fides. The woman turned to me and said, 'Now is the time to give it up, truly.'

With a sigh I reached into my pocket for the only connection I had with the Governor of the State of Louisiana. Miss Pardoner snatched the paper from me and flourished scarce an inch from Garroway's nose. He peered at the paper, blinking several times.

'Ain't got muh eye-glasses.'

Miss Pardoner pointed at the Governor's seal. 'Huh, guess that's jes' dandy.'

And, if these words meant that it was acceptable, it most assuredly was, since Miss Pardoner had, I believed, quite deliberately held the paper upside down.

Miss Pardoner and I followed our host through a door whose glaziery had long been replaced by a dirty material which might have been serge but I doubted it were so. If I had been told that the inside of this low dwelling had been used to house a herd of swine, I should have believed it without hesitation. Foodstuffs, paper and smashed crockery covered the splintered floorboards. There was no indication that this house had ever pretended to the status of hovel, much less the abode of a rich and influential family. Garroway seized a tallow-fat candle from the ruin of some repast that had taken place yesterday or a year before. Its dull light scarcely improved the general gloom, by which I do not mean the simple darkness of night, although it was soon to fall, rather the building seemed full of miasmas and had an atmosphere tending to blur the edges of the sharpest outline. In short, it was as though we all three suffered the weakness of vision that Garroway had earlier claimed.

The fellow peered around the room – it might have been a dining room or a scullery – his pursed mouth moved several times before he spoke, 'Less go tuh the par-luh, y'all 'll fahnd it mo' comf'table.'

This proved an overestimation on his part, for the parlour contained no furniture whatever, only several packing crates and two enormous velvet cushions. I wondered at the mentality of a man who would burn fine furniture before wooden boxes.

We took our seats on the rough wood of the boxes, being most careful to place a cushion between our posterior parts and the splintered surface. Garroway remained standing. This enabled him to look either of us in the eye without straining his neck upward like an ugly swan. He attempted a jut of the jaw, which merely made his pinched mouth all the more ridiculous. 'Guvnuh's a friend of ma'hn, surprises me, ah don't recall yoah name, suh!'

I winked at Miss Pardoner, 'Mudsill, John Mudsill.'

'It cain't be! It cain't be!'

The man seemed as overcome as a Baptist on meeting the Messiah, and I reflected that in the actual and hypothetical cases, he indeed had the right of it, and it couldn't be so. Miss Pardoner appeared to be chewing the inside of a cheek and I must admit it cost me dear to stifle my laughter at the sight of our host hopping and skipping like a child in need of his chamber-pot. Perhaps our sight had trumped our other four senses at first, for after a few moments I noted that the perfume exuding from our host was quite unpleasant at close quarters. I exchanged glances with my confederate. Ishmael, about whom I had quite forgotten, chose this moment to enter the parlour, 'Hell, if'n that don't smell worse than the Pequod's bilges!'

Perhaps it did: what was clear was that our host had more than the lingering traces of his horse's ordure about him and that his own diet was surely not all it might have been.

In the interests of politeness toward our host, I gave Ishmael a cuff about the ear, but truly I confess my heart was not in it. In any event, I needed to return my palm to my nose and mouth *celeriter*, as I was on the point of disgracing myself. Miss Pardoner had turned quite green too.

I cleared my throat and said at a gallop, without pause for breath, 'Well, sir, I am – you might say – performing a census not to say an inventory of property portable, *vis-a-vis*, in particular, slaves in the environs of New Orleans, for and on behalf of the Governor.'

I clasped my palm over my nose and mouth instanter. Miss Pardoner's eyes widened, and she appeared to be in the grip of a choking fit and I guessed she was full of admiration and surprise at my invention. Ishmael, perhaps because of his intimacy with the nether parts of seagoing vessels, was able –

without recourse to covering nostrils and mouth – to rush to Miss Pardoner's side in order to aid her recovery.

In the meantime, Garroway had begun to laugh, a high-pitched sound as piercing as something made by some exotic bird. He came to himself betimes, at least sufficiently to cough out, 'Ain't a single slave left here but cain't walk or has a child too small to take with a runaway, Mistuh.'

Miss Pardoner looked quite shocked. I wondered how much silver could be borne away from the mint in such circumstances. Still there was nothing for it but to inform Garroway that, as he might have put it, 'It made no never mind and the business of the state would be done no matter what.' Moreover, I wished to be out of the stifling fug of the parlour and the house itself.

Outside, I was struck once more by the relatively good condition of the stables and the other barn-like buildings. Nevertheless, these last were missing slates in large degree. Not one door successfully filled a frame and the empty windows allowed all of nature's furies to enter at will. I could not say that I was greatly surprised that these three outbuildings turned out to be the slave-quarters. We all four, including Ishmael, entered the nearest edifice to the bonfire of furniture. At first glance, it appeared that the master of Molasses had understated the seriousness of the situation. The single, long room contained a pot-bellied stove, which looked as though it had remained unlit since it had lost one of its supporting legs. The unpainted metal marking its absence was as rusted as a discarded horseshoe-nail. There were over fifty bunk-beds and, though night had fallen, barely ten were occupied. There were two youngish men of less than thirty years that I could see. Each was in the midst of a racking fit of coughing, which suggested that neither would see their fourth decade's beginning.

The remaining beds contained suckling mothers and

slaves past their sixtieth year. One old woman moaned inces-
santly, calling by turns for Moses and the Lord and petitioning
for deliverance. I could not help but think that it would not
be long in coming. No bed, however, empty or occupied,
enjoyed the benefit of linen, the sick and the old were covered
by fragments of threadbare carpet or moth-devoured horse-
blankets. I made a pretence of counting these less than able-
bodied assets, but Garroway must have seen something in my
face, 'Yaller Fever, suh,' he said. 'Done buried two hunnert
slaves in two months, 'bout fifty run. Prob'ly died in the
swamps.'

He heaved his round shoulders and attempted to
straighten his back. 'T'aint no never mind, suh, I gotta horse.'

A visit to the remaining dormitories gave me a count of
twenty-three nursing mothers, eight adult males between sixty
and seventy, six younger adult males who would not last the
week and twenty-five women past child-bearing age but not
yet in their dotage. Age was ascertained by appearance, as few
were able to offer an age to within less than a decade, refer-
ring mainly to events long past in the history of the plantation,
to which events Garroway would not, or could not, supply a
year of the Christian calendar. I asked him why he remained at
Molasses, to which he repeated his watchwords, 'I gotta horse.'

Miss Pardoner raised a finger and pointed to the exterior.
'I find I need some fresh air,' she said.

Ishmael naturally made to follow her out of the door. I
bade him keep our host company, although he stood motionless, daydreaming of winning some prize atop the beautiful
black stallion, which was all that remained of his fortune. For
myself, I took Miss Pardoner by the elbow and escorted her to
the stables, thinking that the cool of the night might be better borne in the only building on the whole plantation which
seemed entire and intact. Of course, but one stall was occupied

within. The black beast rolled its eyes at us as it stamped, pawed and kicked in rage at his confinement.

'Magnificent!' My companion said.

'Magnificent folly, as are many obsessions, Ellen.'

She made no direct reply, merely saying, 'Well, Moffat, a pretty situation. What do you propose?'

'We cannot move much silver bullion with bodies such as these.'

She bit her lip and looked downward at the dirty straw. When she opened her mouth to speak I held up my hand.

'Do not demean yourself, woman. I'll not risk hanging for some half-sick women and decrepit old men.'

Her eyes narrowed and her lips grew thin and for the first time I saw how she would look in extreme old age. Bitter and alone. It must have been the only time I didn't feel the old urges in her presence.

'There will be others, do not worry. We are to meet with others between here and the mint. You will get your thirty pieces of silver!'

I was reminded of the hissing and spitting of a cat.

The least infirm of the thirty-year-old men gave his name as Compair Lapin. I remarked it seemed a strange name for a slave. He, in turn, observed that a man had a right to his own name, whatever a slave-owner called him. Although he did not put himself forward, and indeed seemed reluctant when I instructed him to do so, he made a start on rounding up the slaves with a clear tenor voice. Miss Pardoner busied herself with the nursing women and children, which I found strange. In the meantime, I went in search of the master of Molasses. Having left him mooning in the care of Ishmael, I was more than somewhat surprised to find the both of them rolling around on the floor of the slave-dormitory exchanging curses and blows in equal measure. The red of Garroway's remaining hair was darkened by the blood from a cut on his scalp. Ishmael's remaining teeth were clamped around Galloway's ear and were in the process of removing it from the side of his head. There was a loud clatter as the other side of the master of Molasses' head struck one of the mean cots. Had these furnishings been of better quality and in better condition, the outcome might not have been so convenient. Galloway was knocked more than insensible, but the cot leg sheared and as Ishmael pulled away from him, the sharp wood penetrated Galloway's eye to the depth of several inches.

Ishmael looked at me. The glint of madness in his eye showed more intelligence than ever I had ascertained thus far.

'Durned Catamite! I warn't Queequeg's toy and I ain't his, nossir!'

I found it most unlikely that Garroway had made advances toward Ishmael. We mounted Garroway on his prized possession and sent them both on their way at the cost of only a hefty kick from the stallion to Ishmael's private parts, which I counted a fine bargain. Ellen Pardoner's mouth had set in a firm line and her eyes glistened. The wooden stake in Garroway's eye was visible in silhouette as horse and rider disappeared into the night. In the meantime, Compair Lapin had assembled near seventy prospective passengers for the Underground Railroad in a ragged column, with himself and Miss Ellen Pardoner at the head. Despite his illness, he seemed to have a dignity and presence about him and I grinned at Ellen. 'Go down, Moses,' I whispered.

17

According to my repeater it was midnight by the time our ragged troupe left Molasses bound for New Orleans and the mint. I did not relish the prospect of travelling cross-country with such companions as these, but comforted myself with the image of Jacob Holzbein limping between the stacks of silver bullion.

One of the young men lay down not a mile into our journey. Compair Lapin knelt beside him and offered up some mumbled prayer, before taking the lead once more. I asked Miss Pardoner if she thought he had any idea of the route to our destination, but she merely gave a sigh and shook her head. This route began by crossing some of the cotton fields belonging to the late master of Molasses, but it was not long before we entered the swampland and I wished I had better boots – or even some of the ridiculous type that the westerners wore so proudly.

After several hours of battling through rank water and rotting vegetation, I realised we were at the edge of the swampland. My disappointment was great when I realised we would not be heading for the levee to follow it back to town. Instead, we headed away from it. A quarter of the compass away from the direction in which we had come. It might have been due north or east-south-east, for the night was overcast and there were no stars to be seen and only the merest sliver of moon to appear in any break in the clouds. Compair Lapin and Miss Pardoner stood hugger-mugger some way off to the side of the rutted track we were following away from the levee. They were too far distant for me to overhear their conversation. I had fallen somewhat behind all but the weakest of the slaves, and the ache in my feet was an insistent reminder that a gentleman should never walk. However, they appeared to be in heated discussion, Lapin was most unsuitably proximate to Miss Pardoner and I stirred myself in order to be in a position to intervene. By the time I reached them, Lapin was sitting on a blackened tree stump slapping his thighs and Miss Pardoner's throaty laugh was offering counterpoint to his basso-profundo guffaws.

'I'm glad you find our excursion so diverting, Miss,' I wiped a kerchief over my brow.

'Mr Northrop, you'll find very few as good company as Compair Lapin. Why I think he has a dozen tales you, in particular, would do well to listen to.'

Lapin rolled his eyes and lolled his tongue like a Bedlam loon, before laughing once more.

'They's a way to go, Missuh Northrup, so I done tole the lady a story, thass' all.'

I forebore to enquire further about the matter.

'Where are we going? I assume you are aware that New Orleans – and the mint – lie in another direction?'

This provoked Miss Pardoner to some ill-stifled cackles, which I thought most unbecoming.

'Y'ain't got 'nuff of us, Mistuh Northrup,' said Lapin, and he strode forth, in a manner much more energetic than might have been expected from someone so infirm.

There was nothing for it but to follow, since I was not altogether sure I could have found my way back to the levee, much less to New Orleans itself. Progress was indeed slow. The children and the women often fell, tripped by tree roots or fatigue. Of the males, only myself and Compair Lapin managed to stay upright, for the most part. Miss Pardoner was remarkably sure-footed, although her feet could have been no better shod than my own. Without doubt, that night was one of the longest of my life. Endless tramping, stumbling and cursing, enlivened only by a brief halt by a brackish stream. We drank as if the stream were the nectar of the ancients, but were advised by Lapin to be abstemious in the partaking and to drink only sufficient to slake the thirst. We left one mother and a suckling babe behind shortly after, her body wracked with retching. One of the others kindly left her a sackcloth to keep them warm. The night air was cold, if one remained still and allowed the sweat to dry on one's skin. We left the swampland for something approaching the savannahs more likely to be found on the other side of the Mississippi.

I had slept in the open more than once: in the green fields of Kent and the rolling hills of north Northumberland, in the shelter of a mole in Newport News and many points between. The open grassland on which we found ourselves that night was as comfortless as any of these.

Miss Pardoner's reaction to the intelligence that two bodies in close juxtaposition would generate more heat each for the other lowered the temperature of that cold night several degrees further. Thus, I found myself in the embrace of Compair Lapin, who produced a horse-blanket from I knew not where to cover ourselves – and our entertainments – before we slept.

The morning was grey, with scarce a ray of sunlight to stain the cloud red. I lay alone under the horse-blanket for a time, watching Compair Lapin scurry hither and yon in an effort to encourage our band of ragamuffin runaways into departure. Presently he came over to where I lay, 'Missuh Northrup, we gunna be gone 'thout you all, if'n yuh don't giddap.'

He spat a jet of tobacco juice, which landed just to the side of his own horse-blanket, which perhaps gave a clue as to his opinion of me. I stirred myself, though my joints were stiff and my soul weary.

To my great annoyance, when I had caught up with Miss Pardoner, I found that she had the air of one who had slept in a hotel and in a better example of such than any I had had the fortune to experience in the Americas.

'Where is he taking us?' I asked her.

'There's another plantation a few miles from here. There, I expect.'

I could read no expression on her face and wondered at this passivity that I had hitherto considered no part of her character.

We continued our ragged progress, leaving behind one of the grizzle-headed slaves by the side of the rough track, which we followed. Plainly Compair's plan was to find more slaves to accomplish what we must do in the New Orleans Mint. The whole business seemed like a lunatic scheme devised by the most abject Bedlamite.

At the top of a small hillock our guide held up an arm, and although by this action he brought the column to a standstill, many of our company were barely moving forward at the time in any case. Compair Lapin pointed with a crooked finger into the shallow dale. A plantation less like Molasses would have been difficult to conceive. Wooden outbuildings had had the benefit of a recent coat of paint. These likely slave quarters even had glass in their windows rather than the customary tarpaper even the most liberal of owners provided.

As I looked at the garish colours of the buildings – the bright yellows, greens and reds a seeming homage to the most exotic of parrots – the taste of bitter leaf soup remained in my mouth and I had wished a circumspect refusal of the tin cup, when it had come my way. I turned to Miss Pardoner, 'Still another moon-struck son of first cousins awaits us inside, no doubt.'

Miss Pardoner, after such long – if interrupted – acquaintance, showed that she could yet take me by surprise: she summoned up a huge bolus of phlegm and projected it with venom at her feet. 'Oh no, sir, very far from that.'

The plantation house itself was a fine example of its type, save for the eccentric colour scheme from which neither the Greek-influenced colonnades, nor the Italianate asymmetrical massing, were spared. Marble and stucco had never suffered such chromatic indignities. Still worse, other parts of the building were of wooden construction in a Gothic style. It offered an emetic and dizzying contrast. Some of my distaste may have been revealed in my face. Miss Pardoner raised an eyebrow.

'Striking, is it not? Carpenter Gothic, they call it. Of course, it is less bruising to the eye when painted in the customary white. Naturally, none of these farmers can resist a little Greek and Roman addition to flavour the gumbo.'

'And how is it called, this feat of architectural melange?' I asked.

It startled me when Compair Lapin replied, 'Iss called New Walden, Missuh Northrup,' and he gave a short bark of laughter before leading the way to the plantation house itself. Over the course of our journey, Lapin seemed to grow healthier with every step away from the baleful influence of Campion's plantation.

If Molasses had led me to expect informality and ill-kempt inhabitants from New Walden, it was a pleasant surprise to be greeted – on pulling the bell – by a pair of tall footmen. Elegantly turned out in a style perhaps belonging more to my youth than current tastes, the effect was rather spoiled by the one livery being as yellow as a canary bird and the other as green as the Duke of Devonshire's Emerald.

'Unu ah wekkum, Missus Tremayne de a bat'room. Shi kian com rait nah. Com in, please.'

I was disappointed in my hope of seeing Miss Pardoner looking perplexed at the Jamaican plantation dialect. Moreover, I was amazed when Compair Lapin enunciated, 'We will enter, in that case, and await the end of Mrs Tremayne's indisposition.'

He waved an arm to the interior of the house and gave Miss Pardoner a slow wink.

We followed the malachite and flavous pair through a long passage whose decoration favoured similar colours. The servants led us to a large and somewhat over-furnished parlour whose walls boasted a different colour each. Naturally, green, yellow and red were in evidence; one wall, blessedly, was painted a calm ecru. However, the effect was somewhat spoiled by an enormous flag which covered a large part of it. It was a saltire, the cross being a vibrant red, and two triangles each of the colours sported by the lofty footmen. It was not a flag that I recognised; perhaps it was some sort of snook cocked at the flag of the Confederacy. Or perhaps, like the rest of New Walden, it was merely an insult to good taste.

Compair Lapin stationed himself behind Miss Pardoner, who occupied a peacock chair, which had mercifully been spared the usual palette of colours. Clearly, all three of us were tired, and I presumed that the rest of our party were resting in the oddly painted slave quarters. Miss Pardoner herself took her repose and was soon soughing like the wind through a cornfield, if it were but recently invaded by swine. I felt that I would never cease to be surprised at the incongruities in Ellen Pardoner. Meanwhile I sat on a chaise and was lost to the world for a time.

I was awakened by the clearing of Compair Lapin's throat. As to Miss Pardoner, I could not say whether this same noise caused her return to her senses, but I was gratified to see her look a little confused, if only momentarily. The entrance of the lady plantation owner had occasioned Lapin's peculiar choice of announcement. Peculiar, too, was that woman's attire. My expectations of some bizarre rendition of Parisian fashions in the colours so favoured on and in the plantation buildings were unfounded. The woman had chosen, for colour, materials in a plain and inoffensive cream. However, she wore no skirts of any kind, but rather trousers as had belonged to a man. The absence of any coat or jacket over what could only be named a gentleman's shirt did little to preserve the woman's modesty. Though she cut a fine figure, it was one that should not have appeared in any other location but the music hall – and even in such a place she might have provoked outrage. Miss Pardoner's eyes widened somewhat, but this may indeed have been an effort to shake off the effects of her brief nap. Compair Lapin was as inscrutable as a log.

The strangely dressed woman was not so circumspect: 'Well, what hev we heah? Do declare, Lapin keeps strange-uh comp'ny bah the day!'

Mrs Tremayne was possessed of a most peculiar form of expression. Her accent did not reflect so much the South, although there were certain inflections therein. What was alarming was the rapidity of her speech – and the ferocity with which she bit off each syllable as though with each utterance she intended to imitate the ignition of a string of fireworks.

'I'm heah from Bawston, Nyingland, doncha know? Married Tremayne and he died during the honeymoon. Had the look of a weak-winded horse the day I met him. The lady I'm acquainted with, and Mr Lapin, of course. But you, suh, who might you be?'

She was a most singular woman. It was scarcely surprising that Miss Pardoner rolled her eyes at the dismissive reference to herself. I made some effort at repartee.

'Well, Madam, I might be Anson Northrup.'

She gave a snort and I surmised that she was of the opinion that I might equally not be. Mrs Tremayne turned to Ellen Pardoner and addressed her by the *nom de travail* she was using on this side of the Atlantic Ocean.

'Miss Fitzpatrick. Do tell! What brings you here?'

Compair Lapin's eyes flickered to the left, but he said nothing. Mrs Tremayne received a terse reply: 'Railroad business.'

'Course that's the case. Why wouldn't it be? What exactly now? Details, that's what I like, now, don't you?'

It was truly astounding how the woman spoke without stopping for breath. Her taste for the interrogative was as irritating as it was nugatory, as she clearly expected no answer to any question that fell from her mouth.

'Expect it's my boys you need. Strong arms and strong backs. Power of men. Manpower. I like that. Succinct, shorter, clear: I like that too. Don't you Mr...?'

She threw me a glance and left the title hanging, before prattling further about emancipation, glory and her passion for the cause. At length, she brought herself up short.

'Coffee? Sure you do.'

She rang a bell that she had somehow secreted in her indecent trousers hitherto, thereby summoning a pair of housemaids attired in vermillion and kelly green. I was glad to note that at least there was some variation in shade when it came to the ghastly livery Mrs Tremayne had inflicted on New Walden. The brightly coloured servants were despatched to fetch coffee for three. I tried to catch Compair Lapin's eye, but he remained impassive, as lumber-like as before.

Coffee was served in a deferential – if diffident – manner by the liveried housemaids. The service was silver, and not, thank God, in some yellow, green or scarlet porcelain travesty. Each piece was as fine as any from one of the great houses in England. Their fine sheen was testament to the skill of one or other of the footmen. Sad to say, for cups we were given Wedgewood's finest crudely repainted in the expected scheme. The coffee itself was a greater disappointment still: a viscid, tepid brew that surely must have been made by a native of China or some other country where coffee was a fancy of foreign devils and not to be partaken of, save under dire circumstances.

Mrs Tremayne had at the foul liquid with gusto, drinking six cups to the single exemplars which Ellen Pardoner and I scarcely touched. A gout of phrases burst forth from our hostess once more.

'The silver. It's the silver, isn't it. I said the silver. Told Levi Coffin, himself. We could take a leaf from Henry 'Box' Brown.'

At last, Miss Pardoner was provoked to meaningful response.

'Tremayne, quite apart from the fact we are trying to move a thousand silver bullion bars, the damned fool Brown has spoken too much of his ingenious use of the mails to escape servitude for any others to profit by the same.'

My surprise lay chiefly in that Miss Pardoner had addressed our strange hostess by surname only. Compair Lapin's lip curled, but he may have been stifling a sneeze.

Mrs Tremayne at last was struck almost dumb, and restricted herself to a breathless, 'Bullion.'

Miss Pardoner addressed her acquaintance, 'Tremayne, we need porters, slaves if you like...'

'No slaves. No slaves at New Walden. Freemen of colour. Have to ask them. Obvious, Miss F, isn't it?'

The purported Miss Fitzpatrick's eyes rolled like a baptist preacher's. However, Compair Lapin interjected at this point, once again in the educated tones that had surprised me earlier, 'Your request is expected and we will have sufficient strong backs for our needs.'

Mrs Tremayne added, 'Of course. I mean, surely. It is their choice.'

I was disinclined to believe in her enthusiasm for the matter, due to the wringing of her hands and the twisting of her lips.

Though for the most part of the venture I had felt less than necessary to its success, it occurred to me that there might be some problem with the volunteers we might take to the New Orleans Mint. Therefore, I decided to intervene. I cleared my throat, 'Ahh, If I might be so bold...'

I detected a sneer at Miss Pardoner's lips and a sigh escaped those of Mrs Tremayne – I need not speak of any reaction from Lapin.

'The sla— freemen? Might one assume that they enjoy the benefit of your especial livery, Mrs Tremayne? Do they own other garb?'

The plantation's mistress' mouth made a round 'O'. Lapin spoke quietly, 'They have things put by. We always do, even "freemen of colour".'

From the look in his eyes, it was clear that he thought little of this term and I could not blame him, since the title, in my experience, conferred little of true freedom on the bearer.

'And if found in the company of runaways, what then for freemen of colour?' I asked.

He gave a smile as sad and old as slavery.

'If one man be yet enslaved, how can I be free?'

'For myself, I concur with the Corsican, "Men are moved by two levers only: fear and self-interest." And, my friend, though you may believe in Comte's altruism, I myself believe in that myth no more than in faeries, fauns or federalism.'

Which riposte, to my great pleasure, rendered Compair Lapin speechless, that man restricting himself to a most alarming scowl in response.

At that moment the relative peace of the parlour was interrupted by the two footmen who arrived in a state of agitation. Their formerly pristine livery was in some disarray and mud-stains at knee and elbow. Both began to speak at once; thankfully, whatever their ordeal had entailed, it had shocked them into speaking in plain English, rather than the Jamaican patois, their mistress seemed to insist on.

'Missy, that man? The dirty, sailor man...'

'He did! Didn't he...'

These two utterances being simultaneous and – perhaps scarcely intelligible to anyone but myself, I held up a hand and asked them, 'Where is he?'

Two heads shook from side to side and their voices spoke in unison, 'Don' make us show yuh, Mistuh. He in the barn, past the slave houses.'

The footmen ran out of the room, Mrs Tremayne held a hand to an open mouth and Miss Pardoner followed me outside. I looked back to see Compair Lapin's consoling arm around Mrs Tremayne's shoulders.

In the barn, it became apparent that Ishmael had entered into some altercation with the footmen. However, in sure sign of the man's eccentricity, he seemed once again intent on continuing the brawl in the absence of his erstwhile opponents. Some of the epithets must have been peculiar to the Nantucket whalers, for I could make no sense of what he shouted. So taken up with his imaginary opponents was he that I found it quite a simple matter to quieten him with the aid of a judiciously applied blow from a nearby plank of wood. It occurred to me that, amusing as the drunken fool was, he might indeed be more burdensome than I had first thought. I turned to find Miss Pardoner eyeing me with a most particular look. She passed her tongue over her lips and a little colour rose to her cheeks. For a moment I thought I might revisit long-remembered pleasures, but she stiffened her spine and asked, 'D'you suppose we might need to… tie him up?'

A length of sisal was found. Miss Pardoner and I made Ishmael quite fast. When the last knot was tied, he looked me in the eye and gave a sharp nod. Once again, there was something familiar in it, but I had other, more pressing things to attend to. Ellen took my hand and we lay on the straw of an empty stall. Her enthusiasm in such matters had, if anything, increased in the intervening years and I was exercised as well as any thoroughbred in a very short time. We were both upright and un-flushed by the time Lapin arrived to see what had happened. I was irked by his smile, although his words were harmless enough, 'We travel tomorrow, we meet the others there.'

'Then we are to overnight here?'

'We are,' Lapin replied and he gave a most military half-turn. We were left to follow him back to the house.

My bedroom proved to be as distant from that of Miss Pardoner as it was possible to be, whilst still remaining part of the main building. A knock at her door in the small hours produced not a whit of reaction. The only entertainment offered was that provided by the sight of Mrs Tremayne's attempt to remain invisible by standing completely still on the threshold of Lapin's allocated apartments whilst I returned to my own.

18

The following morning Mrs Tremayne stood on the stoop in male riding attire.

'Doodekleyah, could almost saddl'up and come with yuh! Wouldn't that be a hoot?'

She waved an arm and then blew a kiss, which I knew was meant neither for me nor my female companion. I was most relieved that the owner of New Walden would not accompany our ridiculous cavalcade. There were some forty able-bodied freemen of colour in addition to the ragamuffin slaves who had survived the trek from Molasses. It was to prove the only thing for which I could be thankful respecting our journey of some ten miles overland to the New Orleans Mint. Although it was not in close proximity to the mansions of the wealthy Creoles who inhabited the upper parts of the avenue, neither was it in the splendid isolation that would have rendered the arrival of two white persons in the company of a column of black men and women less conspicuous, at least not in daylight. However, Lapin said that an approach from the rear of the mint would afford us the least likelihood of discovery.

Therefore, after several hours arduous walking, we stopped about a mile from the rear of the building, which aspect looked over open ground, and waited for darkness to fall.

And late it was, by the time the night was truly dark. I confess the twilight gloaming was marred for me by Compair Lapin's interminable tale concerning a rabbit and something called a tar baby, regarding which I had no clue as to what it might be. I watched the entire company, including Miss Pardoner, rock their shoulders in ill-suppressed laughter. Still it kept our band from wandering and blundering thereby into anyone curious enough to venture as far as this desolate place behind the mint.

'We three will go together.' Lapin indicated Miss Pardoner and myself.

I did not cavil, but, perhaps inevitably, Ishmael insisted on coming too. The man had behaved remarkably well since spending the night bound hand and foot in the stables at New Walden. I had seen the strait-waistcoat employed to similar effect many years ago. Lapin offered no objection and neither did I, since I was enjoying Miss Pardoner's discomfiture at the obviously besotted sailor's attentions. We left one of the more responsible of the freemen in nominal charge of our band and urged them all to remain quiet in the field. The four of us approached the rear of the mint building. Continuity of design ensured that the building was as hideous to view from the rear as from the front. The lack of care and consequent dilapidation, which had ensued more than compensated for the lack of columnar atrocities inflicted on the façade.

A large double door offered ingress. It was quite large enough to admit horse-drawn deliveries of raw material and coal. There was, of course, no bell-pull. However, there was a vast iron knocker, which Lapin struggled to lift, but Ishmael grasped and let fly as though it had been made of paper. We waited in silence. The sailor made for the knocker once more only to have the door's opening remove it from his reach. Miss Pardoner, Ishmael and I renewed our recent acquaintance with Holzbein, but Lapin greeted him as a long-lost familiar.

'Ye've come,' he said, his eyebrows rose.

'That we have, and we'd as soon be gone with what we came for,' I replied.

Lapin held a hand palm upward to me; I doubted he had ever come closer to his maker than in that moment. Miss Pardoner laid a hand on my arm and squeezed with the grip of a street-brawler.

'Mr Northrup, have some patience. It might be wiser to wait until the dead of night before we make our way,' Lapin said.

He was quite correct, and his smile told me that he knew it. I asked him if our motley band was to march through New Orleans down to the Public Dock, with none to remark on our passing. Imagine the extent of my surprise, when he informed me that we would be charging our cargo into a vessel moored at the Southern Yacht Club on the shores of Lake Pontchartrain. The man was simply quite mad. We were to carry as much silver bullion as humanly possible to the spiritual home of the rich and foolish New Orleanians who played at sailing in the waters of the lake. I reflected there would be few Abolitionists among their number.

'What about going upriver?'

I was somewhat relieved at Miss Pardoner's interjection, taking comfort that she had as little influence on events as I.

A voice, perhaps as deep as the Mississippi river, emerged from the gloom behind Holzbein.

'We will go on the Old Waters. From the Big Water to The Big River – on the Old Waters.'

The man who stepped out from behind the guardian of

the mint did not look like the 'noble chief' described in Fennimore Cooper's distasteful drivel.

He wore nothing that constituted any form of buckskin. In addition, he sported the boots that most white people I had met in America wore. He was trousered in a conservative plaid and his long-tailed coat – though worn and shabby – was of a very good cut. This he wore over a muted damask waistcoat and a shirt with no collar. The only sartorial concession to his heritage was a long black feather trapped in the silken band of his opera hat. He extended a hand to me.

'Good evening, sir. I am Manifest Destiny, recently of the Caddo tribe, once of the Natchez.'

He executed an adequate bow. Lapin's laughter rang loud in my ear.

'Do not make a fool of our Mr Northrup, John Tecumseh.'

John Tecumseh then gave a click of his booted heels and a nod of the head.

'My little joke, sir. Besides, what's in a name? We are what we do, are we not? '

I resisted the temptation to reply that we 'did not'.

'There are creeks that the Caddo know, we can reach the river outside of New Orleans, upriver.'

I expressed my concerns about how our arrival at the Southern Yacht Club would be received.

'There is no Clubhouse, Mr Northrup.' Compair Lapin, plucked a little lint from his lapel. 'There are a few shanties where the slaves who maintain the marina exist. The overseer has a cabin, but he spends most mornings inside it sleeping off whiskey from his native Tennessee. We may arrive at our leisure.'

'Surely we will not be stealing a yacht?'

John Tecumseh laughed. 'There are flat-bottomed boats at our disposal, they will get us to the river…'

'And then we'll board the river boat near some isolated jetty,' I finished his sentence for him.

'Bravo, Mr Northrup,' the Caddo replied. 'A name, once chosen, should be lived up to, shouldn't it?'

Lapin was for despatching Ishmael to fetch the rest of our party, but I volunteered to go myself. Of course, this resulted in his insistence in accompanying me, proving that virtue was not always its own reward. For my part, I was content that Miss Pardoner was more than a match for a wooden-legged man. Besides, Ishmael would have committed any kind of foolhardiness in the service of the remarkable Miss P. I was reminded of one Jedediah Maccabi, whose devotion to Ellen had been equally firm, when once we all three were in far-off Northumbria.

19

We arrived back at the mint, our brigade of porters in tow, some two hours later. Ishmael had been prevailed upon to keep cave for our return, therefore the great doors to the rear of the building had been opened and we entered without breaking step. The large courtyard, and indeed the mint entire, was silent. The stamps, dies and rolling mills remained motionless. Holzbein noticed my distraction. There was no sign of the Indian.

'They ain't no one else here. The boys are gone. Sent'um over to work down by the shore-side, the State wants 'em 'til the mint opens again. You know'd I had to shut the ole lady down.'

Miss Pardoner looked alarmed, doubtless wondering if what was left of the slaves and freemen would be enough to carry out the hare-brained scheme. For though most freemen had remained with us, many of the slaves from Molasses had fallen by the wayside. Some few had run and I could not blame them for it.

Compair Lapin put his hand on my one-time ward's arm.

'We will take what we can, we can do no more.'

'We got some handcarts.' Holzbein pointed to some

rather decrepit barrows leaning against the wall of the yard. He looked to Lapin, 'Better git on down to the store.'

'Not the vault?' I enquired.

He gave no answer and we were left to follow. The cavernous vestibule seemed no more welcoming when entered from the rear of the building than the front. This time, however, the passage that we took from it led off to the west wing. The floor was rough stone and sloped downward. After about a chain's length a blank wall faced us. Under Holzbein's feet was a large trapdoor. The frame touched the end-wall and both sides of the passage.

'Cain't lift it myself. The boys lef' it open when they went down to the riverside. Slammed it shut when I finished up.'

He stepped nimbly off the trap and our band took several steps backward. Lapin shouted two of the healthiest men forward and they set to opening the heavy wooden door. They pulled and heaved at the chain looped through the iron ring attached to the trap. After much grunting and – it must be said – some highly imaginative cursing, the two men fell back as the door did the same. When my ears had quite finished ringing I was aware that I was being borne downward on some rough stone steps in the company of all, save Holzbein himself and, to my surprise, Ishmael.

The loud crash of the trapdoor's closure and the resultant darkness came as some surprise given Holzbein's earlier remarks. Perhaps the lunatic mariner had helped him.

The chattering began instanter. Only Lapin, Miss Pardoner and I kept our counsel. Of course, I would have stepped forward had not Lapin's voice demanded silence. That the man had presence could not be denied. However, he did not speak further and I felt Ellen Pardoner's hand on my arm and her lips at my ear, which pleasant experience mitigated the import of her words.

'Is it truly possible that Northrup was a turncoat? That he and Mudsill were one and the same?'

I merely smiled into the dark and put my lips to her own ear, 'Your temper gave me to believe you were convinced of it, not so long ago. Does it truly matter? The man is dead and we are trapped, by his confederate.'

Taking her hand, I guided it to the pocket inside my coat.

'The bond and the warrant, remember?'

Lapin seized hold of us both.

'We need to work together. What did you see the last time you were here?'

This last was addressed to me, and so I answered him, 'I have not been in this part of the mint.'

My eyes were growing used to the dark. I could make out the shapes of Lapin and Miss Pardoner who were standing nearest to me in the underground chamber. Movement provided the only clue to the presence of the rest of our troupe.

Lapin called for the assembled men and women's attention once more.

'We need light. If any have tobacco and the makings stored away against the day, now would be the time to ready your matches. First, we must all go to the walls of this place. Perhaps there are gas mantles or some such. Scuff your feet on the floor, there may be straw or rags or some matériel with which we may fashion a torch.'

There were murmurs of assent and I felt the air shift as the men and women moved to do Lapin's bidding. My boot struck something on the dirt floor. I bent carefully and picked up some part of a packing crate, a piece of wood as long as my forearm. At one end it had split and buckled. I reached into a pocket and withdrew the lacy kerchief I had removed from the late Cuffy McGraw's person. This same I wrapped around the damaged end of the wood. Ellen Pardoner proved an unlikely source of ignition when she informed me that she had a lucifer match, since she liked to smoke a pipe when the opportunity arose. The silk and lace burned tolerably well and I could see many frightened faces by the light of my makeshift firebrand.

There was nothing but bare walls. The room was large, and the ceiling rose high above our heads. There were heavy beams supporting the floor above. I wondered what was over our heads, but could not place our location with reference to what I knew of the geography of the mint. Miss Pardoner and Lapin exchanged a glance.

'There appears to be no ventilation whatsoever,' she said. Her breath curled like smoke in the brumal chill of the air.

'There must be, but…' he looked around the faces in the room, so I finished his sentence for him, 'If not we had better limit the number of torches lit, eh, Lapin?'

'Quite correct. Doubtless you wish to keep yours alight?'

I pretended not to have seen the sneer with which he accompanied the question.

'Naturally, I intend to seek some draught by means of guiding my flame around the perimeter of the room.'

'It is to be hoped you find some breath of air, if not I fear…' Then he addressed the company once more and instructed them to huddle together, for it was truly cold in the dank basement.

20

The touch of Miss Pardoner's hand on my sleeve was more than compensation for what I was sure would be the nugatory nature of my task.

'We'll look together,' she said as she cast a glance over her shoulder to where Lapin must have been, though we could not see him. For my light *was* feeble against the caliginous gloom. Miss Pardoner continued to clutch at my arm. Torch in hand, I ran the palm of my other hand along the rough surface of the wall. There was no crevice that was not crammed with a gelatinous moss indicating the ingress of water from some source, although I doubted that we would ever find it. The flame guttered from time to time but not from any movement of air, rather from the secretions which impregnated the kerchief I had used to fashion the flambeau.

I stumbled. Miss Pardoner showed uncommon strength in preventing my fall. We crouched and cast about for the impediment that had brought me low. Of all things it proved to be a clock. A carriage clock.

'I hardly think we are in need of a time-piece here, Miss Pardoner.'

For answer, Miss Pardoner maintained a fierce grip on the handle, though I tried to wrest it from her.

Compair Lapin began leading the rest in song. I confess I found the sound quite comforting although I could not say why. We continued to investigate the damp walls. Finally, I came upon a recess in the rock. Whilst exploring the dimensions of the niche with my hand, I felt the tiniest movement of the hairs on the back of it. The torch's flame flickered as I brought it closer. Miss Pardoner peered at the admittedly neat lines of the recess in the stone. I reflected on the meretricious nature of hope even as my heart beat faster at this feeble indication of a possible route of escape.

'See! Perhaps we can use a knife and excavate a route…'

Even by the dim light I carried, I could see Miss Pardoner attempting to contain her hilarity. She recovered herself sufficiently to push me aside, whereupon she placed the clock in the recess in the stone.

'Hold it closer, man!' She jerked her chin, indicating the light.

I watched her move the hands of the clock to twelve. The ensuing rumble and roar did cause me to take a backward step, although Miss Pardoner made a veritable leap, accompanied by a short shriek. Perhaps I was not so surprised as some to see a huge section of stone grinding slowly inward to reveal a secret passage. No, my astonishment was reserved for the possibility that my female confederate had known all along of its existence. Since my face had ever been more readable by Ellen Pardoner than by any other, she lifted one eyebrow and smiled.

'Holzbein is a complicated character. One day fair, one day foul. He is no more constant than a weather-cock.'

'How did you know?'

'What? The clock?' She laughed and her teeth gleamed in the torchlight. 'However great a leap of faith it might have been, the coincidence of the clock's presence and the dimensions of the recess demanded that I attempt to marry them somehow.'

The words fell from her lips readily enough, but I remained unconvinced, nonetheless.

By this time Lapin and the rest were crowded around the entrance to the passage. Since I carried the flame, I led the way into the passage, closely followed by the divine, if devious, Miss P.

The passage was narrow but straight. The way neither rose nor fell. I tried to remember the lay of the land surrounding the building. I could not recall any evidence of likely deposits of granite, yet this passage was hewn out of rock, which – by any geological estimation – should not have lain under the flat, marshy ground around the mint. We had travelled but fifty feet when my light finally gave out. There was a collective gasp of fright, which at least saved me the embarrassment of acknowledging my own.

Lapin bustled past us, 'Come on, keep going.'

We all followed although none knew what awaited us at the end of the corridor.

21

I, for one, had not noticed the smell until our band spilled out into an open space yet colder than the vault at the other end of the passage. Miss Pardoner and I each clamped a hand over our mouth at the same moment. There was a door in the wall opposite and there were lit torches set in alcoves. Who had lit them I could not say, for there were no others present but cadavers – perhaps as many as two score. There were no skeletal remains, although the depredations of vermin had laid bare muscle and bone in some cases. Lapin let out a sob and there were gasps of shock among the cursing and crying. All the dead were black men, whether slaves or freedmen I could not tell, which proved to me that all men were equal in the face of death, if not in the United States.

Miss Pardoner bent down and removed something from one corpse's eye. She held a gleaming coin up to the light. I recognised it, for I had one about my person. I had discovered it among Northrup's effects along with the Governor's warrant issued to John Mudsill.

'These men are not so long dead.' Lapin pointed at the cadavers.

'We may have done Northrup an injustice, Miss Pardoner. He may not have been Mudsill after all.'

'Anyone may carry a Liberty coin,' she replied.

'Few would carry as many as eighty.' Lapin began collecting all of the copper coins.

'Is the Railroad so short of funds?' I had not thought him avaricious.

Miss Pardoner snorted. Lapin sighed, 'Better no penny than a Copperhead's coin.'

'In any event, surely this means that Northrup was not Mudsill?'

'Perhaps not, when was it that you met him?'

Lapin laughed, 'I knew you for an imposter, the moment you opened your mouth.'

'Which of us is who we seem, Compair Lapin?'

'Answer, nevertheless.'

'A trip up-and-down the Mississippi river ago.'

'There are more than a few north of the Mason-Dixon Line who sympathise with the South.'

'Be that as it may, the coincidence of the mint and the warrant...'

But Miss Pardoner was not to be moved and I saw that any man whom she considered to have betrayed her would await her forgiveness in vain.

Lapin pushed at the door on the far side of the poor departed and beckoned us to follow. The opening allowed some light from above ground. Therefore, we made our way out and up into the fresh air...

22

Where we encountered nary a sign of any rear, front or side elevation of the mint. Having emerged from a hole in some mossy turf we were in woodland, which – if most certainly not a weald – at least deserved better than to be called a copse or spinney. No such woodland had been visible near the mint before we had entered it. John Tecumseh, yet clad in his feathered opera hat, appeared from between two close-bent trees and stepped into the tiny glade in which we stood. He had painted his eye-sockets quite black and whether he had used coal or kohl, it gave him a fearsome look.

'You will come.' He fixed a steady gaze on Compair Lapin, who made to move and signalled to the rest of the men.

'Will we, sir? And why should we do that?'

Miss Pardoner grasped my arm and I shook it off.

'It is nothing to me what you choose to do. You will come if it is to be so, just as I do what is to be done.' I felt this too gnomic a response to leave unchallenged.

'And here you are, manifest and clearly determined to be part of our destiny, Tecumseh. Why?'

He made no answer to me, informing Lapin that the

handcarts lay on the other side of trees, back the way he had come.

I made sure that Miss Pardoner and I fell in behind Lapin, who in his turn was following Tecumseh through the dense undergrowth of the thicket. A tug at the black man's sleeve drew his attention and I sensed a flash of annoyance, though he merely waited for me to speak.

'The dead? Your fellow slaves? Surely you are concerned?'

'They enjoy as much freedom now as they have ever done, sir.'

We continued on our way as we spoke, since the rest were treading close on our heels.

'But Holzbein? Did *he* kill so many?'

'We will deal with Holzbein when necessary.'

At that moment our company emerged from the trees. In front of us were a number of handcarts, far superior to the broken-down barrows in the yard of the mint. There was a sufficiency of them to ensure that two might share the pushing of them once they had been loaded with bullion. However, as to where the mint might be, I was at a loss. I did not recognise the place to which we had come, any more than I knew whence we had come to it.

Tecumseh stood arms folded whilst Lapin directed his men to the carts according to size. That is, he attempted to place a brawnier specimen with a weaker or sicklier type wherever possible. Naturally, Miss Pardoner was not expected to exert herself. It transpired that Lapin and I were to push the same cart.

'Where to now?' I whispered, though perhaps not so quietly as I might have wished.

This prompted an unfolding of the Caddo's arms.

'You have already trod a native path, there are others. All

are invisible to the white men, since they see nothing – and never have.'

He led us along no discernible causeway across wild grass and swamp-dirt. After a half-mile or so, I looked back toward where the trees had been, but was not unduly surprised to see nothing between the rear of our troupe and the flat horizon. Even so, I could not pretend I was not disturbed by the unearthly nature of our journey from beneath the mint. However, there was no engaging either Miss Pardoner and Lapin on the matter, for both fixed their eyes ahead as we continued to follow John Tecumseh along a path only he could see.

For it was indeed a strange journey, even in the woodland there had been no sight or sound of bird or beast. This uncanny silence yet prevailed as the landscape had changed to something akin to what I remembered surrounding the New Orleans Mint. Yet I recognised nothing, not a landmark nor geological feature. Suddenly, John Tecumseh held his hand high. A distracted Lapin continued to push his handle of our shared tumbrel – and therefore tripped – since I did not.

'We must smoke,' was all that Tecumseh said. He made a gesture with his arm as if presenting a substantial table of exquisite cuisine to a crowd of gourmets in a Piccadilly hotel. We all sat. I took my place in the circle beside Miss Pardoner, who had Lapin to her other flank. To my left hand was the blackest man I had yet seen in the Americas. He gave me a nod and a tight smile that did not bare a single tooth, though the beam he granted his fellow freedman to his own left showed many, including, most unusually I thought, an eyetooth of solid gold.

The Caddo Indian had produced a pipe from somewhere about his person, perhaps the pocket of his frock coat. That he filled it from a leathery-looking pouch that had been secreted under his hat was more surprising. What animal's skin had been sacrificed to make the pouch, I could not tell, but Tecumseh's smile as he handled it was most discomfiting. The pipe-bowl itself was of a polished red stone, with a face carved on the outside, where it could be seen by others. The long stem was a dried river-reed decorated with a few short feathers. The tobacco Tecumseh lit looked very coarse and the smell was indeed quite sickly. He took a draw sufficient only to keep the glow in the bowl and handed it to the man on his left. When that man attempted to pass on the pipe after a similarly short inhalation, the Indian motioned that he should take more, before handing it onward. This he did and I fancied I saw him blink very slowly several times.

By the time the pipe had reached my hands, I was determined not to inhale. I would merely feign the drowsiness that had affected all those who had previously done so. Miss Pardoner slumped against Lapin and I envied the man's luck in achieving such intimacy even while unconscious. I handed on the pipe. I could say that it was not opium, for I knew the taste and effects. However, I believed it was some or other substance, which sent those who partook too deeply of it to similarly insensible dreams. Having passed on the pipe, I dissembled. Since my eyes were shut, the pain of the heavy blow to the back of my head was the first indication that Tecumseh wanted us all insensible by whatever means necessary.

23

I had woken with worse headaches in the past, but never without having earned it through debauchery, drink or similar diversions. I lay in one of the handcarts being pushed by a smirking Miss Pardoner and stern-faced Lapin. My transportation came to a halt when I sat upright and my bearers indicated that I should dismount.

'The Indian?'

'Gone. He left an arrow pointing the way.'

Lapin pointed himself, indicating the mint at a distance of about a mile.

'How long was I... indisposed?'

I looked to Miss Pardoner for answer, but it was Lapin who replied, ''Bout an hour more than the rest of us.'

Ellen Pardoner's lips flattened, and it was clear she was – once more – trying to suppress a laugh at my expense.

We continued toward the rear of the mint. My enquiry as to how we had found our way back was met with a shrug from Lapin and a saloon girl's wink from Ellen. There was silence as we approached the rear of the mint building. I could only assume that the others felt as disoriented as I, although I knew that they had not suffered the cranial inconvenience that I had. The large doors at the rear entrance were still open and there was no immediate sign of Holzbein or Ishmael. We wheeled the carts into the courtyard.

Ishmael was nowhere to be seen. Holzbein stood by the dilapidated barrows in one corner of the stone-flagged yard. I made to dash for the old man, but Miss Pardoner's arm held me back. Lapin was looking keenly at the mint's last employee, but he made no move. I began to speak, but Lapin held up a hand for silence, just as Holzbein toppled forward onto the dusty stones. Miss Pardoner was first to the corpse, for Holzbein had expired before our very eyes. She knelt and rolled the cadaver so that his face was uppermost. Lapin knelt beside her, while I preferred to keep my trousers free of dust. Despite this I noted that the deep furrows in Holzbein's face had softened to mere tracery. His eyes, though red, stared upward to the heavens, if not to Paradise. He did look very pallid and I said as much to the others.

'That is on account of the exsanguination.' Miss Pardoner pointed at the pool of blood, which seemed to have flowed out from a hole in the sole of Holzbein's solitary boot. The upper part of his trouser leg was sodden with blood.

'I hardly think someone stabbed him in the leg and left him to bleed.'

Ellen looked up.

'They did not, sir. Kindly remove his boot.'

It was a high boot of the kind favoured by the westerners and it came off most remarkably easily. So much so, that I fell in a heap onto the dust I had been trying to avoid. Furthermore, a large quantity of his vital fluid, hitherto contained in said boot, saturated my own apparel to the degree of his trouser leg.

'Look at the man's veins, sir.'

Lapin and I peered closer at the late Holzbein's lower

limb. The veins were many, raised and angry. I looked at Lapin and shrugged.

Miss Pardoner's exhalation was a measure of her exasperation.

'Varicosity!'

I confess I felt that this might have been a word she had encountered on this side of the Atlantic Ocean, since it sounded quite as outlandish as 'hornswoggle' or 'pale-face'. She must have seen the disbelief writ large on my countenance, for she went on, 'If untreated, a man might easily bleed to death at any moment. Professor Jedermann had a cousin who expired from the very same in Ghent. He showed me the sketches he made of the corpse. Those of his acquaintance in the medical sphere mocked him most roundly, but he claimed he had proven it beyond all doubt with some experiments on indigent seamen.'

Lapin looked up but refrained from inquiry as to who Jedermann might be. I was glad of it, for I rarely cared to think of that lunatic. The polymath dwarf had believed himself to have resurrected me until the very moment of his own fiery demise in the ruins of Gibbous House. Even so, I was struck by just how much my own life had turned on first encountering Ellen Pardoner, although I was not sure whether I felt regret or gratitude.

We removed from the mint's store such bullion as would fit on the ramshackle carts. Four men were assigned to each cart. The rest of our band was instructed to carry two bars of silver each. Lapin raised an eyebrow when I complied but said nothing. Tecumseh appeared in the arched entry to the mint's yard the moment the carts were loaded. He waved an arm in the direction we were to walk and began following a trail invisible to

all other eyes but his. Thus was I spared the pushing of a barrow, but not the burden of Lapin's company. He began a long
anecdote concerning the damned rabbit and I calculated the
number of bullion bars we transported in my head. The native
led us by a route that meandered like a drunk at midnight. We
stopped by the side of a watercourse of the kind I still could
not bring myself to call a creek – or as the local parlance had it,
'crick'. It was an extremely shallow river, scarcely deep enough
to bear the slight draught of the flat-bottomed boats moored
near its banks. There were ten skiff-like watercrafts in all, each
with a native as pilot. Tecumseh boarded the first of the ten and
beckoned to Lapin to join him. I chose to do the same but was
astounded that Miss Pardoner held back. She boarded the vessel
immediately behind. Her smile was as enigmatic as that of any
odalisque.

We arrived suddenly in the outer reaches of the New Orleans
docks. It came as some surprise to me that the *Enterprise* was
berthed next to the *Grand Turk*. Next but one away was a
smaller vessel. It was no kind of paddle steamer, rather a keelboat, with a flat boat in tow behind. Both were dwarfed by the
Enterprise which in turn was inconsequential in comparison to
the *Turk* and the juxtaposition of the three vessels was greatly
to the advantage of the larger paddle boat, making it seem,
for the first time in my acquaintance of it, very nearly grand.
There was little sign of life on any of the four boats. Alongside,
no stevedores were loading or unloading cargo. I saw no passengers or crew either awake – or indeed aboard – any of the
riverboats. It was the Sabbath day. The Indians guided their
vessels between the *Turk* and the *Enterprise*. There was just sufficient space as their respective jetties were to port and star-

board. A loud 'Halloo!' came not from the *Grand Turk* but from the *Enterprise*.

I recognised the imposing figure of George Washington Irving. Perhaps he had been sold to the owners of the smaller vessel. It was not impossible that one company might own two such poor examples of a boat rather than a single more valuable asset, I supposed. Miss Pardoner waved and pointed at the *Grand Turk*, before lifting her shoulders and raising her palms upward. I confess a laugh escaped me as she fell due to the unsteady nature of the flatboats. Washington gave an exaggerated shake of the head and pointed downward at the deck of the *Enterprise*, having realised that discretion would be wiser than discourse at volume in the New Orleans dockyard, however deserted it might seem.

Washington Irving and another man lowered several ropes over the side of the *Enterprise*. It rode as low in the water as I remembered. The larger man, Irving, held up three fingers. Miss Pardoner held up an ingot and Irving shook his head. The leading boat was then left with Tecumseh and Miss Pardoner aboard, since three of the freedmen of colour had begun climbing the ropes to board the *Enterprise*. These three, under Washington Irving's direction, began drawing the ropes up behind them. To these they attached rope-handled canvas bags, which they then lowered over the side. Tecumseh left Miss Pardoner to fill the three bags with bars of silver. The men on board struggled to heave them upward and over the side onto the vessel. Meanwhile, Tecumseh moved the skiff to the rear and the next, with Compair Lapin and I aboard, moved to the front of the queue. The same routine followed. I had just placed the last bar in the bag, when there was a loud scream.

Tecumseh was floundering some distance away in the water. Miss Pardoner was in the process of tacking her skiff to rejoin the rest of them. The Indian must have had designs on Ellen Pardoner, but his attempt to carry her off to his encampment had ended in failure and a dunking in the Mississippi river. At last the silver was loaded onto the *Enterprise*. All scrambled up the ropes to board her. I waited until Miss Pardoner had ascended, as much out of concern for her safety as the desire to steal a look up her skirts.

When I finally arrived on the *Enterprise*'s grubby deck, Lapin, George Washington Irving and Miss Pardoner were in lively conversation.

'That most certainly was not how the scheme was outlined to me!'

Miss Pardoner stamped her foot and I smiled, for it made her look quite ridiculous.

'Nevertheless,' Washington Irving replied, 'it is how we will implement it.'

Lapin was nodding.

'So the silver and human cargo will be travelling separately after all?' I addressed the question to Washington Irving, but it was Miss Pardoner who answered.

'Apparently so,' she sniffed.

'And why is that?'

'The silver is more valuable to the Underground Railroad at this moment in time,' Lapin said.

This time Irving nodded and Miss Pardoner might have pulled her pistol from her reticule had she had it about her person.

'How are we to board the railroad passengers?' I asked. It was no surprise to hear Washington Irving's reply, 'The masters of both vessels are indisposed after a visit to a sporting establishment last night.'

'In any event,' I went on, 'are Messrs Kincaid and Grey in their respective cabins?'

Washington signalled the affirmative.

'Then we should be about it, gentlemen.'

Irving led the freedmen and slaves alike onto the jetty and around to the *Grand Turk*'s gang-plank.

'I think you had better join them, Lapin,' said Ellen Pardoner.

He hesitated.

'I shall ensure that Mr... Northrup does not succumb to any temptation. At least as regards the silver.'

Which hint at a bargain more than whetted my appetite.

Miss Pardoner and I had been allocated what passed for a stateroom. Doubtless it had been arranged by the Underground Railroad, although my companion could not confirm this.

24

Ellen and I were still abed when the *Enterprise* got under way. I should have liked to enjoy the untidy egress of the vessel from its berth, however Miss Pardoner said she felt a little too delicate for further sport. Since a gentleman never forces his attentions on a lady, I left her in the stateroom and took a turn around the deck. Upriver from the *Enterprise*, the *Grand Turk* was making sluggish headway. Did I imagine that it seemed lower in the water than usual? At least only the stowaways had added to the vessel's tare weight. I hoped the *Turk*'s pilot had noted the difference in his vessel's handling and that he would make allowances when the marks were called, it had been worse still were both forms of contraband aboard the same riverboat.

The voice was not above a whisper, though it was as urgent as a snake's hiss. Since the words came from somewhere near the ankle of my boot, I did not discard the possibility of encountering the world's first talking snake.

'Northrup, Northrup.'

The tug at the leg of my breeches disabused me of this herpetological fantasy. Looking down I saw what looked like a pile of discarded tarpaulins on the deck of the *Enterprise*. I should say I was standing about midship. A delicate hand protruded from the pile of cloth and had hold of my trouser with a most determined grip. I squatted to lift the edge of the tarpaulin.

The unpowdered face of Winona Shepherd looked up at me.

'Help. Help me, for pity's sake.'

There was nothing for it but to put my finger to my lips and bundle her over my shoulder in one of the tarpaulins in which she had sequestered herself for who knew how long.

I used the toe of my boot to fashion a kind of knocking at the door of the stateroom. Miss Pardoner's eyes widened only a little when she saw the burden over my shoulder. Her surprise was a little more evident when I placed the bundle on the bed and Winona Shepherd emerged from it.

'We are betrayed, Northrup.'

While I should have expected a fit of tears from the majority of women at this point, Miss Shepherd shook and bit her lip to such an extent that I thought she was suffering from a fit of a quite different kind. Nevertheless, it should have come as no surprise that the emotion that Miss Shepherd fought so hard to contain was rage.

A glance at Miss Pardoner sufficed to deduce her reaction to a young woman of colour on her recently vacated bed. I was disappointed that she preferred the concept of equality more in the abstract than the concrete – I had thought her an independent thinker from the first moment I saw her. I held up a hand.

'Needs must, Ellen. Miss Shepherd is one of the engineers of the scheme we are embarked upon.'

Miss Pardoner took a step backward, being perhaps unable to stifle her surprise completely.

'How are we betrayed, Miss Shepherd?' I asked.

'The Reverend Newberry. The *Grand Turk* is to be met at the dockside.'

Miss Pardoner's hand went to her throat in a gesture I had not expected of her once upon a time.

'We are but moments under way, there is time to think of something, surely?'

'We are to be met at the jetty in Memphis,' said Miss Shepherd.

'The Reverend has left his flock in Hannibal?'

'The silver hidden in the church is as nothing compared to what we have on board the *Enterprise*.'

I forbore to mention that the Reverend would expect the silver to be travelling with the Underground Railroad's passengers. The man of God struck me as one whose reaction to the thwarting of a scheme would be of the Old Testamentary kind.

'Then we have but little time. Where do we dock before Memphis?'

'Baton Rouge, Natchez, one or two places with Ferry in their name. What good will that do us?'

There being no answer that would have satisfied either of them, I gave none.

Winona Shepherd gave a cry. I looked closely at her appearance. She was not passing, and I wondered if she had smuggled herself onto the *Enterprise* in the company of another woman, as before. Ellen Pardoner flapped her hands at me in the manner of a madam at a penniless drunk and shouted, 'Out, man! Out! And bring some liquor and towels back with you!'

Winona Shepherd writhed on the bed, cursing our former confederate the Reverend Erastus Newberry, all his ancestors and any descendants he might one day have. I overheard Miss Pardoner ask what the girl had taken, but did not know what to make of her reply, to whit: 'Madame Restell's Miracle Pills'.

On my return, I was taken aback by the quantity of blood

on the sheets piled on the stateroom floor. Both women were racked with sobs. Miss Pardoner seized the bottle and bade me throw the bundled sheets over the side.

'Come back in an hour, or better still, spend the night elsewhere, Alasdair.'

I was half-way to the saloon bar before I realised she had called me by a name that had been mine for only twenty years, though I had lived more than double that number without it.

There being no danger of a matinee, I made for the relative conviviality of the riverboat's bar-cum-theatrical venue. Imagine my surprise to encounter the self-styled Shiloh Copland at post tending the glassware, spirits and beer. In truth he was a little short to provide the best of service, but since Cattermole and I were his only patrons, I found his efforts more entertainment than discommodity.

The Actor–Manager said nothing, drank steadily and peered at me from the corner of his eye from time to time. I wondered if he would summon up the blood to say whatever it was he had in mind.

At last, he motioned with his head toward the outside and I understood he wished to take a turn around the deck. The sky loured, grey and heavy, in tune with Cattermole's own demeanour.

'Are they aboard? Up ahead?'

He was quite unable to resist a thespian sweep of the arm upriver. The yelp of pain this occasioned him to make when he struck one of the few intact rails on the *Enterprise* rather ruined the effect.

'Who?' I enquired.

'The passengers. The saved.'

'There are some undeclared souls on board,' I admitted.

'And you would leave them to their fate at Hannibal?'

'It is out of my hands, Cattermole, besides what do you care about the fate of some escaping slaves?'

'Every man is the equal of another. You English may not believe it, but we Irish do.'

'I am as American as you are and furthermore, I know that I am the equal of any man.'

'I think you may be the former, sir, since we are all immigrants here, the red man excepted. As to the latter, perhaps I should have said that every race is the equal of another, though certain exemplars of any may do them little credit.'

Not for the first time, I noted the peculiar effect of the Irish navvy's diction and the Johnsonian vocabulary.

'I repeat, Cattermole, what is the fate of these poor wretches to you?'

The actor mustered a dignity I had thought beyond him and replied, 'I cannot recognize as *my* government one which is the *slave's* government also,' which phrase sounded so familiar that I could almost believe it might be an opinion shared by almost everyone employed on the riverboats, save the masters in charge of them.

'So, am I surrounded by shepherds?'

Cattermole laughed, 'Yes, Mr Northrup, and you are the shepherds' crook.'

On our return to the saloon bar, Cattermole and I matched each other drink for drink until I could see two of him and he could see nothing at all by dint of being supine on the saloon floor, as near dead as the drunk can be without actually surrendering the vital spark. I staggered onto the deck determined to make my way back to Miss Pardoner and her charge. Never had I seen so many stars, although this may have been due to the diplopia induced by the excess in which I had so recently indulged. It must have been an oversight, but Miss

Pardoner had locked the door and both ladies must surely have taken a sleeping draught, for there was no reaction to my fist's assault on the stateroom door. I slept on the threshold like a Viking's dog on his funeral boat.

25

When I awoke, I wished that someone *had* set fire to the *Enterprise*, for my sorry head had no place on the shoulders of a living man. I resumed my assault on the door. Its sudden opening caused me to fall inward in a less than graceful manner. At least it was pleasant to hear Miss Pardoner's laughter, though it had been at my expense. There seemed no prospect of cheer from the figure in the stateroom's bed. Winona Shepherd's face was un-powdered, yet still she was pale under her natural colour. She lay quite still and silent. I looked to Miss Pardoner; she shook her head.

'No, sir, she lives yet. Though she has not moved or spoken since...'

Perhaps there were worse things than crapulence after all.

Miss Pardoner beckoned me away from the bedside of the invalid.

'I have a plan.'

'And what is your plan?'

Even had I felt in the best of fettle she could not have uttered words more dreaded. I was hard put not to eject the contents of my stomach as the paddle steamer rocked a little, although Miss Pardoner seemed strangely unaffected.

'The Reverend's interest is in the silver, is it not?'

I did not observe that I found this quite understandable and merely nodded, though I wished I had not.

'He will expect you to travel with the most valuable cargo, therefore, we will transfer to the *Grand Turk* at the earliest opportunity,' she paused, and though I could not encourage her to continue, she did so nevertheless, 'He will expect me to keep an eye on you. Do you see?'

I saw that it would leave the silver unguarded on the *Enterprise* and that it would end in the slaves' recapture, since Newberry's attention would be on the *Turk*. To me it seemed the worst of all possible outcomes. Miss Pardoner went on.

'I believe that Newberry will come with suborned policemen or militia; they will have no interest in the slaves. Indeed, the Reverend may ensure that he is alone when searching certain parts of the vessel.'

'Gamble,' was my only utterance before I blundered out of the cabin and towards the taffrail, wherein I relieved myself of a great burden, leaving me only with the thunderous headache of the drunkard. I was yet draped over said rail, when Miss Pardoner came out of the cabin.

'We are next to dock in Natchez, you are to offer the master of the *Grand Turk* sufficient money to transfer such passengers as he may have to transfer to the *Enterprise*. Furthermore, you will ensure that the *Grand Turk* makes a grand dash for St Louis. We will announce that we are making an attempt at the river record from Natchez to St Lou. I am sure you will have no trouble in persuading Captain Grey where his interests lie.'

Her smile was most enraging, though my state of health did not permit me to inform her of it. Instead, I asked her what influence I could possibly have over Captain Grey.

'Really, sir! Do you honestly believe that Bilhah is not a part of our network of shepherds and conductors?'

Clearly it was to be a matter of bribery *and* blackmail. Well, I could not say that I was inexperienced in such matters. Instead, I broached the subject of Winona Shepherd.

'And the patient? Is she to be bundled from one vessel to another?'

'Miss Shepherd will do her duty. You, sir, will ascertain whether we will dock in Natchez before noon.'

Miss Pardoner stepped backward into the cabin, doubtless to minister to her patient's indisposition. I went forward, to the pilot house. Again, there was no pilot on duty. At the wheel was Captain Jubal Kincaid, his one eye fixed on the horizon. Despite this, he greeted me as 'Northrop' and spat his usual gout of tobacco juice toward the chamber pot, which was as malodorous as I remembered it.

'Good morning, Captain Kincaid. Are you well?'

'Better 'n some, no worse 'n others.' There was something simian in his utterance.

I had kept a Copperhead coin from the macabre find in the New Orleans Mint. I retrieved it from my pocket and placed it on the pedestal of the ship's wheel.

Kincaid looked down at the coin then removed a hand from one of the handles.

'Take the wheel, Northrop, steady as she goes.'

The riverman stepped away and I took his place, believing that steering the boat could not be so difficult if both Kincaid and Grey had sufficient intelligence to master it.

The Captain found a clay pipe from some not immediately obvious pocket in his strange attire and lit his smoke, after striking a lucifer on the stubble of his chin.

'Watcha want? Must 'a' come here fer sumthin'.'

I turned to look at him.

'Keep yer eyes on the river, might could be a sandbar up ahead.'

Indeed, an obstacle hove into view, if indeed heaving were what such things did. It was the wreckage of a small boat.

'Tole yuh. An eighth turn to starboard. Seven-an'-a-haff minutes clockwise, if'n yuh like that better.'

I asked him if we'd make Natchez by noon.

'Reckon so, long as I don' leave you at the wheel too long.'

There was a fit of cackles and coughs before he lapsed into a ruminative silence whilst he finished his pipe. I concentrated on piloting the boat around the remains of the fisherman's smack.

Kincaid took the wheel once more.

'Gonna be war, fer shure.'

'Is it? Is it really? Surely squabbles amongst yourselves will encourage the British once more.'

'Ain't complainin' if'n' they do. Johnny Frenchman kin help if he wants.'

I considered both interventions highly unlikely and told him so.

'King Cotton. The Britishers needs it and we got it.'

He had a point, but I had heard that grain from the Union was far more important to Britannia than Confederate cotton for its flags, though I did not tell him so. The Captain picked up the Copperhead coin and flicked it with his thumb toward my face. I caught it with my left hand.

'Card sharp needs reflexes, huh?'

'My party will be leaving the *Enterprise* in Natchez, Captain. We'll be boarding the *Grand Turk*. I have a different sort of enterprise in mind. Good day.'

'Suit yourself,' he said before depositing another gobbet in his bordello-purloined spittoon.

My pocket watch displayed a quarter of eleven and the blacksmiths forging a thousand swords in my head showed no inclination to desist. Therefore, I resolved to make for the saloon bar, there being no recourse but to try the ancient Pliny's remedy, viz. a hair of the dog. In all honesty I would have preferred to drink what was left of the drummer's samples in my carpetbag. Since the hideous portmanteau remained in what the *Enterprise* was pleased to name a stateroom, that is to say the sanatorium of Miss Winona Shepherd and her nurse, I could not do so.

The crouch-back was at his station and the saloon bar was bereft of custom save my own. I offered a silent prayer of thanks that Cattermole's condition had kept him to his bunk. Shiloh Copland, or Coble or whoever he was, paused in his shuffling of bottles of spirits on one of the lower shelves behind the bar-counter.

'A beer? Perhaps not. Something stronger, I'll warrant,' he lifted a bottle of murky spirits as like as to a Suffolk pond's water as to encourage me to ask if he had such a thing as a bottle of brandy. I was quite astounded when he produced from who knew where a bottle of quite acceptable Armagnac. Copland poured me a sufficiency for me to discern at least the half of Cardinal du Four's forty virtues in one glass.

Copland looked from side to side and over my shoulder. The bar was quite deserted save for his presence and mine own.

'Put the case – and I admit to nothing – that you and I *had* met before. That we both had other names to go by. Do you find it strange? What age am I? What age are you?'

His diction was pure, and he did not sound drunk.

'What do I care how many years your footprints have marked the earth?'

'You do not, naturally enough. Miss Pardoner, for it is she, what age might she be now?'

'Why, on a good day she might pass for thirty. What of it?'

Copland smiled and refilled my glass before pouring one for himself.

'She is of the family Jedermann, remember.'

I took another fierce swallow. Truly it was a crime to treat such a fine cognac so.

'There are several families like theirs. Mine is one such. So, I ask you again. How old am I?'

The man's face was no more wrinkled than it had been in London more than a dozen years ago. It meant nothing; some were wizened by life before they reached thirty. If I had been inclined to answer him I might have said that he was past sixty, although sprightly for it. I gave a shrug and drank again.

He nodded. 'I see. Would you like me to describe the storming of the Bastille? We played catch with De Launay's head before we put it on the pike. Or would you like me to tell you of the time I met Nicolas Flamel the day after he erected his own tombstone?'

I shook my head at the man's haverings and gestured for another measure of spirits.

'Again, I put the case, that had you and I met before, I should be most surprised that you looked no older than you did on that putative first encounter.' He gestured at the glass before me. 'After all, you are no abstainer from strong drink, and, I'll warrant, life has not been easy for you here in the United States.'

In the latter, he was quite correct. However, who is so vain that they spend their days before the mirror, counting the signs of their mortality? Besides, I had no clue as to what he was trying to convey. I resolved to remain only as long as the Armagnac lasted.

Copland placed his glass carefully on the bar.

'You see, Mr Moffat, there are families like the Jedermanns and like mine... and there is you. We follow you, with good reason. Where do you come from? Did those foolish experiments really do something? Did Enoch make someone like ourselves by accident!'

His voice had risen in volume to great degree and he was near foaming at the mouth.

'I doubt very much that I am anything like you, sir,' I said, and left the bar.

Winona Shepherd, in some different clothes and a coating of face powder, was upright and steady on her feet, although Miss Pardoner held her by the elbow. She handed me my carpetbag and we headed toward the gangplank amidships as the *Enterprise* headed toward the jetty, whilst the *Turk* was already tied up at the mole further along the riverbank. We walked along the river to board the *Grand Turk*. At the foot of the gangplank was a familiar figure with a notebook and pen in hand and a copy of a Memphis newspaper in his pocket.

'Ha! I knowed you was a man of prospects, sir. Are yuh fer makin' a river run! Do you have a sportin' sum involved with someone 'r other? I need it fer the local press, they love a gamblin' story.'

'What if I have? I thought you had gone to Nevada. With your brother.'

'Reckon Orion will have calmed down b'now. I'll catch him before he reaches Nevada, for sure.'

Despite myself, I enquired, 'Calmed down?'

Clemens looked down at the ground. 'Shot his hat off just

outside St Louis, when I was showing a Miss Eugenia Calabash, of Tunica, Mississippi, my Smith & Wesson.'

'How unfortunate!' I said.

'Aw, it's nuthin'. Orion gets his temper pretty soon after the bandages come off, in general.'

Perhaps my sigh persuaded him to return to the point.

'So, are yuh makin' a sportin' venture, or no, Mistuh M–Northrup?

I answered somewhat curtly in the affirmative and brushed past the man whilst escorting the by now impatient ladies onto the vessel. The man gave a low whistle and stage-whispered, 'Two damned fine women, that's jest greedy, Mister.'

Quite how Mr Clemens had heard about the river record attempt, I did not know. Be that as it might, there was no doubt that Newberry would think twice about any assault on the *Turk*, thanks to any publicity which the reporter pro tem might provide. Whichever representatives of the local law Newberry brought with him would doubtless be more circumspect also. I was most nervous about the silver being in the hands of Compair Lapin, but what could I do?

Miss Pardoner saw to it that we had accommodation suitable for the remainder of the trip upriver. It was time to remake the acquaintance of the master of the *Grand Turk*. We left Miss Shepherd to her own devices. It was quite dispiriting to see such a characterful woman brought so low. Miss Pardoner and I made our way forward to the pilot house of the boat. I felt a breeze in my face and, I admit it, a certain pleasure in the company of Miss Pardoner. I had bidden her farewell by the burning wreck of Gibbous House in North Northumberland. Little had I thought to be involved in yet another arcane scheme so many years later.

Pilot Ireland was at the wheel. Captain Grey was nowhere to be seen. I cleared my throat; the Pilot turned his head in the most miniscule amount necessary to acknowledge our presence.

'Howd' ye do?'

'Capital, capital, is the Captain indisposed?'

'He's in thuh cabin, cain't speak to t'other.'

'Might we disturb him, d'you think?'

'I reckon you might at that, if'n ye've a mind to go lookin' for him there.'

He turned his head fully toward us for the duration of a singularly lascivious wink.

Miss Pardoner and I made for the Captain's bunk. A hearty application of my fist to the door occasioned grunts and epithets in equal measure, before the door was unlocked and opened by the beauteous Bilhah.

'It's the card sharp. Going by Northrup, Cap'n.' She called this over her shoulder whilst keeping the door no more than slightly ajar.

Miss Pardoner's hand was thrust past me into this gap and it was grasped in the collegiate style of a banker by the Captain's personal servant.

'You must be Bilhah, I am Eileen, sometimes Ellen, always a shepherd.'

This glib sign was met with what I presumed was its countersign.

'We care for the flock, not the fleece.'

Nevertheless, it was sufficient to gain us both admission to Captain Grey's inner sanctum.

The master of the *Grand Turk* was abed, bed linen drawn up to his chin and a mob-cap adorning his head. I preferred not to speculate as to his attire beneath the patchwork counterpane. I fully expected Miss Pardoner to take the initiative in broaching the matter of the Natchez–St Louis River Passage Record and our prospective attempt at breaking it – at least until the sharp application of her elbow to my ribs.

'Ah… Captain Grey. You may have heard. I wish for the *Grand Turk* to make an attempt on the speed record from Natchez to St Louis.'

The man groaned, a sound of deep despair.

'Ain't no such record.'

'Then we will set one. I imagine there will be opportunities for side-betting.'

Grey let out another moan.

'We require that such passengers as are willing to transfer to the *Enterprise* do so. Those who do stay must contribute to the prize money as they will be hazarding the loss of my own.'

This elicited a further groan still, which might well have emerged from a place still more dire than the previous sloughs of despond. Bilhah responded on her master's behalf.

'That'll be fine, Mister. Most are gettin' awf. They figure to wait for the next but one boat along. Guess we can all understand that.'

Which utterance I took to mean that my opinion of the *Enterprise* was shared the length of the Mississippi river. I enquired as to whether the Captain's indisposition would interfere with an attempt on the river run. This elicited a snort from Bilhah.

'If'n y'all think anyone but the Pilot is master of this boat, y'all're a bigger fool than yuh look. Though ah cain't hardly credit that mahself.'

She stared at Miss Pardoner for a moment and then busied herself with preparing the Captain's toilette. I offered an arm to Miss Pardoner. She gave a tut and pushed me toward the stateroom door. She was most derisive when I asked why the Pilot had sent me to see the Captain, if he was in charge all along.

'He might be in charge of the boat, sir, but Bilhah is in charge of this particular stretch of the railroad.'

We stood beside the railing, watching the passengers troop off. Of course, they passed the *Enterprise* by, who would not have done so? But I did espy one figure boarding the tub. I pointed the (until recently) disappeared Ishmael out to Miss P, but perhaps she was a little blinded by the sun, for she claimed to be unable to see anyone. However, the sun was almost directly overhead, and we, from the deck of the *Turk*, were looking down on both the jetty and Kincaid's *Enterprise*.

A bare quarter hour later I found myself alone with Winona Shepherd in the cabin. Miss Pardoner had intimated that she had a secondary mission on the *Turk* and that I would be such a hindrance as could only distract her from the task. Since she was adamant in her refusal to enlighten me as to what task that might be, I presumed it could only be something to my own detriment. Miss Shepherd looked a little better. I felt the powder and pallor combined had showed her fine features at some disadvantage and was pleased to see her *au naturel*. I enquired after her well-being.

'I am as well as can be expected, Mr Imposter.'

'Who of us is who we seem, Miss Shepherd?'

She did not reply.

'You trust that woman, the one you keep calling Miz Pardoner?'

'Trust? We have, and have had in the past, interests in common.'

'She does not trust you, sir.'

'I've never been a man to be trusted.'

'You will not flirt with me, Northrup – or whoever you are.'

She neither held up a hand, nor turned away, nor indeed did she do anything but remain seated on the chair by the cot, but it was clear to me that there would be no trifling with this woman. I could not believe that she had found herself in her earlier predicament save by her own choice.

'Miss Pardoner's distrust, does it pertain to some particular aspect of our scheme?'

She laughed, 'Our scheme? You hope to make off with some, if not all, of the silver by some subterfuge. That forms no part of any scheme of mine or indeed Miss Pardoner's, come to that.'

A knife appeared in Miss Shepherd's hand; it was no dainty thing.

'Take care, sir. If you betray my people, I will gut you and watch you die.'

I had been on the point of asking her to accompany me to the saloon bar for a convivial drink or two, but thought better of it and went on deck.

By four in the afternoon, Captain Grey, Ellen Pardoner, a newly powdered Winona Shepherd and I stood at the taffrail. Bilhah, as was her wont, stood a few scant feet away from the Captain in the lee of the *Grand Turk*'s Texas. A body of around a dozen men were attempting to march, and play battered instruments, along the quayside. Dressed in cast-off military clothing, which belied the name uniform in every respect, this rag-tag and bob-tail militia's marching band was searching for the lost chord amongst a thousand discords. Their rendition of a tune that had lately become ever more popular was even less tuneful than the whistled versions of 'Dixie' heard in every bar and saloon.

Thankfully the sound became more bearable as the distance from its source increased.

Captain Grey was waving his peaked cap high in the air. Miss Pardoner indicated that I should make some similar acknowledgement of what was, in truth, a rather small crowd considering we were about to race the river.

The Pilot had visited the saloon earlier and had a couple of stiff ones. I asked him if he thought we could actually set an unbeatable record.

'Oh, shore… If'n we had a better boat.'

I'd replied that the *Turk* wasn't so bad. And indeed it was a much better vessel than the *Enterprise*. The Pilot was unmoved.

'On the N'worleans tuh Cairo run, the *J.M.White* had no cargo, they stripped her down. Hardly a bit of superstructure left 'cept the pilot house and the funnel. But one stop on the way upriver. And they weighed anchor at dawn. They hit fog onc't, but durin' the day. That record is near as dammit seventeen years old. Someone'll break it one day, but we won't. Course they did the whole run, we're startin' frum heah. Might could be a record, but only 'cause ain't nobody else tried. Mebbe we might take a crack at the fastest mean speed on the river. Cain't see but whut the sport is mahself.'

Which lengthy speech was the longest I ever heard pass his lips. He put his whiskey glass down and went forward to his post.

I saw Bilhah's eyes dart toward the bow-end of the *Turk*. She was acknowledged by Miss Shepherd. I thought to follow but Miss Pardoner, ever the breaker of convention, placed the flat of her gloved hand on my chest. I watched the Captain, his servant and Winona Shepherd head off, presumably to the Captain's cabin.

'We might as well go forward too. I want to see just how fast the *Turk* can go.'

There was a familiar gleam in her eye, and that was sufficient reason for me to comply with her suggestion.

The discovery that Miss Pardoner merely intended to watch some of our progress from the very prow of the *Grand Turk* was most disappointing. She leaned out over the rail. I imagined she was safe enough. Save the striking of a submerged sandbar, I doubted the Mississippi held many dangers for the riverboat. In spite of this a bellow came from the pilot house:

'Git that dang fool woman outta the way!'

I wondered whether the Pilot would have phrased this request in quite that fashion had he encountered Ellen Pardoner beforehand. She had clearly heard the shout, and I moved to intercept her on her way to upbraid the river pilot. I attempted to grasp her elbow, but she shook me off.

'We should perhaps defer to the man's greater experience of the river, Ellen.'

She gave me a sharp look, 'What harm Moffat? What harm to observe the boat's battle with the Great River?'

'It must be dangerous, Ellen, else why...'

I was not permitted to finish.

'Dangerous? And should it not be so? What do you remember of me and mine? Nothing?'

Frankly, there was much I wished to forget in my dealings with the Family Jedermann, which reply I thought better of giving.

'How old am I, Moffat?'

It had ever been my experience that answering such a question was quite as risky as perching at the prow of any vessel, even were it an ocean-going ship. I made some mental calculation and realising that she must have seen at least forty summers said, 'Thirty-five?'

I was most diverted at the conflict so easily shown on her face. However, I may have been mistaken as to the cause of it for she merely said, 'Oh Moffat, you are such a purblind fool.'

Rather than give any pithy retort, I remarked that perhaps the best place from which to observe what a river race might involve was surely the pilot house. I was in no way influenced by the fact that it was a place in which it was remarkably easy to come by food, even if it were only the Captain's beloved chops.

26

Pilot Ireland was at the wheel. Captain Grey was nowhere to be seen. I asked the Pilot if he thought we would even be close to the record. His expectoration was loud and emphatic. His answer was less so:

'Tole yuh afore. Others had lotsa 'vantages over the *Turk*. Might could get close if it weren't for the fog.'

Miss Pardoner and I looked through the pilot house's glazing. The sky was blue and the sun was a lemon-coloured disc. Fog looked as probable as a politician telling the truth. To save Miss Pardoner doing so, I asked, 'What fog?'

'Be here in a haff-hour, you betcha.'

'How do you know?' Miss Pardoner enquired.

'The river has its own mind.'

''Tis June, man!' I could not help myself.

The veteran of the river placed another chaw of tobacco in his mouth and answered, 'Ayuh, it is.'

He looked at Miss Pardoner. 'Seems ah spoilt yer fun up ahead. Like to take the wheel?'

She grasped the wheel fiercely for a moment or two, then relaxed.

'That's it, Ma'am. People say treat a boat like a woman,

Miss. But them as do don't know what in tarnation they's talkin' bout. You gotta treat a boat like a child. An ignorant one at that. Won't do nothin' less'n you tell it. Treat it mean an'… well, let's jest say that only works for a while, so treat it gentle but firm.'

And she handled the *Grand Turk* as to the manner born. We negotiated a rotting hulk and a slow ferry, crossing our bow with no great difficulty. Ireland rang the bell to ask for less steam as we approached the tiny flat-bottomed vessel, but it was Miss Pardoner who noted that it should be done.

I felt as useful as a pessary in a convent, and as out of place. The Americas were as strange a place to me as when I had first washed up upon their shores. What good to pretend to higher status, when it seemed to matter not a jot to society at large? I could as easily have begun my colonial life under that long forgotten Scottish boy's name, as kept Moffat or stolen Northrup. No, it was only the unlucky likes of Winona Shepherd for whom an assumed identity brought benefit in America.

Miss Pardoner asked the Pilot how fast the vessel might go. The Pilot's eyes narrowed, whether because he had not expected the question or because he was pondering his answer to it, I could not say. He let out an exhalation of tobacco breath.

'Well ma'am, we might reach a mean speed of eleven knots for the stretch of the river we mean to race.'

'And is that enough?'

'It'd mean we'd make about the same average time as the *J.M. White.*'

'And what does that mean?'

'It means we'd have broken the record seventeen years ago, but not this year.'

'Who holds the record now?' I interjected.

'The same owner and vessel as will hold it by the time we finish our danged fool's attempt, Mister.'

'You mean we've no chance at all?'

'Nope, and fer whatever reason yer makin' the attempt, which by the way, I cain't see what that is, it cain't be done on this here boat. And I don't want to know, neither.'

'Then we shall not tell you, Pilot. Is there nothing we can do, to win this gentleman's wager?' Miss Pardoner kept her eyes on the river – though it looked calm enough. I could see the slightest movement at the corner of her mouth.

'Could throw any baggage y'all have overboard. Doubt the crew have much with 'em. Danged if I have. Buy a whole new outfit eftuh ah'm paid off, as a rule.'

I opened my mouth to speak, but the helmswoman advised me not to make any jest concerning her own conversion into jetsam. I was about to ask more about the holder of the record, when the fog fell. I had passed not a few years in London as a younger man and in the circles in which I moved this kind of fog was named a London Particular, after a Madeira wine popular at the time, though I knew not why. Only the yellowish hue that gave the metropolitan brume its alternative soubriquet was absent. The mist on the Mississippi was every bit as dense as cotton wool.

The Pilot had shouldered Ellen aside and gave me a glare as I moved to upbraid him for the assault. Ellen slapped at my arm and told me not to be more a fool than she already knew me to be. We none of us could see further ahead than the prow of the vessel. One of the crew ran past the pilot house toward the rail, adopting a position far more precarious than that which my companion had earlier taken up. The Texas Tender, or Tom, was bent over the rail like a jack-knife, peering downward and forward by turns, holding on by one hand or the other as he made signals to steer to port or starboard as necessary. The Pilot stared past him into the fog. Miss Pardoner's eyes gleamed. Two further crew members had lit oil lamps and stood, according to the colour of their glass, port and starboard of the pilot house. Finally, one more deck hand stood behind Tom, his own hurricane lamp aloft although its light was neither reflected nor refracted, merely absorbed. At one moment Tom made a circling motion with his right hand. The Pilot pulled on a lever and chain affair and the blast of the *Grand Turk*'s horn nigh made my ears bleed. At the self-same moment, the man holding the forward lantern began opening and closing a shutter, so that the light flashed at rapid intervals. The Pilot bellowed at him to slow the signal. Even such a lubber as I knew this meant we would be passing a vessel to starboard, rather than port as was the norm. Easily enough done on a clear day, but a rather more ticklish affair in 'the danged fog', as the Pilot himself put it.

I could make out a single light to our left. The dim outline moved slowly, as we were doing. I formed the impression of a vessel of cleaner, simpler lines: smaller, perhaps a cargo boat bound for any of the towns further downriver. There was a slight bump toward the stern on the starboard side, followed by a scream. Poor Tom had lost his balance.

'Belay that, sir' the Pilot said. My arms were out of my coat and I was halfway out of the pilot house.

He must have seen the colour rise in my face, for he went on.

'Tom is gone. He'll have gone under the keel, if he's lucky.'

He did not have to say that the alternative was the paddle to port or starboard.

'But can he swim?' Miss Pardoner's mouth was a tight line.

''Tain't more of a handful of rivermen who can, Ma'am.

It's considered unlucky to know how, just like on a whaler or a battleship.'

I did not say that I found it damned foolish not to. And still the Captain remained in his cabin.

'Poor Tom,' said Miss Pardoner.

The Pilot removed his cap and the fog lifted, as suddenly as it had come.

The sunlight glinted on the river; the sky was as blue as smalt. The dense brume seemed no more than a memory from another day. It was a sky that should have been adorned with swallows. The only birds visible were corvidae of various kinds, known to follow the riverboats in the hope of juicy offal and waste thrown overboard from the galley. Even the ever-dynamic Miss Pardoner seemed held still by the strange equili-brant rhythm of the river. I repaired to the saloon bar, unable to bear the monotony as others clearly could.

The peace of solitude was not to be found. A roundhouse bare-knuckle fight was in progress. Most of the onlookers were at the stage of drunkenness where not even their mother's funeral would occasion their speaking below the level of a bel-low. I was surprised to see that a round dozen males and a com-parable number of ladies had remained on board the *Turk*. The ring was marked out with sand on the deal boards of the deck. It was more or less square, and, given the cramped confines of the saloon bar, served well enough. There were two bloodied figures coming up to the mark and the sluggish movement of their limbs indicated that the prize-fight had begun more than several minutes ago. One of the men in the ring was Com-pair Lapin, whom I had last seen when I departed from the *Enterprise*. The other I did not recognise, but he was a large, blond figure with the crazed aspect of a lunatic or a Bowery drunk. Lapin had several cuts to his handsome brow and his knuckles already looked swollen. Furthermore, his eyes were just beginning to swell shut and his breathing would forever be easier through his mouth from that day. As for his opponent, he was missing teeth but only a pair of them were recent of departure. The sporting onlookers bellowed encouragement and increased their wagers at similar volume. Who should be the sport busy in the acceptance of said wagers, but Shiloh Copland?

I had neither seen him leave the *Enterprise*, nor board the *Turk*, but then why should I have done so? From what I could see, the bout was going the Nordic fellow's way.

'Fifty dollars, Copland. What odds on the black?'

'As it's you, I'll give you plus 200, Mr...'

'Two to one? You are a robber, sir! You'll give me four to one and like it!'

A gout of blood flew from Lapin's left eyebrow.

Copland nodded and wrote my name down in his pocket book; I wondered which name it was.

Lapin's foe appeared to have two seconds: short, swarthy types. One carried a grimy towel and the other was armed with a pail and a still grimier rag. As for Compair Lapin, there were none to second him. A similar pail, doubtless with a similar rag in bloodied water, stood unattended beside a crumpled towel on the opposite side of the ring.

I went to stand alongside Lapin's bucket. My voice was barely strong enough to shout over the hubbub.

'Copland, Copland! Is it Broughton's rules?'

Copland nodded, vigorously.

I shouted again, 'Lapin!'

He looked toward me and took a fierce blow to the chin.

'Take a knee, man! Take a knee!'

The watch I had acquired from the late Reverend

Parminter was blessed with a four-wheel movement and had the benefit of a seconds-hand, I held it aloft, brandishing it at the crowd, such as it was.

'Thirty seconds, my man has thirty seconds.'

I had hold of the pail and the towel over my arm. I hoped it would not stain my coat too badly. I bent down and – with the rag covering my hand – I grasped the bridge of Lapin's nose and gave it a fearsome tweak. The tears started from his eyes and I said to him, 'Dance, Lapin, dance with him. Do not leave him lay a hand on you. He will tire and then you must strike.'

It was not sure if any of this counsel had penetrated. The seconds had ticked away and I withdrew. Lapin stood and walked to the mark. A momentary hush fell on the sporting assembly... and Lapin felled the man. With one blow. The huge brute lay senseless on the deal planks. The crowd were considerably more animated. Clearly the vanquished had been the favourite. Lapin, Copland and I ran out of the bar and made for my cabin.

Having locked the door behind us, I turned to see Miss Winona Shepherd languishing on the bed. At least until she espied Lapin. Needless to say, at the same time as she began examining his injuries, she began to berate me as though I had been more than a concerned observer in the matter of his injuries. I felt I had almost disabused her of this belief when, of course, Copland mentioned my winnings. Lapin was in no position to enlighten her as to the matter, as he had fallen insensible on the tiny bed, staining the bedspread quite irremediably.

I grasped Copland by his scrawny throat and induced him to hand over my winnings. Once I had placed sundry silver dollars and other scrip about my person, I asked him about the bout.

'Lapin came to me, earlier today. Imagine my surprise when he proposed a prize fight. He even had an opponent in mind.'

'How did he get on board? Last I saw he was on the *Enterprise*.'

'There are plenty of lighters and smaller boats on the river and plenty on board who would have thrown him a line to clamber aboard.'

'So simple?' I feinted to grasp his throat.

'Well, yes, of course. So many things are much simpler than they look.'

Which piffling finally did encourage me to shake him by the neck until the eyes turned up in his head. Miss Shepherd shrank from me and attempted to cover Lapin's dormant form at one and the same time.

'He will be fine, woman! He is far too amusing to throttle to death. His prattle becomes annoying from time to time, that's all.'

Lapin appeared still insensible. I replied that I did not know to Miss Shepherd's inquiry as to just how many blows he had taken to the head. On my asking what Mr Lapin was to her I received a most disconcerting answer:

'He is my brother.'

This I found hard to believe and it must have shown in my face, for Winona Shepherd rolled her eyes and tutted.

'Persons of colour are no more of one hue than they are of one character no matter how your kind care to paint us, sir. My brother cannot pass, as I can, and though a free man of colour he risks more for the Railroad than many a white fellow traveller.

I shook Lapin's prize-money from Copland and threw it on the cot. Then I sent the latter on his way.

'Why did he fight? To what end?' I asked.

'Because he wanted to.'

It was no answer at all. All the sporting crowd were as white as Lapin's opponent. Our escape had had to be made at the moment we made it. There would have been more blood spilled else and I had had no intention that any of it should be mine. Still, it was a strange thing for this cultured man to agree to, and I respected him the more for it. However, I could not let the matter lie. I have been but rarely curious for curiosity's sake, but events in my past had proven beyond doubt that – *pace* the untimely death of any felines – a lack of curiosity might be quite as fatal as a surfeit thereof. My inquiry into how far Copland's responsibility for the bout's organisation extended was greeted with a curt reply of, 'It doesn't take a Philadelphia lawyer to see *that* man might be behind all manner a'things, Mister.'

I did wonder if the lady knew how true that might be and resolved to take the matter up with Copland, when next I saw him. At that moment, Compair Lapin sat bolt upright and asked if he had won. I emptied my pockets of his share of the purse onto the cot.

'I think we both did.'

'Thanks for the advice,' he said, and I knew that the terrible blows he had received to his head had not damaged his intellect, nor his taste for mockery.

Out on deck, the river was serene save for the dull throb of the *Grand Turk*'s engines. Was it fancy, or was the *Turk* making faster progress, despite the Pilot's pessimism? Miss Pardoner smiled and though my fervent hope was that it was directed at me, I suspected that it was not. My remark that she had concluded her other business quite rapidly was only sufficient to make her smile as wide as the river.

Her next words chilled me to the marrow, not for the first time.

'I have a plan.'

27

Of course, Miss Pardoner and I had endeavoured to achieve common goals in the past and, on balance, I believed that she had been more ally than enemy, if one judged by the final outcome of events rather than the events themselves. I had been drugged, electrified and made the butt of the most insane scheme engendered by the Jedermann family's desire to keep their own secrets from the gaze of others. Nevertheless, I felt a bond with Ellen Pardoner that a dozen years and an ocean between us had failed to unravel.

'Is our situation not complicated enough?' I failed to contain a sharp tone.

'What is complicated? We shall not stop at Memphis. The Reverend Newberry will assume that the silver travels with us.' Miss P's rejoinder was equally pointed.

'And who is travelling with the silver?'

'Lapin, of course.'

'Lapin is in our stateroom having recently felled some brute of a fellow in a prize fight in the saloon bar.'

She had the grace to assume an expression conveying a modicum of perplexity: to whit, a charming line bisecting her brow. I found it all the more so since I had but rarely placed that formidable woman in such a non-plus.

'Why? Why did he do that?'

I replied that I had put that question to his sister, and deduced from Miss Pardoner's lack of surprise that the familial connection between Lapin and Miss Shepherd had been just one more secret kept from me. She gave me an old-fashioned look and stung me to reply, 'I don't know. Maybe he is so tired of waiting to strike a metaphorical blow he thought he might land a few physical ones.'

That at least made her laugh and my joy in that fact was palpable. I put the question that I was sure she had formulated herself, if but silently.

'Can we trust George Washington Irving?'

'We must,' was her only reply.

We walked to the stern of the *Grand Turk* and looked down the river. Already the *Enterprise* was out of sight, and it had been so since before the fog had descended.

'What will Newberry do?' I asked.

'We had better ask Miss Shepherd.' There was a familiar tightening of Ellen's lips and I realised that her relationship with Winona Shepherd was at best a convenient alliance, rather than a meeting of minds.

On our return to the cramped stateroom, we were unable to make inquisition of Miss Shepherd. Both Lapin and his sister had gone, as had his prize-money. A solitary coin lay on the cot and my carpetbag had been taken too. I picked up the coin, it was a Copperhead penny. I noted that surely this must be another of Lapin's little jokes, as we had been agreed that John Mudsill and the real Northrup had been one and the same person since our visit to the New Orleans Mint and our grisly discoveries therein.

'Is it though?' she breathed a heavy sigh. 'I find you may be right, Alasdair, the situation is complicated, as it ever is when you are involved, I fear.'

Which sentiment I felt in equal degree, although, for my part, it was she who complicated matters.

One would think it easy to find such a pair as Lapin and Miss Shepherd within the confines of a riverboat even of such moderately large size as the *Grand Turk*. The public facilities such as the restaurant and the saloon bar were simple enough to search, especially at that time in the evening. It was not yet the hour to dine and as for the bar, there were but a few grizzled faces of either sex. Of course, it was unlikely that Lapin would have been seen in the restaurant in any other capacity other than dishwasher or waiter. As for the bar, since his last appearance there had ended in our flight therefrom, I surmised that Lapin would be in no hurry to return. I was on the point of ordering a whiskey, when Miss Pardoner suggested that we might prevail upon the Captain via the agency of Bilhah to allow us a search of the *Turk*'s passenger accommodation. Thirst unquenched, we sought the Captain out in his cabin, where Bilhah welcomed me somewhat less effusively than she did Miss Pardoner. The latter wasted no time.

'Shepherd, Lapin. Are they so trusted by the Railroad?'

She bit off every word as though it were some of the beef jerky the younger Mr Clemens had offered me during our stagecoach ride. For the first time I realised the extent of her antipathy towards Miss Shepherd.

'Miz Shepherd is known for her devotion to the cause. She vouched for Compair Lapin, as has Mrs Tremayne in the past,' Bilhah spoke slowly, as if to a child.

Miss Pardoner stamped her foot; I scarcely escaped the

consequences and stumbled a little as I moved my own out of its way.

'Show her, M–, Northrup.'

Bilhah looked from Ellen to me and gave a slow nod. I gathered Miss Pardoner wanted me to show the woman the coin we had found on the bed.

'They are hiding on the boat somewhere. This's what they left behind.'

I was holding the tiny copper coin at arm's length, between the index finger and thumb of my left hand. Bilhah let out a word I had last heard from the sailors arguing over whorehouses and mothers-in-law on the night I first encountered the name Northrup.

'Quite,' Miss Pardoner said, and pulling off her gloves with her teeth.

'We have been too trusting. Compair Lapin is one name of The Trickster, after all.'

'What does that mean?' Miss Pardoner was quicker than I to enquire.

'Compair Lapin's jest a character in stories. They're African stories, we tell'em for entertainment, for hope, for the hopeless. The Trickster gets the better of the hyena and the fox jes' like we dream of doin' to the White Man. For a man to go by that name and betray his own is to be lower than a damn snake.'

'Perhaps it is a message rather than merely a provocation?'

The two women turned to look at me as though I had spoken in Hottentot or perhaps the Caddo of John Tecumseh. Bilhah merely lifted her apron and handed Ellen a large ring of keys that hung from a chatelaine that glittered like gold.

'Find them,' she hissed. 'I will have an explanation, an' retribution to follow.'

Most staterooms, cabins and bunks were empty, as was expected when so many had disembarked in Natchez. I suggested a search of the secret compartments where the Underground Railroad passengers were hiding. Miss Pardoner shook her head with vigour.

'They will not take refuge there.' I proposed to check on my own initiative later, if necessary. Finally, we came upon the third class longroom, this was little better than the crewmen's quarters in the *Enterprise*, so I did fervently hope that we encountered the fugitives there and could abandon the search before we had to enter crew's quarters on the *Turk*. We did not find Compair Lapin, though we found the relict of Winona Shepherd. She lay in a pool of her own blood, which had seeped from beneath her skirts and was slowly drying on the deal boards of the deck.

I knelt beside the woman, lifted her head, but could feel no evidence of having been struck a fatal blow.

'You are looking in quite the wrong place for the cause of Miss Shepherd's death, Alasdair.'

Miss Pardoner's eyes were shining and I sensed the incipience of tears equally as likely to be of rage as sorrow.

'The miracle pills? This is no murder then?'

'It is society that has murdered this woman, that all would shun for having a child out of wedlock.'

'Could she not have borne the child?'

'And risk the arrival of one of darker hue than her own?'

'I had thought the father might be…'

'It does not seem to matter who fathers a child. Still less who inflicts the state of gravity on someone who passes, it is a cruel God who punishes the most vulnerable, is it not?'

I thought of the popinjay politician in whose company I had seen Miss Shepherd in the grounds of the Louisiana Capitol and reflected that whatever the right of Lapin's behaviour might be, his sister had sacrificed more than enough for the Underground Railroad. We wrapped the young woman in the bedlinen and a poor shroud it made her. Neither of us made to say any words over the corpse. We would leave that to the Captain, and I hoped Miss Shepherd's corpse would not suffer the indignity of being thrown over the side. Miss Pardoner's gaze was fixed at some distance beyond the walls of the third class accommodation. I had never seen her so still.

'Ellen, we must keep looking for Lapin, if only to eliminate the possibility of his continued presence on board.'

Her gaze turned on me.

'We sometimes call ourselves Hyperboreans, make jest that we come from the back of the North Wind, although, of course, we do not. Antimachus of Colophon believed that Hyperboreans were Celts, Moffat. Did you know that?'

'Lapin—'

'Gone. You will tell me your age, Moffat. I no longer care as my family still do who you might be, but you will tell me how old you are.'

It may seem strange but truly I did not consider the matter often. I should have known my answer to the effect that I was 'in the prime of life' would prove unacceptable.

'How many summers have you seen?'

'Why, fifty-six.'

'I am older than you, Moffat, though by our looks you are no more than five years my senior. What do you think of that?'

She smoothed down her skirts and said, 'Come, "Mr Northrup", we must advise Bilhah of Winona Shepherd's demise.'

To my surprise, Captain Holden Grey was absent from his stateroom. Bilhah admitted us both amid plumes of cigar-smoke. I somehow doubted his absence or presence would have influenced her in the matter of her partaking of a smoke to any degree at all. I declined the offer of a puro of my own, which Miss Pardoner did not.

'Lapin has left the *Grand Turk*. Winona Shepherd is dead.' Miss Pardoner exhaled a plume of smoke and watched its ascent toward the darkened planks of the cabin's ceiling.

Bilhah sighed, 'Gone to the Lord.' Her face darkened, 'Are these news connected? Surely not?'

'They are not. Miss Shepherd bled to her death and not from any wound.'

Bilhah looked askance. Ellen Pardoner raised an eyebrow and shrugged.

I could not let this pass and said to Bilhah, that I believed Miss Shepherd's delicate condition was attained in pursuit of the Railroad's goals. As, indeed, it might have been, among the State Capitol's garden groves in Baton Rouge. Miss Pardoner gave a tut.

'Lucky are they who may still attain such a state.'

Exactly what she meant by that I could not say.

Bilhah came to practicalities, 'We will surely reach Cairo in under two days, it's a matter of findin' somewhere cool is all.'

'I suspect there is no ice-house on this vessel, Miss.'

'Call me Bilhah, Mister Whoever-You-Are. T'aint more 'n a slave name anyhow.'

'I shall call you by whatever name you prefer.' Which effort at gallantry was roundly ignored.

'No, sir, there's no ice-house, but there's a space below the water-line in the stern, we got no Underground Railroad passengers in it. It's only for desperate cases, ain't been used but once and that for an eight-year-old girl who died on her way upriver. Folks don't like it. I guess Winona might be good company for the ghost of that other dead girl.'

Bilhah made for the bell-board above the Captain's bed, but I told her I would carry Miss Shepherd to her temporary place of rest, if I were but shown the way.

Bilhah sounded the bell marked 'Deck-Hands'.

I was escorted aft by a young man of an age with the late Tom Jefferson. A singular young man not least because he exhibited no trace of servility in his demeanour.

'Northrup, huh? Thawt you wuz a fairy tale. Sumpin' to keep people hopin'. Jes' a man after all.'

We were walking towards the long bunkroom, and I asked him his name. He stopped, made sure I was looking him in the eye, and said, 'Lapin.'

'Oh really? Is it so very common a name, then?'

'Reckon a man might call himself anythin', if'n he'd a mind to.'

Since I knew the truth of that, I agreed with him.

'The Underground Railroad is a good thing, ain't no doubt. But some people thinks we should be more active, do somethin'. We go by Lapin. They ain't many of us, but there'll be more, one day. Maybe we're like Northrups only...'

'Only black?'

We had reached the corpse; I put Miss Shepherd over my shoulder. The deck hand gave a nod as if he'd confirmed some suspicion that he had had concerning me. We continued aft to a small square hatch. I had almost tripped over it when the *Grand Turk* had got underway, what seemed like days ago, although it had been a matter of hours. I laid the poor girl on the deck whilst the deck hand removed the hatch. There was a short ladder to a space with barely enough room for one person, much less two.

'I'll go down, you hand her down to me.'

He nodded. I crouched in the tiny box-shaped space.

'You a trustin' type?'

He slid the corpse down towards me. I was forced to embrace the late Miss Shepherd and all went black when the hatch was slid into place. The noise of the bar sliding across it was as dispiriting as the prospect of sharing such a confined space with a cadaver, however appealing she had been in life.

28

More as a matter of form than in the hope of achieving a prompt release, I ascended a few rungs of the ladder and smote the underside of the hatch-cover repeatedly. My knuckles smarting, I peered around the dark and damp space. There was some sacking in one corner and I placed it over my fellow, if dead, captive. Something, or several things, gleamed in the corner where the sacking had been. They dispersed and rolled about the deck into the corpse and around my boots. I bent down and picked up a piece. It was a marble. I retrieved the rest of them, ten in all. Two flints, a cloudy and the rest taws. Perhaps they had belonged to the little girl who had died in this river-borne oubliette. Doubtless Miss Pardoner would have assumed they were an ingenious key to my freedom from my cell, but no one could be so fortunate twice. Nevertheless, I put them in my coat pocket, for luck, if not for any sensible reason.

Compair Lapin had left the *Turk*; a second 'Lapin' had locked me in this place with Lapin's sister's body. I surmised that Miss Shepherd's brother had gone over the stern of the boat and intended to board the following *Enterprise*. The riverboat carrying the silver had been out of sight for some time, but it could have been but one bend of the river away. Or twenty. Of course, there were any number of lighters and small boats to pick him up, any of which could turn about and let the river current take him downstream to the smaller paddle-ship. I could scarcely credit a band of 'Lapins' with their own designs on the silver, though surely that was the case, since they could not possibly wish for any other outcome than the runaways' successful debarking at the Underground Railroad's terminus, could they? It was a puzzle, though not as bewildering as the hints and gnomic utterances I had endured from both Shiloh Copland and Miss Pardoner herself regarding longevity and youth. For despite events at Gibbous House, I had never for one moment believed that Jedermann's fantastical tale of long-lived Carpathian counts and dukes was true. However, the per-suasive evidence of Miss Pardoner's youthful appearance was difficult to deny. I wished I had asked Copland whether he *had* met Robespierre, as my education at the hands and other bodily parts of another man once known as Moffat had engendered a fascination for this unscrupulous zealot. A man of whom it was said, 'It's not enough for him to be master, he has to be God,' must have had a sense of his place in the world.

I remembered little of my boyhood in far-off Scotland. The unfortunate fate of my sibling was no more than she deserved. My parents had delivered me to the Edinburgh Asy-lum, and whether they lived still, I did not care, though I would have been most surprised to hear it. What I remembered most about my earliest years was the feeling that I was but a changeling left with a dull, minor laird and his equally dull wife by malevolent fairies or sprites. My younger sister had wailed and grizzled for as long as she was alive. One would have thought my parents would have been relieved at its end-ing. I put no bolster over the screaming babe's head. I merely watched while she screamed herself into a fatal fit. My mother arrived apace after the babe's caterwauling stopped for the final time. The silence did not last long. I was delivered by both my parents to Edinburgh the day after the burial, by which time my mother's eyes were dry.

I had taken a marble from my pocket; it was a flint. I sat tossing the little sphere absently, from hand to hand, while I stared into the gloom. Introspection never did sit well with me, or rather, I did not sit well with it. However, on this occasion, even I was forced to consider the events of the last few months. It is a foolish man who regrets what he has done or a decision already taken, but I felt that even the great pleasure in encountering Ellen Pardoner once again did not counterbalance the foolishness in which I, thanks to the unwise despatch of Mr Northrup and the still less prudent assumption of his identity, had become involved. I felt sympathy for the Underground Railroad's cause, of course I did; to misappropriate the words of the Ayshire Poet, 'A man's a man for a' that'. Besides, such a sprawling organisation – in terms of geography as much as society – could not but have infiltrators and spies throughout. I was at a loss to identify them. Indeed, I was not sure that Miss Pardoner was a wholly disinterested party to the current scheme. Furthermore, the poor relict with whom I shared this narrow space had been the most dedicated of those involved and she had paid the heaviest price for it. It was not beyond belief that none of the players were wholly dedicated to the rescue of the few dozen slaves we were attempting to deliver to the free North, if not to Canada. The incomplete sketch-map and tabulary notes hidden in my carpetbag showed only a prospective route out of the Union; I doubted that any of these brave souls would reach St Paul, much less the Great Lakes.

I gave a greater start than ever in my life when Miss Shepherd's 'cadaver' sat bolt upright and let out a long and echoing belch.

'How do, Mr Northrup?' She wiped the back of her hand across her mouth, removing some of the white powder from her face thereby. I was breathing like an alderman riding a Cheapside brothel jade and therefore did not reply. Miss Shepherd rummaged in a pocket and handed me a familiar card. It showed a horned devil atop a shallow-walled well, flanked by two child-imps chained to a ring at the front of the well. Still unable to speak, I fumbled in my pocket for the identical card, which I carried in my pocket. Miss Shepherd laughed, when I held it up to show her.

'Voudoun is powerful, Mr Name-beginning-with-M, have you never seen the Zombie trick?'

Finally I found my voice. 'The pills, Madame Restall's Miracle Pills?'

'I took 'em and they worked, over a week ago. Today I have the flowers in, and I had some pig's blood from the galley, which is enough to fool any man and evidently your lady friend too. I took a powder I learned how to make from Márie Laveau herself. People are easy to fool. I guess you know that.'

'But why?'

'Somethin' ain't right. My brother's been like a cat with shingles since New Orleans. Your friend is up to somethin' too.'

Though I inwardly acknowledged the truth of this, I merely said that I had little insight into the workings of the said lady's mind.

'Beggin' your pardon, Mister Imposter, I don't reckon you got much insight into anythin' at all. We'll be out of here soon enough, meanwhile you can make yourself useful.'

So I obliged, and though some might have found it distasteful, I most assuredly did not.

Afterwards, Miss Shepherd was kind enough to permit me the use of one leg of her drawers to clean my person whilst she employed the other to a similar end. She placed the soiled garment in the sacking and let out a long sigh.

'Lord, I'm tired.'

'I am somewhat surprised a practitioner of Voudoun invokes the name of the Lord so easily.'

'Voudoun is no more a religion than it is magic. Mostly, anyhow. Wise women have been using 'erbs and plants since you white men were clubbing animals and throwing spears. 'Course sometimes it pays to have a little mystery and rite around such things. Any church is mighty jealous of those, though. Ain't so long ago women got burned for a little knowledge. 'Sides, the magic is all trickery, there are no miracles, not even the Carpenter's are real.'

'And the card, what does it mean?'

She looked at me for a moment or two. 'Márie Laveau is a capricious woman, perhaps she liked you for seeing through the flummery.'

Winona Shepherd's manner of speech was a charming admixture of the demotic and the educated, as if below, in the dark, she could stand with a foot in both worlds; whereas up above, in the light, she must powder her face and tread carefully whilst she passed.

'We see what we expect to see. Even in the mirror.'

She laughed. It was a happy sound, so I laughed too.

Miss Shepherd gave a start, which I felt as much as saw, in the confined space. There was a sound as though someone were struggling with the hatch overhead. My fellow captive took a breath and held it, as did I. I clapped my hands over my eyes and Miss Shepherd did the same, thereby proving once again her bona fides in the matter of being in Márie Laveau's confidence.

It proved to be an unlikely rescuer who opened the hatch. Having recovered from the blast of alcoholic breath, which greeted me once the hatch was opened and I had removed one hand from my eyes, I was absolutely dumbfounded to be greeted by the grizzled visage of Ishmael with the words, 'Ho-ro, my nut-brown maiden!', which words I presumed were not meant for me but Winona Shepherd. I helped her to egress our floating dungeon, then followed her out on deck. I fancied that Ishmael held himself a little more erect and that the glint of lunacy in his eye had faded somewhat.

'Well met, Ishmael!' I said and I meant it. For answer I received a grunt and a snigger. Though I should have known better than to enquire how he had changed vessels in the time since I had glimpsed him on the jetty in Natchez.

'Lighter, longboat or sailin' ship. Ah kin con 'em all. You're a danged fool, Mistuh Moffat.'

He began to laugh and I found something familiar in it, the echo of another's laughter from years before. However, I could not place it. Perhaps this showed to some degree in my face, for Ishmael laughed all the harder.

'Ye'll be fine jest now, Mistuh Moffat. Ah got other mat-tuhs to see to.'

With that he clambered once again over the taffrail, pre-sumably descending by rope into whatever skiff had borne him from the *Enterprise* to the *Turk*. As for me, I was so discom-fited by the very idea that Ishmael might have any matters at all to 'see to' that I quite failed to notice the impossibility of his knowing that I once went by the name of 'Moffat'. Moreover, the sight of Miss Shepherd clambering over the side after him gave me more than a little pause too. I stepped to the rail and looked over the side. Miss Shepherd's pointed toe had barely touched the planks of the little barque when Ishmael cast off the rope used to board the *Turk* and fasten his boat to it. He began to row in a vigorous manner, quite out of tune with the aspect he had hitherto shown since first I'd encountered him. Then Miss Shepherd took over the oars and Ishmael stood, seeming to grow inches merely by standing erect. He passed the sleeve of his coat over his face as if wiping the sweat of heavy toil from it. When he looked upward I saw a face I should never have expected to see; that of Jedediah Maccabi, still handsome, and still with the harsh and dissonant laugh that was the only unattractive thing about him.

I determined to brace Miss Pardoner on the matter of Ishmael's true identity without delay. With this in mind I made my way forward to the Captain's cabin, thinking to find her in the company of Bilhah.

No entrance thereto being possible, due to the door being locked from the inside, I belaboured the wood until my knuckles reddened like a prizefighter's, but there was no answer. I wondered what kind of discussion could be so deeply engrossing as to prevent their hearing such a knock.

At the pilot house the Pilot and Captain Grey were engaged in some philosophical discourse of their own. A civilised drink was in order: however, the relative difficulty of obtaining such, Copland's Armagnac aside, on this side of the Atlantic Ocean almost made me wish for the cornucopia of wines, spirits and sundry other libations I had enjoyed at Gibbous House. Almost. On entry into the pilot's domain, the man himself gave a curt nod and Grey's bluster faded to a mumbled, 'Good day, Mr Northrup.'

'Good day, Captain Grey, I wonder if I might trouble you for some of that fine "Brandy from Paree".'

'S'in the cabin, Northrup.'

'Well, I'm sure the Pilot has everything well in hand.'

Confirmation from this quarter was signalled by the clang resulting from the Pilot's unerring aim at the spittoon to the right of the Captain's left boot.

'Cain't go, Bilhah's busy.'

'You are the master of this tub, are you not, sir?' I confess, in my frustration, I merely wished to humiliate the man still further.

'Yore a Yankee, suh and yuh jest don't understand, nossuh.'

I rather thought that I did and was on the point of telling him so, when Miss Pardoner arrived. She sported a flush on her cheeks, which I should admit that I found familiar.

'Doubtless it was yourself playing the marching drum at the cabin door, M– Northrup.'

It was a sign of just how out of temper she was that she had almost made a slip with my *nom de jou*.

For answer I held up my reddened knuckles. Miss Pardoner gave a sniff.

'Well, what was it that was so urgent?'

'It is a private matter.' The Pilot snorted, but this may have been an involuntary consequence of his addiction to chewing tobacco.

Miss Pardoner raised her eyebrows at Captain Grey and his answer took the form of a shrug, before he turned to look over the Pilot's shoulder at the grey waters of the Mississippi river.

In the cabin, bedlinen lay heaped on the floor but there was nary a sign of Bilhah. I asked Miss Pardoner if she were acquainted with the whereabouts of the Captain's brandy supply.

'As well as you yourself, I venture,' she said, as she retrieved two cheap glasses and the bottle I had sampled before, or one very like it. Miss Pardoner poured us both a generous measure and handed me a glass.

'Well, Moffat? What was so urgent? I'm sure you realise we... had better things to do.'

I did not doubt it but decided against saying so. Instead, I related the tale of Miss Shepherd's deception and her escape, most likely to the *Enterprise*, in the company of 'Ishmael'. Thereupon, I asked, 'Did you know? From the beginning?'

She smiled and it was as provoking as ever was.

'Do you mean Ishmael?'

Had she been on the stage, the audience would have applauded her delivery. And mocked the fool to whom she delivered the line.

'Well, did you?'

'Jedediah's lot is still thrown in with the Family Jedermann. Mine is not.'

This was quite as great a facer as the discovery that the drunken sailor had been Jedediah Maccabi, and that I had not once suspected it, though we all three had been more than close in Northumberland. That being the case, I posed the obvious question, 'In God's name, why?'

'Exactly so, might be an answer, though I confess it may be more complex than that.'

'I have found very little to be simple where you Jedermanns are concerned.'

'One thing is simple. Others like us are—' She stopped, patted her hair absently in a move that was the very opposite of coquettish.

'Rare?' I offered.

'Not so rare as you might think. We like to know where they are. Who they are. How they will react to finding out the truth about themselves. I was sent to find out about Márie Laveau.'

She took the last of her brandy at a gulp.

'And what did you find?'

'The same fraudulent hocus pocus that you did.'

I had thought that she would have returned to wherever she had come from thereafter and said so.

'I found that we were looking in the wrong place.'

She poured us both another measure, though my glass was a third full.

'Indeed?'

'Indeed yes; Miss Winona Shepherd is forty-two years old. She looks twenty. Her delicate condition came as some surprise to me.' She took a more considered sip of her brandy.

'Whilst the Jedermanns will be pleased at her use of the Miracle Pills, *I* believe we should care for our blooms wherever we find them.'

She raised a kerchief to the corner of her eye although I felt no dust moving in the air.

'You, sir, I imagine have ploughed many a furrow in your time on earth. Your seed must have produced some crops. Most likely you have not considered such an eventuality.'

The woman was most assuredly correct. Though I had never made great efforts to ascertain the existence of any progeny of mine, I had no issue on either side of the Atlantic – as far as I knew. Miss Pardoner went on.

'We are not barren, sir, but we are not as fecund as we might be. Our longevity does not increase our child-bearing years. We are lucky if our numbers do not decrease from one year to the next. So we look. We search for others like us. Some believe the colour of the skin matters. I do not. I have not heard of a quickening among us past the age of thirty-five. We must tend our shoots in whichever garden they grow.'

Perhaps I should have enquired further as to why she believed this, but at that moment, the cabin door burst open, and I turned to see the Captain enter. Always florid, he had turned quite puce, with the look of a man about to succumb to a fit of apoplexy. He was attempting to speak, but his efforts sounded like the dying breaths of a severely wounded buffalo. Ellen took the Captain's arm and sat him on the rumpled bed. She pointed toward the bell board and urged me to ring for Bilhah. She arrived instanter, smiling broadly until she caught sight of me. Her scowl changed to an expression of tender concern on seeing the Captain's distress.

For he was yet spluttering. The jerking and spasms were worse than the grandest of mals ever suffered. His eyes looked as though they had been replaced by white china marbles; their contrast with the colour of his face was most alarming. Bilhah pointed to the cabinet which held the drink, and hissed, 'Stick!'

I snatched a carved wooden dowel of about six inches in length and a half-an-inch in diameter. The carving was intricate but badly damaged, as though it had been chewed by a hound. This item was snatched in turn by Bilhah from me. She nodded at Miss Pardoner, who grasped the stricken man's lower jaw, whilst the other woman forced the upper mandible away from it, before forcing the dowel as far to the back of the jaw's hinge as she could. The most likely outcome of this seemed to me to be a broken jaw, if the man did not choke first. Bilhah grasped at Ellen Pardoner's hand, ran her fingers over each digit and then kissed each one. She turned to me.

'Hold him down! On the bed!'

Whilst I forced him down, after laying tight hold of his shoulders, Bilhah produced a needle from a reticule, pulled down the man's trousers with some difficulty and plunged the metal spike into a pale and flaccid buttock.

The effect was instant, if not the intended one. He became as still as stone.

Bilhah's hands went to her mouth as she attempted to stifle a scream. Ellen Pardoner bent over the Captain, her ear to his mouth, for a moment or two. She stood erect and shook her head.

The scream escaped and was transformed into sobbing. I had not thought the Captain to be held so dear in her affections. However, it later turned it out that he was not. Bilhah's tears were for the freed slaves aboard the *Enterprise*, as she recognised our over-elaborate scheme for the house of cards that it had been from its inception. Miss Pardoner slapped Bilhah, who returned the blow, but at least the howls stopped. The noise had been too loud by far for me to bear much longer. She spoke in a whisper. 'What are we to do?'

Miss Pardoner bade me assist her in putting the Captain to his bed.

'The Captain's death, though inconvenient, need not be insurmountable. We have only to reach Cairo.'

I enquired as to when we might do so. Miss Pardoner sighed.

'We will be in Cairo at dawn. The Pilot is a capable man, and sympathetic to our cause. After the authorities search the boat we will carry on upriver and the *Enterprise* may follow on behind. We might even travel slowly the rest of the way.'

'What about the Captain?'

I looked at his corpse. He was so recently dead as to seem merely asleep, but I wondered what changes twelve hours might wreak on the relict. It was Bilhah who answered, 'If they extend their search to the Captain's cabin and find him dead, so be it. We shall say he has suffered the final indisposition.'

She laughed, as did we, and all three of us went forward to the pilot house.

The taciturn pilot was at his post, enjoying his own company, whistling a tune I did not recognise, when we arrived to fill the space to the point of intimacy. He gave the ladies the benefit of a nod and reserved a brief but steady gaze for me. Bilhah spoke. 'The Cap'n won't be out of his bed for twenty-four hours. He's took a bad turn.'

The Pilot nodded.

Miss Pardoner informed him that he had charge of the boat. He showed no surprise that she should take it upon herself to inform him of this, confining himself to another nod. Perhaps he did not care for anything other than the navigation of the river.

'When will we arrive?' I asked him. 'Will we set a record?'

'First light, maybe six in the mornin'. Might, if'n we're as lucky as a warren-ful of rabbit's feet.'

It occurred to me that it might be better if I lost my money, the swifter to pursue the other riverboat upriver and recover the silver in... where? I realised that I had not been privy to this part of the plan, or indeed to anything beyond a sketch of an outline of a plan. Miss Pardoner was not disposed to discuss anything with me in the presence of the Pilot, so I resolved to quiz her as soon as I could.

29

The first opportunity came an hour before dawn. I had slept but little, but Miss Pardoner suffered no such discomforts. I was rolling the flint sphere between my fingers; my dexterity had suffered in recent weeks and I doubted whether I could relieve even the least sensible dotard of a watch or wallet unnoticed. Miss Pardoner awoke with a start.

'A child's toy, Moffat? How very... peculiar.'

Ellen Pardoner looked none the worse for her *déshabillé*; I knew from experience that this was not always the way, but perhaps that was more a reflection on those women with whom I customarily consorted.

'No more peculiar than our scheme, about which I know very little, beyond our arrival in Natchez, and that I wish I had known about these "Lapins".'

It was clumsy badinage, but I had never been the soul of wit in the early hours.

'I know little of that group. I thought them happy with the Underground Railroads plan. Surely you see that our Compair is their leader, in any case? What else do you need to know, Moffat? So long as you get your silver, I should think you could not care less where you alight with it.'

'Since the silver remains with our runaways, I would prefer to know where they will disembark.'

'We hoped to reach St Paul or perhaps thereabouts.'

At the rate at which we were travelling that would have taken another three weeks, and I was sure that the *Grand Turk* would not be able to keep anywhere near the pace we were attempting as far as Hannibal.

'Thereabouts?'

She gave smile, tight and flat.

'We'll go as far north as we can.'

'Hannibal? St Louis? It could take us a week to get just as far as that.'

'Our rescued must reach real freedom. We must debark no further south than Hannibal.'

I shuddered at the thought of visiting the Clemens brothers' hometown once again. Then I enquired whether Newberry was truly waiting for us in Memphis and not in Hannibal, where I had met him in his guise as the shepherd of his Parish of the Church of St Onesimus.

'Newberry's plan is as we told you. And we will stop in Memphis after all.'

I asked her if she thought Newberry acquainted with the old army game with three shells and a pea, but was rewarded only with a look of indulgent puzzlement. By my calculation we were one shell, in the shape of a riverboat, short. Therefore, my own belief was that our subterfuge would not fool anyone of as nefarious a bent as I believed Erastus Newberry to be – that is to say – quite as much as I was. We performed our toilet and dressed in silence, before going out on deck, in expectation of our arrival in Memphis and whatever awaited us there.

We stood at the rail on the port side, a little aft of the pilot house; I wondered when, or indeed if, the Pilot slept. The sun was on its way; the sky remained a mulberry colour due to the unseasonably dark clouds overhead. In the distance I could see the wharves and jetties of Memphis on the banks of the river. There were fewer lights in the town itself, perhaps the arrival of our 'record-breaking' riverboat was not the sensation – not to say distraction – we had been hoping for. Crewmen brushed past, with less deference than usual, intent on reaching their posts further forward ready to throw lines to people waiting on the jetty. For they had to check the ropes and the points at which they were anchored to the deck. Perhaps they were nervous, remembering how Tom, the Texas Tender, had met his end. There were shouts across the deck from port to starboard, unintelligible to me. I looked at my companion. Miss Pardoner's gaze was quite fixed on the land beyond the jetty, scouring it for any sign of the Reverend and his officers of the law, or paid ruffians, whichever he intended to bring.

The *Grand Turk* edged to port, seemingly drifting towards its appointed jetty, although I could hear the engine and the paddle's concomitant racket quite clearly. Miss Pardoner stiffened, as one might on spying a poisonous snake in the corner of a room. She threw out an arm, her gloved forefinger extended towards the shore, 'Look!'

I squinted, shaded my eyes with a hand, although there was no light to speak of: it seemed the thing to do, though I could see nothing.

'There!'

Perhaps I had got used to the environing light, for I soon saw a group of a dozen or so men, with a thin figure at its head. It could not but be the treacherous clergyman, looking for all the world like some long-legged, wading bird of a most unlikely black colour. Once again, an ad-hoc group of Americans had felt the need to wear items of uniform, but in no uniform style. It was as though they had rather be individuals in a volunteer militia than a soldier in anyone's regular army. I saw hats in the kepi style and bully-cocked, one fellow even wore an opera hat, though its spring no longer functioned well. Most carried weapons: long-barrelled rifles, doubtless firing the minié ball in the main; two men carried a pair of handguns which they brandished in the air as they drew closer to the river. The Reverend was unarmed, unless he had secreted some example of small arms about his person. He did, however, have a small book, which he held aloft as though it were some torch to ward off bats in a darkened cave. I presumed it was a Bible, but it could as easily have been the accounts of a policy shop in New York.

'He is here, then.'

'And he will be disappointed,' Miss Pardoner replied.

The *Grand Turk* approached the jetty. The pilot rang the order to cut the engines, whereupon the crew, with the help of the men on the wharf, made the riverboat fast in short order. The gang-planks were laid out ready for deployment, a short man unhooked a chain and held it coiled in his hand. However, we were not the only people above decks aside from the deck hands. We stood cheek by jowl with Bilhah, whilst several of the galley hands and boiler-room stokers had taken the opportunity to enjoy some air outside of their cramped and foetid workplaces.

The *Grand Turk* finally sat flush alongside the jetty – even the record attempt had not been enough to ensure us a berth alongside one of the more well-appointed wharves, despite the newspaper story almost certainly telegraphed by Clemens to *The Memphis Daily Eagle* and *Enquirer*. We were finally connected to the jetty and the gangplanks were in place. There were but two passengers alighting at Memphis: a married couple of indeterminate age and greenish complexion, whom I supposed not to have enjoyed their trip along the big river. If they had been expecting the Captain to say farewell as they disembarked, they showed no disappointment at his failure to appear.

Newberry boarded first, a malevolent crow at the head of his small flock of starlings. The Bible, if such it were, was now clutched to his chest. I suspected he might use it to keep me at bay were I to step forward to meet him.

'Where is Miss Shepherd?' The Reverend peered forward and aft, craning his neck as if to see whether the young woman was lending a hand to the crew.

'She is no longer with us,' I said.

'A pity. No matter. I have brought these men to help me search this vessel.'

'On whose authority,' Miss Pardoner asked.

Erastus Newberry gave a smile that stretched thin lips but showed nary a glimpse of a tooth.

'Oh, the highest of all,' he waved his Bible in my face. I grasped his wrist and tore the little book from his grip.

'Render unto Caesar,' I opened the book to look at the title page and laughed. '"An Essay on Woman", Newberry? I think we'll keep this, it's not healthy reading for a man of God.'

Newberry bristled, 'I mean to search this vessel.' I shot a glance at both Bilhah and Miss Pardoner, before enjoining the Reverend to search away. 'Ere he went any further he held out a closed fist, fingers down, towards me. 'Take it,' he said. I opened my palm below his fist, and he dropped a small copper coin into it, whereupon he and his men divided into two groups and headed into the riverboat's accommodations, above and below decks. I held up the Copperhead towards my co-conspirators. Bilhah shook her head, whilst Miss Pardoner said, 'Even fools can be useful. Let's hope he searches thoroughly and takes his time about it.'

I asked the obvious question, to which Bilhah gave the reply, 'C'mon, let's go aft and look downriver.'

Miss Pardoner and I followed her to the stern-rail. A riverboat was making slow progress upriver. The sun was finally up and shining in our eyes as the stern of the *Grand Turk* was facing east. A moment or two later the riverboat passed us by. Someone, most likely the pilot of the other vessel, blew the steam whistle as she passed. I saw Compair Lapin waving from the deck.

And I understood; it did not matter how far or how fast the *Grand Turk* travelled upriver, as long as all eyes were kept from the *Enterprise*. Perhaps it might be possible to gull the flats with only two shells to hide the pea after all.

Bilhah straightened her back, the only acknowledgement any of us made of either Lapin's salutation or the passage of the *Enterprise*.

'We'd better see if the Reverend has got as far as the Cap'n's cabin.'

She led and we followed.

30

The size of Captain Grey's accommodations were sufficient to allow room for all six of Newberry's section of his search party, and we three. If the disarray in which we found the cabin were an indication of how long they had been searching, it was surprising that no one had attempted to wake the 'sleeping' master of the *Grand Turk*. No one was more surprised than I when Bilhah let out a most piercing scream. During our short acquaintance I had formed the opinion that there was nothing that might disturb the woman's equilibrium. She fell on Newberry and beat at his shoulders with her fists, even though I was quite sure she could have managed a blow as mighty as the one with which Compair Lapin had ended his prize fight in the *Turk*'s saloon bar. The woman gave me a slow wink over the Reverend's shoulder.

'You kilt him, you kilt him,' Bilhah began to bellow.

I made an effort at covering my amusement with a simulated sneeze or two. Ellen Pardoner remained quite stony-faced and I felt glad to have made her acquaintance across the green baize of a card table but the once, many years ago, in a humbling game of skat. Bilhah relented, hid her face with her hands whilst her shoulders heaved.

Newberry had recovered sufficiently from the assault to open his mouth, but very little of sense came out of it. In summary, he swore that the Captain had been dead when the searchers had entered the cabin. Though this was the most unvarnished of truths, we did not acknowledge it as such. However, Miss Pardoner declared, 'There is nothing for it; there must be an investigation.'

Newberry's crest fell further than that of a loser in a cock-fight. I was no more cock-a-hoop than he. Whilst I lamented the likely loss of my wager in the matter of the river run, I wondered just how much further up the river the bullion would be before we could think of catching it.

Miss Pardoner touched my arm and nodded at the Reverend, 'Brace him.' I stepped towards him, but he offered no resistance. His retinue fled, doubtless warning the other half of the search party to do the same.

Newberry cleared his throat, 'Ah... I'd rather not... you can't think?' His eyes remained fixed on Ellen Pardoner, he would not look at Bilhah, but it was she who answered.

'Tain't what we think, Reverend. S'what the local law might think, ain't it?'

The Reverend Erastus Newberry's reply was addressed to the wooden boards of the deck.

'There will be no need for the law.'

His voice was far from the stentorian bellow he had affected when I first met him at the Church of St Onesimus. We could put him ashore and be on our way, albeit with the dead captain still on board. I played the bum-bailiff with him to the end of the gangplank, Bilhah having instructed the crew to cast off without delay. Newberry remained on the jetty and fixed his gaze on the *Grand Turk* as we turned to starboard and headed upriver. I watched him myself until he was no more than a charcoaled stick figure on the landscape's canvas, all the while wondering that he had not played his trump card of the runaways hidden about the vessel. I supposed the truth was that he truly did not care whether men lived in servitude or not. Besides, I suspected he might have had earlier experiences of penal servitude, which discouraged him from risking a further dose.

I intended to pass the remaining days until St Louis and the end of the supposed record-breaking run in my own company. I took to wandering about the deck, hoping for a glimpse of the *Enterprise*. I thought perhaps it might heave to at one of the ludicrous little stops that were little more than a single jetty, which the Pilot had assured me were called such descriptive but unlikely names as Catfish Bend or Turpentine. However, it must have been a better vessel than it looked, for though I expected to see its slovenly lines around every bend, I was disappointed. As for Miss Pardoner, I would leave her to the comforts of the cabin provided for us both, whatever purpose she put them to. For want of anything better to do, I entered the *Grand Turk*'s restaurant 'salon' in pursuit of something resembling breakfast. The only occupied table was wreathed in a cloud of smoke. It was so dense as to hide the identity of the person responsible for it. Occasionally, a hand holding a clay pipe disturbed the fug like a Vatican priest's thurible on the feast of Saint Bernadino, the patron saint of bowel disorders. I must have stared a little too hard and a little too long, for a croaking voice enounced with the extreme care of the habitual drunkard, 'May as well set down, if 'n' yer goin' 'member me right.'

It was such a strange invitation that I chose to accept it, out of curiosity.

We were attended to by a white woman of middle years,

who brought the person behind the acrid nebula a whiskey and then enquired of me, 'Your pleasure, suh?'

'Might one break fast at this hour?' As it was nine, I harboured hopes of doing so.

'Y'all kin eat, f' that's what yuh mean.'

'Breakfast. Do you have breakfast?'

'We got oatmeal and we got grits.'

I had not eaten porridge since I was a very young man and as for the other, whenever I had seen others eating it, I was inclined to think even Dickens' larcenous orphan would not have wanted more. Ergo, I ordered a whiskey, which duly arrived, and proved to be of such strength as to be able to remain in its dusty tumbler despite the ferocity with which the woman placed it on the table.

'Aw, fergoodnesssake, kin yuh jest put out the fires for a minute or two, it's like workin' nextuh a gol-durned volcaner,' she drawled, before flouncing off with a movement I had heard termed as a 'sasshay'.

One fume-enshrouded arm waved away the smoke while the other's hand tapped the clay-pipe against the heel of a boot until the bowl broke away from the stem. A loud sigh served to disperse the last of the smoke and finally my breakfast companion was revealed. Rather than any standing on ceremony, a hand was extended across the table by a distinctly androgynous figure only a little past their prime. Large blue eyes were magnified by thick-lensed spectacles. My confusion was apparent for the introduction ran as follows:

'Deee-lighted to meecha, Mister. Ma name is Jane Stevenson, though some calls me Seymour. Seymour Clearly. Hah. Some folks think that's funny.' Her index finger pointed towards her spectacles. Her voice was a pleasant contralto, neither overly mannish nor feminine.

'Northrup, Anson Northrup, the pleasure is all mine.'

'Northrup, yuh say?' She gave a slow nod and so did I.

'That's right.'

'Tain't the commonest of names.'

I did not reply. Meanwhile, she patted the outside of her coat down and then reached inside to draw out another clay pipe, looking at it for a moment before laying it on the table before her.

'Whut's in a name? That Shakespeare feller said that, din't he?'

I could scarce imagine in what circumstances Jane or Seymour might have encountered the works of the Bard of Avon. Then I reflected that Cattermole was murdering Macbeth up and down the Mississippi and supposed that anything was possible.

Jane Stevenson was dressed in much the same manner as the card-players I had met on the river: item, a coat which might better be termed a jacket, it being shorter than the more elegant frock coat preferred by gentlemen; item, britches which left no doubt as to the muscular nature of her inferior limbs; item, the knee-boots so beloved by every man Jonathan. In short, she dressed like a man, it had been a bold thing to do in London, but here I did not find it so strange. There was much that was practical in the Americas; besides I found it strangely attractive.

I allowed that Sweet William had indeed written such a thing. However, Mistress Stevenson was not yet finished.

'Been called worse, ya know. A calamity, I been called. S'what the Sawbones said, anyhow. My maw took it up. Ah don't answer to such now.'

'Calamity? How so?'

'Like in a bad surprise. Ah don't consider any surprise bad, myself.'

She gave me a wink and then laughed so hard she spilled some whiskey.

'Donch'y'all fuss. I ain't fer that stuff n'more.' She paused, 'But you ain't Anson Northrup, least not the one I knew.'

How was it possible that I should meet two persons of such distinct character and quality who would know the late Anson Northrup? I did not remember breaking more than one mirror in Gibbous House though it had an entire hall of them. I emptied my whiskey and signalled to the woman for two more.

'And this Anson Northrup, who was he?'

'Card-sharper, mostly, did a bit o'whiskey-drummin' though I hear he drank most of it.'

In fact, his last box of samples had been emptied chiefly by Jedediah Maccabi in his guise as the drunken sailor Ishmael. Perhaps it was this debauchery which had thrown me off the scent so, for of all those I encountered at Gibbous House, Maccabi had been the most abstemious.

'I have grown fonder of whiskey over time, it's true.'

Jane Stevenson rummaged once again through her pockets, before holding up a small coin before one lens of her spectacles like a jeweller inspecting a gemstone.

'Useta carry one a'these.'

Like a flat at the army game, I had been thoroughly misdirected: Jane Stevenson was also pointing a pistol across the table at me. A tiny thing that had doubtless been concealed in the sleeve of her jacket, in a contraption similar to that of Northrup's own, which I had singularly failed to master.

The waitress arrived with two more tumblers of whiskey. The advantage of height which standing gave her over the seated woman allowed her to throw the contents of both downward, behind Miss Stevenson's spectacles. I hurled myself to the side and the derringer's discharge damaged only the back of the chair in which I had been sitting.

I felt a little sympathy for Miss Stevenson who must never have been less suited to the nickname Seymour. Obligation led me to thank the woman who had put the water of life to such good use and, out of politeness, I asked her name.

'Hepzibah Whitlow, most folks call me Felon, on account I been to jail onc't.'

'Well, Hepzibah, you have done me a service indeed. Would that I could reward you in some way.'

'Y'all can git the silver to where it's goin', not furgettin' the railroad's real cargo too. She wuz right, you ain't Northrup, are yuh?'

'It's as good a name as any.'

'He was a damned turncoat, never did understand why Miss Shepherd 'r any of 'um couldn't see that.'

'I assure you my allegiance never changes,' I said, and it was no lie.

There remained the matter of what to do with the Copperhead spy. Hepzibah was for throwing the woman over the side. I thought we should be more circumspect, at least in so far as to wait for nightfall, before trying anything so drastic.

Jane Stevenson remained incapacitated by her grain spirit eyewash; Hepzibah Whitlow nodded at the stricken woman.

'That there woman is kin to Anson Northrup, cousin 'r sump'n'. Ah figure yuh might take that into considerashun, all things bein' equal.'

Miss Whitlow bent down, one hand at her back whilst the other reached for the derringer Miss Stevenson had dropped on the deck. When she stood up again the barrel was pointing at me.

'Go ask the fellah in there for the length a'rope by the coal bucket.'

She jerked a thumb towards the doubtless tiny space where such vittles as were on offer for passengers were prepared. I returned with a length of dirty bucket-rope. 'Felon' Whitlow nodded at the still distressed woman in the chair.

'Reckon yuh kin tie a square knot, even if yuh ain't a sailor. Leave her arms move frum the elbow.'

The prisoner did not protest as I made her fast to the chair, leaving her arms free as ordered. The whites of her eyes had turned the solid red of a British soldier's tunic and she was whimpering like a well-beaten dog. Felon handed me the tiny gun. A wicked little blade had appeared in her other hand. Any thought that Felon was being merciful in regard to allowing the prisoner to attempt to wipe her eyes from time to time was soon banished.

'Put 'cher hand on the table, Miz; splay those fingers.'

The knife thudded straight through the whiskey-stained linen into the wood. It was a short overhand lunge downwards and it landed between the thumb and index finger of Stevenson's left hand. Naturally the hand closed with a flinch. The blade was so keen that both digits were cut. The blood mixed with the whiskey-stains, but at least the whimpering had stopped.

'What do you want for God's sake?'

'You in with Newberry?' Felon snarled.

'Newberry's just a greedy fool.'

I surmised that Stevenson had slipped on-board with Newberry's rag-tag little company.

The knife came out easily and slammed down again, this time between the thumb and forefinger of the right hand. This time Stevenson's hand flinched but remained splayed on the tablecloth.

'Why in H-E-L-L are yuh on the *Turk*, 'at case?'

I pointed at the Copperhead penny still on the table, 'One

would suppose that the Copperheads' interest in our affairs remains keen, despite the death of their spy.'

Both Stevenson and Felon started at that.

Having been presented with an opportunity to sow some confusion, I continued, 'Northrup also went by John Mudsill, though I suppose only a few knew him by that name.'

The knife was at my throat in an instant. Felon had lost interest in the captive, who seemed to have lost interest in everything, being in a dead faint.

'I knew yuh wasn't him, Mister.'

The knife really was most awfully sharp, and my voice must have sounded a little strained.

'All the better that I am not, since I am no turncoat, nor secretly working with the Copperheads.'

She withdrew the knife a little.

'Mudsill, yuh say?'

'I found papers in that name on his person when he died.'

Felon Whitlow nodded, but a revived Stevenson seemed surprised.

'But—he—it—we decided…'

Which incoherence neither Whitlow nor I could fathom, however it had the effect of the knife's point returning to menace Stevenson.

'Whut? Whut didja decide?'

'I was to be John Mudsill.'

A flick of the knife urged her to continue.

'At the mint. Plan weren't no different from yours, I reckon. 'Ceptin' there wouldn't be no slaves freed, no how.'

I failed to see the point of transporting the bullion northward and said so.

'See-cession Mister. We take that silver north to like-minded people and we can raise a militia in northern states. Cain't fight a war on two fronts.'

A truism which Napoleon had disregarded to his cost; which remark I might have offered if I had thought either party had ever heard of the Corsican. What I did observe was that that boat had already sailed, in more senses than one. Then I asked her, 'How then to move the silver? Were you to carry it north alone, on your shoulders? A brick at a time, always supposing that you had managed to "requisition" it?'

'I had volunteers, true patriots. A message came for John Mudsill at my hotel. We weren't so many, but we coulda got some, or at least enough. When we got to the vault, it was empty. The old fellah was lyin' there, dead, not long since neither.'

'And then?'

'Caught this boat out of New Orleans.'

And I started to laugh. It was pure coincidence that she and I were travelling on the same boat, since I had begun the trip upriver on the *Enterprise*. It was a more error-strewn comedy than any of the Bard's efforts involving assumed identities. I was grateful that thus far I had come across no confusing twins at all. Both parties looked put out by my fit of hilarity, but it was Jane Stevenson who spoke, 'I figured you musta been to the mint, 'stead o' my cousin.'

'Where is the silver then?' I enquired.

Whitlow looked from me to the captive and the knife-point wavered again.

'You ain't got it, and it ain't here,' Stevenson sighed.

Felon's shoulders relaxed, although the knife-hand retained a firm grip. I had thought that Lapin or one of his acolytes might have used the Stevenson woman as a dupe, but it seemed that the coin he had left behind was mere provocation after all.

'I think we can dispense with the knife, Felon, if you'll just check for any further weapons.'

The still-blinded woman sat passive, whilst the other recovered two knives: a longish one with a curved blade and a shorter one, which would have been called a popper in my youth. A small billy club completed her small collection of treasures.

I looked around at the deserted dining room and instructed Felon to keep her eye on the other woman. Her eyes would recover soon enough. I had known a fellow in London who had regularly attempted to get drunk by rubbing gin on his eyes; it took him years to go blind, but the gin was of very poor quality in those days. Such appetite as I had earlier had by now deserted me, so I went in search of Ellen Pardoner.

31

The cabin being empty, I thought to try further forward. Perhaps Miss Pardoner was teetering dangerously over the prow of the ship, though I sincerely hoped not. My fears were unfounded, for she was not there. Nor was she in the pilot house, where the Pilot gave me a nod somewhere between an acknowledgement and a dismissal. I crossed the deck to the rear of the pilot house and turned towards the stern, where I could see two figures. Before I reached them the shorter of the two scrambled towards the port side of the riverboat and was lost to view behind the funnels. The other was, of course, Miss Pardoner. I asked if her friend had a previous engagement. She smiled and said that we were all busy.

'How so?' I asked. 'I for one am quite at my leisure, save for being marooned on this damned boat.'

'The marooned are usually on some desert isle and might sacrifice much for the arrival even of a vessel such as this.'

'As well on a desert isle as on this benighted tub, I say.'

'And yet we are in broad daylight; how so then "benighted", sir?'

She was and had ever been a vexatious minx.

'Very well, I am bored, Mistress. Bored, almost beyond distraction.'

'Then let me distract you, Moffat. Walk me around the deck.' She offered me her arm and I linked my own with it.

The Mississippi's water was that indeterminate colour between grey and brown and offered no approximation of the blue of the skies overhead. Above the engine's racket I could hear the variegated cries of sundry birds. For myself, I could not tell a coot from a double-crested cormorant, but one sound was as like that of the creak of a rusted cemetery gate as to have one looking to the riverbank in search of tombstones.

My companion turned to look at me out of the corner of her eye.

'Cambion. Does that mean anything to you, Moffat?'

'It sounds French. Is it some poetaster?'

'It has been a surname, though not, to my knowledge, of any French man.'

'I would think you would know me for a man not overly enamoured of riddles, Ma'amselle.'

'Very well, I shall allow it is a word of French origin.'

I gave her a look meant to convey that I should be grateful for a more interesting subject for our conversation.

'Do you even remember your given name, Alasdair?'

'I have not heard it in many a year, but no I do not forget it.'

'And what is your name?'

I was about to answer but the loudest blast I had ever heard prevented my reply. My ears rang. Whether it was a crack of thunder from an innocent-blue sky, or the report of some huge cannon, I could not say. I only knew that the noise appeared to have originated further upriver around the next or a still more distant bend. We both rushed forward, glancing in at the Pilot, who was shaking his head. As yet there was nothing to see from the prow. The Pilot bellowed at us to stand aside. We returned to the pilot house, where the Pilot managed to keep his eyes fixed on the scene in front of him whilst continuing to shake his head. I pointed upriver, 'What happened? Surely that was no thunderclap?'

'No, 't'weren't. Reckon as some families'll feel a lightnin' strike, fer certain sure.'

'What do you mean, Pilot?' Miss Pardoner asked.

'At's the sound of a boiler blow. Ain't heard it but once before, mahself. But every steamboatman whut recognises 'at sound is glad that he does, fer it means he ain't on board no boiler blown boat hisself.'

The Pilot continued to scan the scene in front of him, muttering and shaking his head all the while. We rounded the bend some ten minutes later.

'Ain't no hope o' that record now.'

It wanted a few minutes more before my own eyes made out what the sharp-eyed pilot's had seen. Flotsam. Wood, supplies and cargo. Up ahead the *Enterprise* was afire, the vessel's stack looked like a defective squib. The formerly cylindrical metal now held the shape of a child-drawn bloom. To the *Turk*'s port side, a solitary traveller's trunk circled the river's surface, sinking by degrees until, for an instant, its luggage label stood proud of the water, flapping in the breeze. The *Enterprise* began to heel to starboard. We were chugging forward slowly. The Pilot blew the whistle: one short, two long, though most hands were already on deck scanning for survivors. A lone figure leapt into the water.

Miss Pardoner put my own thoughts into words, 'Where are the survivors?'

For there were none, save whoever had just leapt into the water.

The person in the water made some inelegant, if ineffective progress through it. Still, by dint of the *Grand Turk*'s forward motion, the distance between themselves and the vessel diminished until I could make out the identity of the swimmer.

Two deck hands threw down a life belt into the water and began hauling a woman clad only in her underclothing. The water of the Mississippi had had a cleansing effect and Miss Winona Shepherd most definitely was not passing.

'Did no others escape?' Miss Pardoner's mouth turned down at the sides.

'No, ma'am. Some was trapped below and anyone near the boiler room isn't much more than shivers and smithers now, I'm sure.'

'What about the pilot? And Captain Kincaid?' Miss Pardoner's questions were not the ones I had been on the point of asking.

'Still on the boat when I...'

'What about the...'

Both women eyed me as though I were a drunk at a Temperance Society meeting. I raised my eyebrows and lifted my hands palm upward.

'What? I merely wanted to know about the clandestine cargo.'

'The bullion is gone, sir,' replied Winona Shepherd.

'And the Underground Railroad's passengers?'

'All gone.'

She shivered and Miss Pardoner placed an arm around her shoulders to guide her back to the cabin.

Not everyone had gone: a head and a pair of shoulders appeared from the surface, around a chain's length from the *Turk*'s bow. The same two riverboatmen hauled in the lifeline again. Jedediah Maccabi had shed all vestiges of the drunken sailor Ishmael. His river-sodden clothes were such as a gentleman of reduced means might have worn, were he reduced so far as to be wearing hand-me-downs. There was no denying it was an improvement, for the reek of the clothes he had worn in his guise as Ishmael had smelled worse than the Mississippi at its most foetid. Maccabi collapsed, retching, on the deck. Miss Shepherd and I stepped backward to avoid the splashes. Ellen Pardoner cradled the man's head and asked him if any more had survived. Maccabi struggled to enunciate a, 'No'. Then Miss Pardoner gave his neck a twist until it broke. This manoeuvre she effected as though she were an Ottoman *Delibaş* inflicting the Istanbul Twist on a luckless brothel keeper, instead of a lady passenger on a Mississippi riverboat. Winona Shepherd looked relieved, rather than dismayed. Even though Maccabi had borne her off to the *Enterprise* and Lapin.

I was taken aback still further, when Miss Pardoner bade me shove Jedediah over the side.

She greeted the splash with the observation, 'At least there'll be no bearing of tales back to the Family Jedermann.'

Truly, I could not say that she had surprised me. I had considered the woman to be a kindred spirit from the moment that I had first met her, in that far distant vicarage on the island of Lindisfarne. However, I did not expect her to show me something she had taken from Maccabi's pocket; to wit, an oilskin wrapped very tightly around contents about the size of a small book. Though I doubted they had survived its dunking in the river, Miss Pardoner withdrew from the sodden packet a box which looked to be of tinned iron. Inside there were folded documents, but from the bottom of the little sheaf she brought out a filthy and ancient piece of vellum. She handed it to me.

'Read it, sir. Read it and weep… Or laugh, as you please.'

I unfolded the paper. The faded ink was barely discernible amongst the smuts and stains decorating it. It read as follows:

We leave the care of this bairn to the laird. He is none of ours from this day.

We have named him Cambion, but care not what he is called from this day forth.

MacJoyce and Wife

Their Marks

XX

This 31st Day of October, 1800

My hands shook a little, as I placed the paper in my pocket. MacJoyce? It was not a name I had ever heard, but the date and my own long-held conviction that the laird and his wife had not been my parents seemed to offer confirmation that I – and none other – was the bairn referred to in the note. More diverting was the appellation Cambion, which word, despite what I had said to Miss Pardoner earlier, I *had* encountered in a copy of Malleus Maleficarum. That book and another had been all I had taken with me from the Edinburgh Asylum, long after I had first become Moffat. Clearly, I was the offspring of illiterates, though whether the husband had been the father of the 'bairn' I had my doubts. Nor did I believe myself the progeny of an incubus, whatever was written in Henricus's ancient book. It was far more likely that they had wanted to inflict the alternative name of the Catchfly flower upon me, but the notary had mistaken the P of Campion for a B. As for what any of it all meant in terms of who or what I was, I believed my experiences had made me, not my birthright. Campion MacJoyce; it sounded like the name of some effete poet or a minor character in a Walter Scott novel.

Miss Pardoner eyed me as though she were expecting some exclamation of surprise at the contents of the note.

'Superstition is the explanation of the inexplicable,' she said.

'I had rather thought that to be the role of science.'

'And for those without science? What of them?'

'Enlightenment will come for all, one day.'

Which noble sentiment I thought most unlikely.

'And in the meantime, there is voudoun?' I laughed, Ellen Pardoner did not, though Miss Shepherd allowed herself a smile.

'We will know everything, one day. Everything.'

'At which time we will have found God, and God will be ourselves, Miss Shepherd.'

'And the Devil too, sir, the Devil too.'

Miss Pardoner rolled her eyes at this, but I thought that Winona Shepherd had the right of it, in truth.

All the while the four of us, the Pilot included, had swept the river ahead, searching for what would surely be lifeless bodies floating on the surface of the water. There were none. I thought it sad that Cattermole's rag-tag troupe would no longer sail up and down the Mississippi, murdering Macbeth and music in equal degree. Neither was there more luggage. This was no great surprise, for there had been few passengers left aboard the *Enterprise* when we left it.

And now the silver bullion and the freed slaves who had done the carrying of it lay in the mud of the Mississippi riverbed. I asked Miss Pardoner what she planned to do; she gave a shrug and said she would leave the *Turk* at St Louis.

'Bilhah and the Pilot will see to the arrangements over the Captain's remains.'

'I fancy he will be a little high by that time.'

'He'll be fine below the waterline; didn't you notice how cold it was?' Miss Shepherd asked.

'I did not, I had other things to think about. Besides, we kept ourselves warm later.'

Miss Shepherd had the good grace to blush a little. Miss Pardoner's mouth set in a thin line. It quite made my day.

I took my leave of the company and said that I would knock on every cabin door until I found one unoccupied and sleep therein until whatever time I chose. It was scarce mid-afternoon but I was as tired as I had ever been in my life. I had barely lain down on a cot devoid of linen than I remembered two things: Galloway of Molasses's first name had been Campion, and Ellen Pardoner's reaction to his demise had been more marked than I had expected at the time.

Two hours later I was awake, if not entirely alert. I was, however, pondering how long it would take to reach St Louis, and what I would do there. Conversation with the Pilot had elicited that our speed would average fourteen miles per hour – a little over twelve knots. Therefore sixty hours would have been a good time made to establish a record from Natchez to St Louis. But we had been delayed by fog and the explosion on the *Enterprise*. I spent another day and a night in this fashion, in a funk of deep despond.

The *Grand Turk* pulled alongside in St Louis. There had been little traffic on the river. We left the Pilot and Bilhah to deal with the matter of the Captain's demise. As for the escapees, whilst I wished them no ill, they were no longer my concern. Another master would be found for the *Grand Turk* and they would continue upriver. Miss Shepherd, Miss Pardoner and I made for the Yaller House, the former intimating that perhaps we should inform its owner of the failure of our scheme, at least in the matter of the bullion. The door was answered in familiar fashion and we were permitted to enter the main salon. It was early in the day, and few of the couches or chaises were occupied. The proprietress greeted us with a smile, as though the fiasco of our scheme were no more than a pitcher of milk spilled.

'Mr Northrup, as might have been.'

The woman had the composure of a countess. There was an embrace of great warmth exchanged with Miss Shepherd and I noted a resemblance between them now that I saw them together. I raised an eyebrow at Ellen Pardoner, which expression she reciprocated.

'You will have heard about the accident,' Winona Shepherd said.

Zoe Terrebonne smiled, 'It was fate.'

Miss Pardoner shook her head at this. 'There were some on board with the bullion. George Washington Irving, Compair Lapin, for good or ill.'

The owner of the Yaller House continued smiling and offered us a drink, which I was not about to decline. Though it was yet early I requested some of Miss Terrebonne's excellent brandy. Miss Pardoner declined any refreshment at all and Miss Shepherd asked for a shot of rotgut. Miss Terrebonne waved a hand at an invisible retainer and Muskrat Jaw Jean appeared carrying a silver tray. She was dressed in the manner of a servant in a very different kind of house. Miss Terrebonne looked at me.

'I run this house, sir. And none earn their money on their backs save that they wish to. Some leave straightway, some learn other skills here before moving on and some, like Jean, stay in other capacities.'

The drinks were served and Jean withdrew, as dignified as a dowager duchess. She had been a most talented horizontale and I silently wished her luck. We remained standing in the empty salon; I could not fathom why we had not been invited to sit. Miss Shepherd had been recounting Newberry's treachery for Zoe Terrebonne's benefit, perhaps expecting some commiseration for the loss of the bullion or even the fact that our elaborate subterfuge had saved not one of the Underground Railroad's passengers. The madam remained serene, sipping from a glass of clear water. Presently the wall-eyed footman arrived carrying a folding table of the type seen at county fairs, where there are fools to be fleeced. This same retainer produced three small cups, apparently made of bone.

Miss Terrebonne clapped her hands, 'For sport. Just for sport. Now does anyone have anything suitable?'

The shell game lacked its pea. Miss Shepherd said, 'I believe Moffat has a few playthings about his person.'

I still carried the marbles found when incarcerated with Winona Shepherd. I chose the flint, though not because I expected the game to be anything but rigged. No, I had counted flints as lucky ever since childhood. Miss Terrebonne held out a palm; I dropped the little sphere into it.

'Miss Shepherd, would you care to demonstrate?'

She put one cup aside, on the furthest corner of the baize-covered table from herself. Was she going to attempt the game with only two shells? It was a nonsense. Taking the flint, Winona Shepherd placed it with exaggerated slowness under the cup to her left. I had never seen the game so badly played; she appeared beyond clumsy in her manipulation of the cups and marble. On being asked to choose a cup, Ellen Pardoner pointed at the cup the marble had been placed under in the first place, that is the one to Miss Shepherd's left. Well, of course it was there. Ellen was in the role of confederate. The conjuress affected a cry of surprise. Then she placed the flint under the cup on the right. Again there was the artless rigmarole. When she had quite finished, she looked at me and then jerked her chin upward. I pointed at the right cup. She lifted it and there was no flint, of course. Then she lifted the cup on the left. The marble was gone. Miss Shepherd lifted both arms to the level of her shoulders.

'You are welcome to attempt to find the marble, Mr Moffat.'

However, Ellen Pardoner intervened, 'That won't be necessary, will it, Miss Terrebonne?'

Whereupon the Yaller House Madam lifted the bone cup on the corner of the table, and gave the flint a flick with an elegant finger, and as it rolled towards me Winona Shepherd swooped upon it and replaced it in the pocket of my coat.

'A carriage awaits you outside, sir. Do you stay, Miss Shepherd? Miss Pardoner?'

Ellen Pardoner allowed that she did not mind accompanying me to wherever I was going, but that she suspected she knew where that might be. Miss Shepherd said that she might stay a while. For all I know she might be there still.

The carriage was handsome, though no landau or brougham. It was equipped with lamps and the bench seat was comfortable if worn. It was open to the elements, the breeze was pleasant and the company more so. We wound through the streets at a leisurely pace. The driver was silent, and Miss Pardoner seemed distracted. It was not long before I realised we were doing no more or less than retracing our journey from the riverside docks to the Yaller House. Miss Pardoner nodded at me as if she had read my mind and she smiled for the rest of our little jaunt.

The driver bade the horse to halt and alighted to open the door for us to do so too. There was a crowd on the jetty by the *Grand Turk*. An assembly of ne'er do wells and patrons of nearby bars had come to gawk at the spectacle of Captain Holden being borne away from his boat on a litter carried by men I did not recognise, although they might as well have been medical orderlies as policemen from their attire. Bilhah was looking down from the deck of the riverboat, either extremely stoic in grief or unmoved by her charge's departure. I waved but was ignored. Miss Pardoner laughed.

She fastened her grip upon my elbow and bade me move along the dockside, well past the *Turk*'s berth.

'There Moffat, look!'

I followed the direction in which her outstretched arm pointed. There was a scruffy keelboat towing a flatboat in the centre of the river. Ellen produced a spyglass from her bag, a receptacle that was somehow capable of containing more than my own grotesque carpetbag. She drew it out to its fullest extent, looked briefly at the two boats, and then handed it to me.

'Take a closer look.'

A group of several dozen black men and one white man stood in the flatboat, staring at the riverbank. I swept the glass over the keelboat. Familiar figures stood side by side: George Washington Irving, Compair Lapin and, of all people, Cattermole the actor. Did I imagine their smiles? Perhaps I did, perhaps the spyglass was not so powerful as all that.

Miss Pardoner gave an exasperated sigh, and snarled, 'For the love of God, Moffat, look at the name!'

I moved the lens across the freshly painted wood near the prow of the keelboat. I said the words aloud as I read them.

'*La Troisième Coquille…*'

By the time I had taken the eyepiece from my eye, Miss Pardoner was already nowhere to be seen, and I finally realised there had been three shells in the game all along.

Acknowledgements

There are so many to thank.

All of those named in the front and back of this book, of course.

Rugby Glue, which has done so much to stick this book together.

The Unbound Authors' Social Club, without whom I would certainly have given up 'Tub-thumping', AKA crowdfunding.

ABCTales, where Moffat first saw the light of day.

Tony Cook who started it all, by catching someone reading an early version on the train.

Rachael Kerr, who took on the task of reining in Moffat's digressive excursions, for a *second* time.

Unbound, who have always believed in Moffat.

T, for everything.

And you, who are reading this, however you came by the book.

Unbound supporters

Unbound is the world's first crowdfunding publisher, established in 2011.

We believe that wonderful things can happen when you clear a path for people who share a passion. That's why we've built a platform that brings together readers and authors to crowdfund books they believe in – and give fresh ideas that don't fit the traditional mould the chance they deserve.

This book is in your hands because readers made it possible. Everyone who pledged their support is listed at the front of the book and below. Join them by visiting unbound.com and supporting a book today.

Stumpy Cornah
Michael Cranston
Martin Darby
Patrick Davie
Rhiannon Davies
Rachel Deering
Andrew Dove
Jessica Duchen
Alys Earl
James Ellis
Mike Ewing
Paul Fearon
Graham Fernihough
Rob Frisby
Evan Frisby
Emma Frost
Danny Glover
Emma Grae
Mike Graham
Iain Graham
Stuart Grant
Eamonn Griffin
Drew Gummerson
Eileen Harmer
Philip Harvey
Angela Hemlin
Andrew Hill
Paul Holbrook
Paula Hunter
Tim Hutchinson
Martin Hyatt
Flash Jones
Jane Kelly
Dan Kieran
Dave King
Shona Kinsella

Mit Lahiri
Shaun Lane
Robert Lewis
Karen Markwell
Alan McCormick
Erinna Mettler
John Mitchinson
In memory of Geraldine Murphy
with much love
Mike Murtagh
Rhel ná DecVandé
Carlo Navato
Ivy Ngeow
Par Olsson
Jamie Paradise
Bryn Parry
Justin Pollard
Lucy Price
Paul Richardson
Helen Richardson
Ron Scott
Stuart Seaman
Janet Smith
Alex Smith
Angie Stalker
Bobby Stevenson
Tabatha Stirling
Helen Taylor
Andrew Thornton
Greg Thurgo
Vicki Timings-Thompson
Mark Twain
Tom Ward
Paul Waters
Aliya Whiteley
Derek Wilson